ORPHAN
OF THE
SUN

ORPHAN

OF THE

SUN

GILL HARVEY

BLOOMSBURY
CHILDREN'S
BOOKS

Published by Bloomsbury Publishing, New York, London, and Berlin
Distributed to the trade by Holtzbrinck Publishers

Library of Congress Cataloging-in-Publication Data
Harvey, Gill.
Orphan of the sun / by Gill Harvey.—1st U.S. ed.
p.   cm.
Summary: Meryt-Re, a thirteen-year-old orphan living in Set-Maat, Egypt, during
the building of the pharaohs' tombs, tries to come to terms with her ability to see
the truth in dreams while also attempting to determine who is trying to over-
throw the village foreman.
ISBN-10: 1-58234-685-2 • ISBN-13: 978-1-58234-685-4
[1. Dreams—Fiction. 2. Self-realization—Fiction. 3. Orphans—Fiction. 4. Dayr al-
Madinah Site (Egypt)—Fiction. 5. Egypt—History—New Kingdom, ca. 1550-ca.
1070 B.C.—Fiction.] I. Title.
PZ7.H267478Orp 2006   [Fic]—dc22   2005030622

First U.S. Edition 2006
Printed in Great Britain by Clays Ltd, St Ives plc
2 4 6 8 10 9 7 5 3 1

Bloomsbury Publishing, Children's Books, U.S.A.
175 Fifth Avenue, New York, NY 10010

For my mum

 PROLOGUE

*There is an ancient site in Egypt called Deir el Medina:
the 'Monastery of the Town'. It is nestled in an eerie desert
valley, surrounded by sheer limestone cliffs. Few tourists
venture here. There are much more attractive sites on offer,
only a donkey ride away – the mysterious tomb of
Tutankhamun, the magnificent temple of Hatshepsut, the
paintings of the stunning Nefertari. Deir el Medina's
tombs are small, and the site is mostly a network of broken
mud-brick walls, with a neglected temple at one end ... so
why bother visiting?*

*But if you go to Deir el Medina in the evening, when
the sun is slanting on the golden limestone rocks and there
are only a few bored and lonely guards to stare at you suspiciously, you might discover something else. Listen for
the wail of a Muslim muezzin in the distance, calling the
faithful to prayer. As his voice echoes against the rocks,
stay very still. Listen.*

Listen.

*There are other voices here. Voices of children. Voices of
women calling across the narrow, crowded streets. Voices
of water-bringers, and the shrill, squeaking bray of*

*donkeys. And some of the time, there are voices of men,
back from their work on the precious pharaohs' tombs.*

Where do these voices come from?

*From the time when Deir el Medina was called 'Set
Maat', the Place of Truth. When scores of families were
crammed into its tiny houses. When pharaohs ruled this
life and the afterlife, surrounded by a multitude of gods.*

When life was short, scorched by the merciless sun.

CHAPTER ONE

In the cool shade of the courtyard, Senmut the plasterer was reasoning with his niece. She sat cross-legged and listened, but her slender shoulders were hunched in defiance.

'Ramose is a good man,' he was saying. 'He will care for you and provide well for your children. He is a respected stonecutter on the gang. You are lucky to have received an offer from someone like him.'

'I know this, Uncle,' said Meryt-Re quietly. 'But I have no desire to be his wife. Doesn't that count for anything?'

Senmut frowned. 'You are insolent, Meryt,' he commented, his voice rising slightly with anger. 'As you ask, the answer is yes – it does count for something. I can't force you to marry him. But it doesn't count for as much as you think.' He stood up and smoothed his linen kilt with his fingers, then stared at Meryt, batting away a fly.

Meryt-Re lowered her gaze and waited. There was more to come, she could tell. She steeled herself to hear it.

3

Senmut paced around the courtyard, then came to stand in front of her. 'You're thirteen,' he said. 'You'll soon be fourteen. I know you are still young, but my mother had given birth to me by your age. Until you marry, I'm responsible for you, and with another child on the way I have other things to worry about. Ramose will treat you well. You would be foolish to refuse. What makes you so ungrateful?'

'Uncle! I am not ungrateful, believe me,' protested Meryt-Re. 'I understand how much you have done for me. But ...' she trailed off, unable to find the words to justify how she felt.

Senmut crouched down again, nearer to Meryt-Re this time, and lowered his voice. 'You know what they say about you, Meryt, don't you?'

Meryt shook her head, even though she knew what he was going to say. Her uncle continued. 'They say you are under the power of Sekhmet. You see death before it happens. They say no good will ever come of you.'

It was exactly what she expected to hear, but Meryt's heart sank nevertheless. 'Sekhmet is not only the goddess of pestilence and destruction. She also brings healing,' she said in a low voice. 'It would not be so terrible to be under her power – if it were true, that is.'

'That is foolish talk, Meryt,' said Senmut. 'You know what such a rumour can achieve. If it spreads, the likes of Ramose will have no wish to marry you. You will be feared and shunned. Is that the life you wish for?'

Meryt-Re shook her head again. 'No, Uncle, that's

not what I want at all, believe me,' she said. She looked up. 'Please give me time. I will think about Ramose, I promise.'

Senmut was silent. Meryt was suddenly filled with fear, and clutched the amulet that she wore about her neck.

'You don't believe what people say, do you?' she asked him. 'I have only foreseen a death once. People exaggerate. You know that I wish no one any harm.'

'I know what you wish, Meryt,' said Senmut, his voice strained. 'But the gods may be stronger than a young woman's wishes.'

He rose and left the courtyard. Meryt-Re watched him go and fingered her amulet, one of the few items left to her by her father. It was in the shape of a scarab beetle, the creature that was born from a sphere of dung just as the great sun god Re rose as a sphere every morning. Meryt-Re believed it offered her the protection of the gods. In particular, she felt it imparted the warm touch of the sun god, for her name itself meant 'Beloved of Re'.

Even so, her position in Set Maat was precarious. She was dependent on her uncle's goodwill. With no parents of her own, the government made no provision for her. The village existed to house the craftsmen who built the royal tombs; they alone received a wage, which took the form of grain and other foodstuffs. With this they cared for unfortunate relatives as well as their immediate families; so, along with Senmut's children, wife and mother,

Meryt lived off his income. It was adequate – many families in the village were larger and lived on the same. But she knew her uncle well. He was fair, but not greatly generous, and the truth was that he had taken Meryt under his wing only because Tia, his wife, had insisted on it. He would be only too happy to pass her on to a husband. So, as far as he was concerned, Ramose's proposal was an opportunity to be grasped with both hands.

And as for the stories ... Did her uncle really believe them? Or was he simply prepared to use them as a lever against her? The thought made her shiver. She felt very alone.

She glanced up and saw Baki, peering down on to the courtyard from the roof. When Meryt caught his gaze, he gave a gleeful grin, and disappeared back over the edge. Meryt was furious. He had been listening! She knew Baki all too well.

'Baki!' she shouted, jumping to her feet. She leapt up the stairs from the courtyard and chased after her cousin, who was on the verge of leaping on to the roof of their neighbours' house. She caught him by his side-lock of hair just in time.

'Ramose! Ramose! You're going to marry Ramose!' he sang, then gave an enraged yell as Meryt-Re yanked on his hair.

'Don't you *dare* say that,' cried Meryt. She pulled his side-lock harder, so that Baki had to peer up at her sideways. 'Not here, not anywhere. If you say one word to *anyone* ...'

'You'll cast a spell on me?' taunted Baki. He cackled and wriggled around, out of Meryt's grasp. She pounced on him again and they wrestled, falling to the surface of the roof and rolling around in the dust.

Meryt grabbed Baki by the side-lock again, but Baki grasped both her wrists with all his strength and twisted his hands around, burning her skin. Breathless and determined, they clung on to each other. They had always been rivals, from the day that Meryt had entered the household at the age of two. Baki had been only one year old, but even then, his resentment of the new child had been clear.

Things were no better now. In fact, for Meryt they were worse. Although he was a year younger, Baki was getting stronger, and she was finding it difficult to hold her own in their fights. More importantly, as the oldest son, Baki would soon become his father's apprentice in the Great Place, where the kings' magnificent tombs were hewn deep in the limestone cliffs. It was going to his head. As the day of his manhood approached, he became more and more full of himself. And Meryt had nothing to balance against it, because she wasn't even Senmut's own daughter. She was a nobody, and she hated it.

'Yes!' she hissed in Baki's ear. 'I'll find a special curse just for you, if you breathe *one word*.'

Baki gave her wrists a vicious twist. Meryt yelped in pain, and tugged at his hair. They rolled around on the floor again, then Baki broke free and headed for the stairway.

'Wait till I tell Father!' he whooped, as he disappeared down the steps. 'You'll be in for it, Meryt!'

Meryt sat down on the roof, breathing hard. Sometimes she hated Baki with a passion that frightened her. She was often tempted to summon the wrath of the gods against him, but she held them in too much respect. Baki was his father's son, and that was no fault of his. She would do better to beg for an answer to her own predicament.

She stood up and brushed herself down, inspecting her bare brown skin for injuries under the dust. These days, her tussles with Baki were sure to leave her with some. Her right thigh and shoulder were smarting – there were new grazes where they had scraped across the rough surface of the roof. She ran lightly down the steps back into the courtyard and poured some water from one of the water jars on to her hands. She splashed it over her grazes, giving a little gasp as she felt them sting.

'What have you been doing to yourself, Meryt?' chided a voice. It was Naunakht, Senmut's mother. She came into the courtyard and sat down at the linen loom, which stood in one corner. 'Not fighting with Baki again, I hope.'

'No, Nauna,' lied Meryt. 'I tripped on the roof. It's nothing.'

Meryt reached for a rough piece of linen and hurriedly dried herself off. She had no desire to be quizzed by Naunakht. She felt uneasy around the older woman, sensing that Nauna resented her presence in

8

the household; after all, she even resented Tia, and was forever complaining about her daughter-in-law. So it was more than likely that she fuelled her son's desire to get Meryt out of the house. Nauna probably knew all about Ramose and his proposal; she might even have put him up to it. Before the older woman could say any more, Meryt fled through the house, out on to the street.

Senmut's house was situated on the main street, which led from north to south for almost the entire length of the village. Meryt walked south, past the rows of whitewashed houses, then followed the street as it zigzagged south-west. She came to a house that was slightly larger than most of the others, and knocked. The red door was open to allow the air to circulate in the heat, and Meryt peered in while she waited. The front room was empty, but she could hear the murmur of voices further into the shady mud-brick building.

'Dedi!' she called. 'Are you there?'

A beautiful girl appeared and beckoned Meryt inside. Meryt slipped through the door and followed Dedi through the remaining rooms of the house. She nodded a greeting to the three women who sat surrounded by a gaggle of children in the middle room. They were deep in discussion and barely noticed her, so she carried on after Dedi until they reached the courtyard and sunlight once more.

'We'll go up on to the roof,' said Dedi. 'I'm keeping out of the way at the moment.'

9

'Why?' asked Meryt curiously, as they climbed the steps to the roof. 'What's going on?'

'Our neighbour's newborn is dying,' explained Dedi. 'They are discussing how to save him. My mother thinks it's a curse. All three of Tanefru's children have died before their first birthday. She thinks that the goddess Sekhmet is plaguing the household.'

At the mention of Sekhmet, Meryt-Re shivered slightly. Her uncle Senmut's words were still very fresh. *They say you are under the power of Sekhmet ...* Then she pushed the thought to one side. It was all too easy to blame Sekhmet whenever events turned sour. The fearsome goddess was not of their village but of Men Nefer, far to the north, and Meryt's instincts told her that the reasons for things often lay closer to home.

'Tanefru should make an offering to Tawaret,' she said. 'She is there to help the newborn and their mothers. Surely it's more useful to call upon the gods who love us and wish us well than to talk of Sekhmet's curses.'

Dedi looked at her friend strangely. 'You sound like Teti,' she commented. 'That's the sort of thing she'd say.'

Meryt felt confused at this, and said nothing. The day's events were becoming difficult to fathom. There was the proposal from Ramose. There was Senmut's reminder that her reputation was becoming a danger. And now, her best friend was saying that she sounded like Teti, the village *rekhet*, the Knowing One.

The two girls sat down on a piece of reed matting in the shade, and Meryt decided to change the subject. 'Is your lyre up here?' she asked. 'May I play it for a while?'

Dedi shook her head. 'It's down in the storeroom,' she said. 'But I'll fetch it for you. I'll get the sistrum too.'

She scrambled to her feet and disappeared down the steps, leaving Meryt to stare out over the rooftops until she returned. She surveyed the scene. The afternoon heat was just past its peak; the sunlight was mellowing slightly, losing its harsh glare. On the neighbouring roofs, goats and sheep still lay in the shade, their sides fluttering in and out. Smoke from bread-baking ovens rose up in thin plumes in between the houses, then drifted away to the east. Two roofs away, there was a woman breastfeeding a young baby, and a toddler staggering around under her watchful eye, his naked skin golden brown in the sun. Meryt sighed, and stretched herself out on her stomach, waiting for Dedi to return.

Meryt loved and envied her friend Dedi in equal measure. They had known each other for years; they had met as small children, for Dedi's mother often bought the fine, soft linen woven by Tia. Then, they had just been two village girls, playing in the sun; it was only as they had grown older that their differences had become more apparent. Dedi was stunningly beautiful, and delighted everyone who looked at her – especially the young men, who whispered among themselves about her up on the rocks above the village. She was also the only daughter of Nebnufer, one of the two foremen in the Great Place. The foremen were chosen by the king's vizier himself and, as such, they were the most powerful men in the village.

Because of all this, Dedi's future was bright. She would soon be marrying Neben-Maat, the son of Sennedjem, the second foreman, and her status would then allow her to become a musician in the village temple-chapels. Her mother Wab already held this position, as befitted a foreman's wife, and had given her daughter instruments to practise on as she grew up. It was these that Dedi brought up the steps now. Meryt sat up as she approached.

'You took your time,' she said, with a smile.

'I was listening to the women. They are still at it,' said Dedi. She sat down and handed Meryt the lyre, laying the rattle-like sistrum across her own knees. 'They are talking about calling Teti, but also Harmose, the doctor. Tanefru's sister thinks they should call either one or the other but not both, for fear they should disagree. The others are trying to change her mind.'

'They might as well forget Harmose. He is useless with young children,' commented Meryt. 'He cares only about the men who work in the Great Place.'

Dedi smiled. 'Well, that's what he's paid for.'

'What is the child's problem?' asked Meryt. 'Is it fever?'

'He seems to have no will to live,' replied Dedi, with a shrug. 'He has barely taken his mother's milk. He cannot live long like that.'

'No,' agreed Meryt. She looked thoughtful. 'I think that sometimes the gods wish it that way. They summon a child to the next world before he can become too attached to this one.'

A look of apprehension passed over Dedi's face, and Meryt instantly regretted her words. A similar statement was at the root of her reputation. Earlier that year, a neighbour's child had been still-born a month or so too early. But her belly had stopped growing a month before that. Meryt had feared the worst, and had said as much in passing. When she was proved to be right, the rumours had begun to spread. Meryt-Re saw death before it happened – so could she not summon it too?

She smiled at her friend to reassure her, and picked up the lyre. 'Well, I hope they make their minds up soon, for the child's sake,' she said lightly, and began to pluck the strings. Dedi smiled too, and watched her, the sistrum idle in her lap. Neither friend ever talked of it, but the fact was that Meryt was a natural, and drew more beautiful melodies from the lyre than Dedi had ever been able to, despite her mother's training.

Meryt played through all the tunes she had learnt, and then stopped. She placed the lyre by her side and looked out over the rooftops. A donkey brayed close by. She thought of Ramose, and sighed.

'I have received a proposal of marriage,' she announced.

Dedi's eyebrows shot up. 'Meryt!' she exclaimed. 'Who from? Wait – let me guess – Kenna!'

It was Meryt's turn to look surprised. 'Kenna! Dedi, he's our friend!'

'So? He is more *your* friend. He always has been. Such friends can become lovers,' said Dedi confidently.

Meryt flushed. Dedi was much more versed in the ways of love and adulthood. She and Neben-Maat had courted each other for five years – since Dedi was only nine. They were only waiting for Neben to finish building a new house before they became man and wife.

'Well, it's *not* Kenna,' stated Meryt firmly.

Dedi warmed to her game and reeled off a list of names. Meryt shook her head at each one.

'Who, then?' cried Dedi at last, in frustration.

'Ramose,' said Meryt. 'Son of Paneb and Heria.'

Dedi looked puzzled. 'Ramose?' she repeated in wonderment. Meryt felt her heart grow heavy as she imagined what her friend was thinking. Ramose was quiet and solid, a plodding reliable stonecutter. Although only eighteen, he already showed the signs of too much bread and ale. 'Well, he's ...' Dedi trailed off awkwardly.

'Uncle Senmut wants to get rid of me,' Meryt said. 'He wants me to accept.'

'And are you going to?' asked Dedi cautiously.

'No!' cried Meryt. 'How am I ever going to join you as a chapel musician if I accept?'

Astonishment flooded Dedi's fine features all over again. 'But that can't really be what you expect,' she said. 'You would have to marry a scribe, at least – or a foreman! And a well-connected one at that.'

Meryt was silent. *Is that so impossible a notion?* she wanted to ask. But she knew the answer. Dedi hadn't meant to be hurtful. The chances of anyone of high status wanting to marry Meryt were slim. She had nothing to offer and she was only of average beauty.

She caressed the neck of the lyre longingly, then stood up.

'I'd better get back home,' she said. 'I'm supposed to be helping. You know what Nauna's like.'

The sound of Nauna's shrill voice was carrying along the street. Meryt's pace quickened as she approached her home, seeing that the neighbours were peering out in curiosity. She slipped inside and was met with a scene of chaos.

Her aunt Tia was sitting on the floor, crying. Henut, her three-year-old daughter, was clinging to her dress and weeping in harmony, while eight-year-old Mose sat nearby with his head buried in his arms. Nauna was shouting, waving two blackened loaves as she did so, while two neighbours chattered and interjected, inspecting another three loaves that were burnt a charcoal black.

'What is the use of a wife who burns the bread!'

Nauna was crying. 'My son deserves better than this. I deserve better than this, and look at the children. They have nothing but shame for their mother!"

Meryt stood in the doorway, aghast. Nauna spotted her. 'Take the children and comfort them,' she ordered her. 'Take them from this scene of shame!'

Meryt hurried to Mose and put her arm around his shoulder. 'Come, Mose,' she whispered. 'We'll play a good game on the roof.' Mose stood, his face wet and blotchy, and took Meryt's hand. Meryt reached out for Henut, but the little girl howled and clung fiercely to her mother.

'We'll eat some special dates,' Meryt promised her desperately. 'And a pomegranate.'

The tears dried quickly on Henut's face, an expression of greed taking their place. She left Tia's side and held out her grubby hand for Meryt to grasp. Meryt ushered the two children out of the room and through to the courtyard, as Nauna resumed her tirade. She picked out a ripe pomegranate from the fruit pile, and a handful of dates.

'Mama's been bad,' said Henut solemnly, as they climbed the steps.

'No, no, not bad,' Meryt assured the child, her anger with Nauna rising. 'Maybe she made a mistake. That's not bad, sweetheart. Everyone does that sometimes.'

'She left the bread in the oven too long,' said Mose.

'Do you know why, Mose?' asked Meryt, spreading

out a reed mat for them to sit on. Mose was a quiet, thoughtful boy, the opposite of his older brother Baki. He often spoke a surprising amount of sense for someone so young. She sat down, and the children curled up next to her.

'She doesn't know how it happened,' Mose informed her, as Meryt handed him a date. 'Nauna was next door. When she came back, she smelt the bread burning.' He paused, playing with the edge of the mat, his eyes averted. 'Mama says it was Peshedu,' he finished quietly.

Meryt looked at him sharply. 'Is that what she said? Are you sure?' she quizzed him.

Mose turned his honest gaze to Meryt's, and nodded.

Meryt frowned. Peshedu was her own father, and Tia's brother. He had died of the coughing disease when she was only two, leaving Meryt an orphan. Her mother Simut had died in childbirth at the age of fifteen. Meryt had been her first child. It was difficult for Meryt to picture this shadowy, girlish figure, only two years older than she was now, and she rarely thought of her. But Peshedu was different. For as long as Meryt could remember he had been a restless presence in the household – although, as she had grown older, she had come to realise that it was only Tia who sensed him on a regular basis.

It puzzled and worried Meryt. Her father should be enjoying life with the gods in the next world. She knew for a fact that no expense had been spared on his embalming and funeral, and that he lay in the family tomb surrounded by everything he needed. While she did not begrudge it for a moment, it was partly for this reason that Meryt had inherited so little. It made no sense that he had lingered – especially to cause trouble, as Tia often claimed he did. She was beginning to wonder what lay behind it all.

'I expect your mama said that because she was upset,' she said.

'I don't think so,' said Mose gravely. 'I think she meant it.'

Meryt bit into the pomegranate to break its skin, then peeled off a piece to reveal the juicy red fruit.

'I want first bit!' demanded Henut.

Meryt handed her a small section, and Henut took it eagerly, soon happily lost in breaking off the tiny segments, chomping them one by one, and spitting out the seeds.

'Why is Peshedu angry with Mama?' asked Mose.

Meryt felt uneasy. Mose's clear, childlike question echoed the niggling uncertainty in her own mind. 'I don't know, Mose,' she said. 'Maybe he isn't. Not really.'

Mose threw a date stone over the side of the roof. 'He makes her unhappy,' he commented. 'I don't like Mama being unhappy.'

Meryt was momentarily lost for words. She looked up as Tia came up the steps, her footsteps slow and subdued. Her unborn child was growing bigger and she seemed to tire more easily each day. She walked over to the mat and sat down next to them, pulling Henut to her and wrapping her arms around her. Henut wriggled and fed her a piece of pomegranate.

Tia laughed and chewed it, then spat out the seed.

Meryt met her eyes and smiled. 'Have things calmed down?' she asked quietly.

Tia nodded. 'Every wife has a mother-in-law to bear,' she said with a grimace.

But not a dead brother, thought Meryt. *You shouldn't have him to bear too.* She looked at Mose, who had quietly sidled up to Tia and was sitting with his head resting on her arm. It was difficult to read his expression, and Meryt decided to say nothing about Peshedu. She scrambled to her feet, suddenly feeling the need to escape.

'I'll be back to help later,' she said. 'I won't be long.'

Meryt-Re walked quickly to the south gate, where a member of the Medjay police force stood guard at the village wall. He was half asleep, and ignored her as she went past. She soon turned off the path and started up a stony track. The last heat of the sun hit her as she left the shade of the houses, and she followed the track slowly, past the entrances to disused tombs and up the hill that hid Set Maat from the Nile valley. With the tombs behind her, she picked her way carefully over the crumbling limestone to the top.

There, she had a view in all directions. She sat and hugged her knees, facing the River Nile that glittered in the distance to the east. The annual Nile flood had long since receded, leaving behind a rich layer of black silt that was chequered with irrigation channels. It was now the season of *peret*, the 'time of emergence', in which crops were sown and the first shoots poked up their heads. And so, on either side of the river, there was a band of fresh, bright green; but where there was no irrigation, the crops stopped abruptly. After that, there was only desert, where nothing could grow.

She watched as a line of men trudged towards Set Maat, driving donkeys before them that were laden with flagons of water from the river. Without the water-carriers, life in the village could not exist. This was a strange, barren place, a dry desert valley overshadowed by towering limestone cliffs. The cliffs offered a little shade, but otherwise the village had no protection from the scorching Egyptian sun.

Meryt closed her eyes and turned her face to the sun until she felt beads of sweat pricking on her forehead. She loved to do this, for it reminded her of the blessing within her own name: *Beloved of Re*. She imagined the sun-god travelling across the sky in his barque, having once more defeated Apep, the monster of darkness. She smiled, basking in warmth.

The sound of scrambling feet on the rocks made her open her eyes again. She sat still, wondering who could be coming up this lonely track. While Meryt came here often, she rarely encountered anyone else along the way. It was her own special retreat.

She stared as a small figure came into view, head bowed, muttering under her breath.

'Nofret!' called Meryt.

The girl jumped in fright, and stopped. She was perhaps a year younger than Meryt, but seemed younger still. She was a servant girl and had arrived in the village three years earlier, purchased by one of the workmen. Meryt did not know her well, but she saw her often enough, and she had noticed that the younger girl had been looking miserable lately. She had a furtive look, and Meryt had sometimes seen her curled up on her own in shady places.

'How are you?' asked Meryt.

'Why do you ask?' responded Nofret warily.

'I wondered if something was troubling you,' suggested Meryt. 'You don't smile the way you used to.'

Nofret stared at her. 'You don't know anything,' she said defensively, backing away a few steps.

'No. Only that you are unhappy,' said Meryt. 'I am curious, that's all.'

Nofret seemed confused by Meryt's words, and then she backed away further. 'There's nothing wrong,' she muttered. 'I'm fine.'

Meryt-Re shrugged. 'If you say so,' she said.

She looked out towards the Nile again, over the grand mortuary temples. Their brilliant colours were beginning to glow in the late-afternoon sun, and she shaded her eyes. Nofret still stood nearby, watching her. Meryt turned and looked at her again.

'Have you come to sit up here too? Or are you going somewhere?' she asked, wondering what the younger girl was after.

Nofret seemed flustered by the question. 'I'm going … yes, I just came here to sit.'

Uneasily, she perched on a rock, and the two girls lapsed into silence. *She's lying*, Meryt-Re said to herself. *But I can't think why*.

The sun sank lower, and Meryt-Re turned around to face the limestone cliffs that overshadowed the village. They shifted in colour throughout the day, starting golden-pink in the light of dawn, changing to shimmering yellows and whites in the heat of the day, and developing deep orange-gold shadows as the sun moved round behind them to the west. The pattern never changed, except that in winter a few wispy clouds sometimes stretched themselves out across the sky. Rarer still, they released a sprinkling of rain, but the drops dried almost before they hit the ground.

Meryt-Re had heard of other lands where the clouds formed black and angry battalions and the rain lashed the ground in fury, but this might not be true. Who could believe the words of the travelling traders? They were too fond of the tales they told. She gazed as the shadows inched across the valley and imagined water from the sky upon her face.

How strange, how wonderful!

She stood up and smiled at Nofret, who still sat watching her, waiting … for what? For Meryt-Re to go, she was sure.

'Are you coming back down?' asked Meryt.

Nofret shifted on her rock, looking guilty. 'No – no. I'm going to stay and sit for a while.'

Meryt-Re shrugged, smiling, and set off down the track, humming to herself. She reached the disused cemetery again. The ancestors lying here dated from a time that was all but forgotten – from the era of the village founders, the deified king Amenhotep I and his mother Ahmes Nefertari. The mud-brick chapels that stood over the tombs were falling into disrepair, and some had even been dismantled by the villagers for their bricks. Meryt-Re ducked behind one of them, and peered back up the hillside.

She could just see the top of Nofret's head, sitting where Meryt had left her. Then the servant girl stood up, and Meryt flattened herself against the chapel wall, expecting her to soon pass by on the track. She waited. After a few minutes, there were no footsteps and Meryt peered out again. She frowned in surprise. Nofret had disappeared.

So Nofret was heading away from the village via the winding hilltop track that few people used. It was growing late. The sun would soon set. The servant girl was a funny little thing, but this behaviour was odd, all the same. She shouldn't be leaving the village at this hour, especially not by herself. And wherever she was going, she didn't want Meryt-Re to know about it.

But Meryt-Re knew only too well that nothing could remain a secret in Set Maat for long …

 CHAPTER TWO

With the shadows lengthening, Meryt made her way back home reluctantly. Senmut and Baki would be home for the evening meal, and the chances were very high that Baki would have stirred up trouble. Nauna's mood would still be ugly; Tia would be nervous and jumpy. But there was nowhere else to go, and besides, she had promised to do her share of the chores.

'Meryt-Re, come here,' Senmut ordered her, as soon as she stepped inside. 'I want to speak to you.'

Meryt followed him into the front room, but not before catching a glimpse of Baki in the courtyard. He grinned at her and pulled a face.

'What is it, Uncle?' she asked, dread rising inside her as she registered the anger in his eyes.

'You have been threatening Baki,' said Senmut in a low, furious voice. 'You have been speaking the unthinkable in my house. What kind of person brings curses into the house that shelters her?'

'I didn't mean what I said, Uncle,' said Meryt. 'I didn't curse him. I was just teasing. Baki heard you talking about Ramose –'

'Yes! Ramose! There is only one answer, Meryt,' shouted Senmut. 'You will marry him and leave my household in peace!'

Meryt felt her insides go cold. 'You promised me time, Uncle,' she managed to say. 'Please give me that. Baki is a troublemaker …'

Senmut's face darkened further. Meryt began to tremble. Any minute now, her uncle would snap, and strike her.

'Baki is my son,' he thundered. 'You will not speak of him like that, and you will show him the respect that is due to him. Do you hear?'

Senmut turned his back and paced the room for a moment. 'And I will speak to Paneb and Heria in the morning. The arrangements with Ramose will be made. The sooner the better.'

'I will not marry Ramose against the will of the goddess!' gasped Meryt, clutching at straws. 'You cannot make me do that, Uncle!'

Senmut spun around and faced her. He stared at her. 'Which goddess?' he demanded.

'Our goddess Ahmes Nefertari,' stammered Meryt, holding Senmut's gaze despite the thumping of her heart. 'She knows the life of the village, doesn't she? I must ask her if this is her will.'

Senmut looked at Meryt warily, and smoothed his hands over his kilt. His eyebrows were furrowed in a scowl, but Meryt detected something other than anger in his black eyes. She realised with a jolt that it was fear.

'Consult the goddess then,' he muttered. 'Keep further harm from our family.'

Meryt thought quickly. Ahmes Nefertari was not a vengeful goddess but, with her son Amenhotep, she was an arbiter of justice. Meryt did not want to bring fear or judgement into the house. She would do better to consult the goddess Hathor, who was concerned with matters of love and happiness and had never been known to pour wrath on the villagers.

'I will consult Hathor instead, if you prefer,' she offered.

To Meryt's relief, Senmut's features softened. 'Very well. Very well.' He nodded in satisfaction before raising his voice again. 'But be sure to understand that this cannot go on, Meryt. You will respect my son and respect our household. There will be no ill deeds under my roof.'

'Thank you, Uncle,' said Meryt. 'I will do as you say.'

She darted out of the room and went through to the courtyard, where the rest of the family were gathered. She ignored Baki, who was capering around in glee, and sat down next to Tia to help her chop vegetables. Naunakht was gutting three fish, throwing their innards to the two pet cats that appeared out of the shadows to beg. She was clearly still irritable, and snapped at little Henut for getting under her feet. Henut retreated to Tia, glaring resentfully at the older woman, until her attention strayed to the cats and she chased after them, giggling.

27

'How much longer?' asked Senmut, appearing in the doorway. 'I'm as hungry as Ammut the devourer.'

'About an hour,' said Tia. 'Maybe less.' She shot a nervous glance at Nauna, who nodded briefly.

Senmut stepped into the courtyard and picked up a jar of beer and a strainer. 'Pass me a cup, Baki.'

Baki obliged, and held it for his father as he poured out the gloopy ale. The strainer soon filled with residue – lumps of soggy barley bread – which Senmut fed to the family goat. He took the cup from Baki and swigged noisily, then noticed the pile of blackened loaves in the corner. 'What happened to the bread?' he asked.

Meryt saw Tia flinch. She raised her head. 'I burnt it,' she admitted miserably, her shoulders hunched and tense.

But despite Nauna's constant complaints, Senmut was not given to chiding his wife. It was one of his better qualities. He bent and touched her arm. 'These things happen,' he said. 'And we are lucky that it happened at a good time. We don't need to make any offerings or gifts tomorrow. Or the day after.'

But Meryt saw that guilt was still etched on Tia's face, all the same.

The meal was a subdued affair. The family ate in a circle on the floor, mopping up the fish stew with hunks of the lesser-burnt bread. Meryt ate little, trying to avoid drawing attention to herself. As soon as she could, she lit a lamp from the embers of the bread oven and slipped away up on to the roof, hoping that Baki would not follow and pester her.

For once, he did not. Meryt placed the lamp by the edge of the roof, where the mud-brick wall sheltered the flame from the wind. She sat for a few moments lost in thought, watching the lighted wick flicker in the oil. Then she crossed the roof and uncovered a little pile of ostraca, or limestone flakes. Next to them lay an old scribe's palette that had once belonged to her father, Peshedu – two little blocks of pigment, red and black, in a wooden base. With it were a papyrus brush and a little water pot.

Peshedu had been a sculptor, not a scribe, but along with many men in the village he had received a little schooling. If he had lived, he might have paid for Meryt to have some instruction too, for she was his only child. But as it was, Senmut would not dream of such an indulgence. Hori, the scribe who lived two doors down, held classes for boys who were not the sons of scribes; but only at a price. Baki had not studied for long and had quickly moved on to learning his father's art of plastering. Little Mose, on the other hand, loved learning his letters, and with Tia's encouragement, Senmut sent him to Hori whenever he had some spare grain. But Meryt only knew what she had managed to glean from Mose.

She selected a nice flat ostracon about the size of her palm and, with the palette and brush, took it back to the circle of light around the lamp. She pulled the stopper from the water pot and moistened the black block, then filled the brush with ink. Carefully, she drew the face of a woman – but not just any woman. This woman's ears pointed out, like those of a cow, and a heavy wig curled into her neck as far as her shoulders.

Above the face, Meryt drew the hieroglyphic symbols that spelt out the goddess's name. *Hathor*. Then, in one corner, she drew the little image of a man wearing a linen kilt, his face turned towards the goddess. She waited for the ink to dry, then tilted her completed drawing into the lamplight and studied it. Smiling in satisfaction at her work, she picked it up and, with the lamp in her other hand, headed back down the stairs.

Naunakht had already retired to bed in the back room, while Senmut and Tia sat together in the middle room, talking in low voices. Henut was asleep, cuddled up to Tia, and Baki was absorbed in a round of the board game *senet* with Mose. Only Tia looked up briefly as Meryt slipped quietly through to the front room.

This room had a large raised altar-bed in one corner, which was where Tia gave birth. There were five niches in its walls. Meryt went to one of them and brought out a little packet of incense, wrapped carefully in linen. It was her own personal supply and she treasured it, only using it on special occasions. From the same niche, she brought out a copper incense burner and carefully placed some of the precious substance inside it.

She looked around the room. The largest niche, above the altar-bed, had in it an engraving of Bes, the grotesque lion-maned dwarf who protected women through childbirth. In the next one there was an image of the god Ptah, Senmut's favourite, for he was the patron of craftsmen. There was another across the room that contained an engraving of Tawaret, the half-hippopotamus, half-crocodile goddess who also cared for women and children in their homes. In the last niche stood a bust of Peshedu, Meryt's father, to whom Tia made regular offerings.

Meryt approached this niche and balanced her own little ostracon against the bust. Then, with the wick from the lamp, she lit the incense and knelt before the niche.

'I give praise to you, Hathor, Lady of Heaven, Mistress of all the Gods,' she murmured, swinging the incense burner. 'May life, prosperity, health be yours. I turn to you as your humble servant, Meryt-Re, daughter of Peshedu and Simut. Answer my prayer: must I marry Ramose against my will?'

She repeated the prayer seven times, wafting the burner gently to and fro and breathing in the heady scent. Then she sat in silence as the incense burnt out, leaving nothing but a few blackened scraps. Meryt put the burner away, then picked up the lamp and the ostracon and padded back through the house and up on to the roof once more. The colder end of the year was approaching and the desert nights were growing cool, but it was still just warm enough to sleep out. Meryt lay on one of the reed mats and pulled a linen sheet over her, then lay staring at her ostracon in the darkness.

She had never made such a request before. Of course, she had made offerings to the gods and her father out of respect, along with everyone else, and the presence of the god Re had warmed her for as long as she could remember. But she had never needed to ask anything of this nature, and she was unsure what would happen next. She thought for a few moments, then placed the ostracon near her head. Perhaps it would be in her dreams that the goddess would answer her.

The night was still. Meryt could hear the murmur of voices from the surrounding houses, and the yelp of a dog, somewhere down towards the river valley. At the far end of the village someone was throwing a party, and the strains of music and laughter floated over the rooftops. Meryt lay and looked up at the stars, mulling over the day's events.

A voice broke into her thoughts, calling from the street below.

'Meryt!'

Meryt threw off the sheet and got up to peer over the wall. It was her friend Kenna who stood there, grinning and staring up at her. 'Kenna! What is it?' she whispered.

'I am going to trade some grain for my father in the morning,' he told her. 'We are having guests tomorrow night, and he wants me to exchange it for some extra fish in the market. Will you come with me?'

'I'd love to!' exclaimed Meryt. 'Are you leaving early?'

'Just after dawn,' said Kenna. 'Father says we can take the donkey. I'll come and wake you.'

Meryt grinned and nodded. 'See you then.'

A noisy gaggle of geese flying overhead woke Meryt before Kenna returned. She sat up and looked to the east, where the pink light of dawn was spreading. Meryt waited for the first glimmer of sunlight before standing to stretch and yawn. As she did so, she caught sight of her ostracon, and frowned. She racked her brains for images, but no – there was nothing. Her sleep had been dreamless. Meryt swallowed her disappointment and ripped off a piece of linen from the sheet. She was wrapping it around the ostracon when she heard Kenna's voice, calling softly from below.

'Coming!' she called back, and hastily hid the ostracon under the mats in the corner. Then she skipped silently down the steps and into the courtyard. She took a hunk of bread and two leeks from the store, then hurried through the house, where the rest of the family still lay sleeping.

Kenna was sitting astride his father's donkey. He grinned at Meryt and grabbed her elbow as she hoisted herself up lightly behind him. Kenna tapped the donkey with a stick and they set off at a trot, taking the main street to the northern gate of the village, then the wide road that led down to the grand mortuary temples of the plain.

Once away from the village, Meryt began to relax. Trips to the market were always fun, especially with Kenna, who had been a friend from the day when Meryt had been chased up the street by a maddened dog at the age of six. Kenna, then nine, had shooed the creature off with a big stick, and Meryt had been awed by his bravery. Kenna was now sixteen. As the fourth son in his family, he could not become his father's apprentice and learn the craft of carpentry in the tombs. He had picked up a few skills, but essentially he had no craft of his own. He ran messages to and from the tombs and the village, did general odd jobs for his family, and made little sets of the game *senet*. His uncertain future didn't seem to concern him, for he was always easy-going and sunny; but Meryt was becoming aware that his father felt differently. She worried for her friend sometimes.

They passed near the walls of the massive temple of Ramesses II, which shone in brilliant hues in the morning sun, the paintwork still relatively unaffected by the sands that blew across the valley. Following the temple canals, they rode on to the temple of Amenhotep III, one of the oldest on the plain, and beyond, down to the river.

The early morning market was already in full swing. Kenna and Meryt dismounted and wandered along on foot, looking at what was on offer. Some women sat selling produce from gardens – much in demand until the main crop was harvested; others offered reams of fine linen and clothing. The date harvest had begun and mounds of the mud-gold fruit lay everywhere, graded according to quality.

The sight made Meryt hungry and she offered Kenna some of her coarse brown bread. Kenna looked at it in disgust.

'What happened to that?'

'Tia burnt it,' said Meryt, with a giggle. 'Have some. It's tasty, anyway.'

She ripped off a piece and handed it to him. Kenna took it and chewed it, grimacing. Meryt laughed at him, and handed him a leek. They ate a mouthful of each in turn, heading for the area where the fishermen sat with baskets of their shining catch.

Kenna waved as they approached. Two of the fishermen were well known in Set Maat. They visited often, because they were employed by the government to supply the villagers with a weekly ration of fish, which formed part of the craftsmen's wages. Once the fishermen had enough for the ration, they were free to sell whatever else they caught.

The two men shook their heads as Kenna and Meryt approached. 'Go away,' said one, with a grin. 'We haven't caught enough yet. We're just heading out in the boats again.'

Kenna laughed. 'Go on,' he said. 'I only want six.'

'Six!' The fisherman shook his head in mock

dismay. 'Well, as it's you …'

He tipped his basket so that Kenna could see inside. Kenna picked out six of the biggest with an expert eye, and handed over his grain for the man to measure out his payment.

'What's the news from the east bank, and the north?' Kenna asked him, as the man measured out enough grain, handed back the surplus and wrapped the fish in fronds of fresh papyrus.

'Another of the king's sons died last week,' said the fisherman. 'That's what I heard. That's two in the last month. They'll all be coming down for the funerals – the king and half the court.'

'Must be good for business,' Kenna commented.

The fisherman shrugged. 'I don't see that end of things, Kenna,' he said. He smiled. 'I still have to catch the right amount of fish whatever happens. You're the hoity-toity lot who get all the bonuses.'

Kenna looked slightly embarrassed. He placed the fish and the remainder of the grain in his bag. It was true that the families of Set Maat were better off than most, for the craftsmen's work was valued highly by the king, and their wages reflected that. In the eyes of the peasants who farmed the land or fished in the river, they were rich. 'Bonuses from the king are good for everyone in the long run,' he said. 'We come and buy your surplus, don't we?'

'True, true,' laughed the fisherman. 'You have to look on the bright side.'

Slinging his bag over the donkey's withers, Kenna

turned to Meryt. 'I've some grain left over. Let's buy some dates.'

With a big handful of dates each, they began to lead the donkey back towards the village. When they reached the temple of Amenhotep III, they decided to rest for a while. The king's shrine was now neglected, as he faded from people's memory; so the area around this temple was often deserted. Kenna hobbled the donkey and they sat in the shade of the temple walls to finish the dates.

'So what's your news?' asked Kenna, idly throwing the date stones at a pecking hoopoe. 'Any gossip?'

Meryt bit into another date, not sure how to answer. A strange feeling crept over her. There was, of course, the proposal from Ramose, but she held back from speaking of it. Dedi's strange suggestion about Kenna came back to her and she found herself blushing. *Such friends can become lovers ...*

'Nothing much,' she said.

'I don't believe it,' said Kenna, with a laugh. 'There's always plenty of gossip to report.' He looked at her quizzically.

'Tanefru's newborn is sick,' said Meryt hurriedly, for something to say.

Kenna leant back against the temple wall. 'Another sick child. This is nothing new.'

'True.' Meryt leant back beside him, and they lapsed into silence. Another hoopoe flew down to join its mate, making a flutter of its brilliant feathers as it landed. Meryt watched it, thinking about Ramose, and her devotional ostracon. She wondered how long it would take the goddess to answer her. A few days? A few weeks? It was impossible to know.

A movement caught her eye, and she looked up. She nudged Kenna. 'Look. It's Nofret,' she whispered.

Nofret was scurrying past the temple, and seemed to be making her way towards the river. Her head was bowed, and it was clear that she hadn't seen them.

'I caught her heading out of the village last night, on her own,' said Meryt. 'She wouldn't say where she was going.'

Kenna snorted. 'It's no big secret,' he said. 'Userkaf has hired her out, that's all. How come you didn't know?'

'Hired her out?' demanded Meryt-Re. 'Who to? Someone outside the village?'

Kenna nodded. 'She's working as a servant girl in the embalmers' workshops in the Fields of Djame.'

'The Fields of Djame!' Meryt was astonished. The Fields surrounded the great mortuary temple of King Ramesses III, and as such were part of the main administrative centre for this side of the river. The king himself would be embalmed there, and in the meantime it was wealthy officials and royalty who kept the embalmers busy. 'How ever did Userkaf manage that?'

'You know what he's like,' said Kenna, with a

shrug. 'He's always done things differently. He's ambitious, and makes friends in high places. He probably knows the chief embalmer or something.'

It was true. Userkaf was a vibrant character in the village, a draughtsman by trade but an unlikely one: his flamboyant behaviour was at odds with the fine concentration and precision required in his work. He was fond of wine and beer and was always first to appear at parties. Rumour had it that he was fond of other men's wives too, but that was harder to prove.

'But she looks so nervous all the time,' commented Meryt. 'She's been miserable for weeks.'

'You would be too,' said Kenna. 'The embalmers' workshops are gruesome places. They're filled with the stench of flesh and natron and sickly incense and balms. It's a messy business.'

Meryt-Re wasn't convinced. There was no need for the girl to be so miserable, just because of her workplace. 'Well, perhaps,' she agreed, doubtfully. 'But if that's the problem, her step should lighten when she leaves.'

The sun was rising higher in the sky. Its heat was intensifying, so Meryt and Kenna clambered back on to the donkey and trotted up to Set Maat before the fish could begin to rot. There, they went to their separate homes.

The smell of burning incense greeted Meryt as soon as she stepped inside: the smell of an offering in the first room. Tia was there, alone, burning incense before the bust of Peshedu. She jumped when she heard Meryt, and turned guiltily.

'I'm just …' she started, then trailed off, swinging the burner nervously.

Meryt moved into the room and squatted by her aunt. 'Is Peshedu troubling you?' she asked.

Tia nodded. 'It was he who burnt the bread yesterday,' she told Meryt. 'I had only left it for the usual amount of time. I am trying to appease him. Baki has his ritual next weekend – I should hate there to be any trouble.'

Meryt frowned. Much as she hated Baki, she could not see any reason why Peshedu should interfere with his rite of passage to manhood. 'Why would my father make trouble for Baki?' she asked. 'I thought he was a good man. You have always told me he was.'

'Oh!' said Tia hurriedly. 'You need not fear about that. Peshedu *was* a good man. I loved him so much – he could not have been a better brother to me. He …' she trailed off again, her voice trembling. She stood, and gained control of herself. 'We just need to keep him happy, that's all,' she said firmly. 'When I neglect him, he quickly reminds me of his presence.'

The subject was clearly closed. Tia went out to the courtyard and Meryt followed her, puzzled. Her aunt sat down at the loom and started to weave, an expression of determined concentration on her face. Meryt picked up a handful of flax strands from the pile in the corner of the courtyard. She sat down next to Tia and began to tease them into thread with the spindle. The two worked in silence for a while.

'Where is everyone?' asked Meryt, when she grew bored.

'Henut is sleeping,' Tia answered her. 'Mose went with Nauna to deliver the kilts to Harmose's wife. They'll be back later.'

Weaving and sewing provided the family with extra income, and, like Dedi's mother, Wab, Harmose the doctor could easily afford an extra kilt or two. Meryt enjoyed joining in with the whole process, for it made her feel less of a burden on the household.

'Senmut has gone to work,' continued Tia. 'He has taken Baki with him. They are staying over at the tomb huts until the weekend. Senmut wants to make sure that Baki is ready for the ritual.'

Meryt nodded, and concentrated on the spinning, thinking of Baki. The ritual he would undergo was welcomed and dreaded in equal measure by boys of his age. Their side-lock was shaved off, to allow a full head of hair to grow in its place; but far more painful was circumcision, the removal of the foreskin, an operation carried out by a priest of Amen-Re. Meryt shuddered to think of it. She was glad that girls did not have to suffer anything similar – apart from childbirth, of course.

She worked steadily for an hour, then she and Tia ate some bread and lay down in the cool of the back room to sleep through the midday heat. Before doing so, Meryt went and fetched her ostracon, and laid it next to her head.

Tia looked at it curiously. 'What's that?' she asked.

Meryt showed her the painting and Tia studied it thoughtfully. 'It's the goddess Hathor,' explained Meryt. 'I am consulting her about Ramose.'

Tia nodded, and Meryt realised she did not know her aunt's view on the matter; so her next words came as a surprise. 'Whatever happens, you will always have a place here – if I can help it,' said Tia quietly.

Meryt was astonished, and touched. She smiled at her aunt. 'Thank you, Tia,' she murmured. 'But I know such a thing is out of your hands.'

'Perhaps not so much as you might think,' said Tia, with a little jut of her jaw. 'But we shall see.'

They lay down, and Meryt stroked the ostracon gently before dozing off. *Send me a message, my goddess*, she thought, as sleep overcame her.

This time she dreamt. She was looking out through a window to the rocky hillside above the village – the Peak of the West, home of the snake goddess Meretseger. There was a figure standing there, his kilt billowed by a strong, hot wind blowing in from the desert. He turned and toiled up the narrow path that led over the cliffs to the Great Place, his lean body curled against the sand-filled blasts. In her dream Meryt left the window and struggled after him, calling, but the wind whipped away her words and the figure battled on ahead of her. She knew it was her father, Peshedu, but he seemed forever beyond her reach.

She paused to gasp for breath. Then, as she looked up to see how far he had progressed, she saw another figure descending the path in the opposite direction. He was wrapped in a linen shawl to protect him from the wind and sand, but Meryt recognised him nonetheless. It was Ramose.

Her father stopped. The men greeted each other, and they embraced. Then, as Meryt began her pursuit once more, Ramose turned in his tracks and accompanied her father, using his linen shawl to wrap around them both as they hurried on, back to the Great Place ...

Meryt woke, her heart pounding. She sat upright and stared at the ostracon. It lay there innocently, giving nothing away. She looked around the room, which was quiet but for Tia's gentle breathing. Her mouth dry, she rose and went out to the courtyard for a drink of water. As she lifted the cup to her lips, she realised that her hand was trembling.

Was this a message? She had no way of knowing, but the dream had been so vivid, unlike the usual jumble of images. If it was, what was Peshedu doing with Ramose? Was her father answering her prayer on behalf of the goddess? Was he trying to say that he approved their marriage? Meryt felt cold and desolate. What other meaning could the dream suggest? Could she really trust the appearance of Peshedu, when Tia was so sure that he was the troublemaker in their household ...? Meryt did not wish to believe such a thing of her own father, but now she found herself hoping it was true.

She decided to head to her favourite spot, up on the limestone hill that overlooked the Nile. She hurried through the village, her head bowed, and didn't see a figure approaching in the opposite direction. She cannoned into him.

'Meryt-Re!' he exclaimed.

Meryt looked up. 'Ramose,' she managed to say.

For an instant, their eyes locked and they gazed at each other. Meryt took in his plump, solid frame, his heavy jowls that were furred with two days' stubble, and his dull, doe-like eyes. It was too much. Instinctively, she took flight and ran.

'Meryt!' Ramose called after her. 'Wait! I would like to talk to you ...'

But Meryt didn't stop. Gasping for breath, she ran until she reached the edge of the village, only slowing to pick her way between the yellow-white boulders of the hillside. She reached the top and flopped down on to a boulder, almost crying with exertion and distress. She buried her head in her lap.

Slowly, she grew calmer. Her fate was not yet sealed. The goddess seemed to have sent her a dream, but its meaning was by no means clear. Her heart lightened as another interpretation occurred to her – that her father had turned Ramose in his tracks, and was taking him away from her ... it was so far impossible to say. She must wait. If the goddess had spoken to her once, she would surely do so again.

She sat in the sunlight, throwing limestone

44

pebbles from one hand to the other, her golden skin lightened by the white dust. It was peaceful here, with a gentle warm wind blowing and the view of the Nile valley stretching out below. It was where she always came if she was troubled. She wished she could stay longer, but she realised that the hour was getting late, and that Tia would be expecting help. She stood up and had just started to descend when a small figure appeared behind her, leaping down the path, scattering stones in front of her.

Meryt stopped. 'Nofret!' she greeted her.

Nofret stopped too, and gave a hostile glare. 'Why do you keep appearing wherever I go?' she hissed. 'Are you following me?'

Meryt-Re was taken aback. 'Of course not,' she protested. 'I came up here anyway. I was just going back.' She hunted for something else to say. 'I hear you have a job in the royal embalmers' workshops.'

'And what if I do?' asked Nofret defiantly. She started walking down the path again, and tried to push past Meryt-Re.

'Don't go,' said Meryt. She reached out to touch the other girl's arm, but Nofret shied away from her. The path was narrow, and she slipped sideways on to a boulder, crying out as she fell.

Something dropped from her hand and Meryt picked it up. It was a small object, with rough linen wrappings that had begun to unravel. Meryt could see clearly what it was. She gasped as Nofret scrambled to her feet and snatched it back from her furiously.

'Nofret …' exclaimed Meryt, horrified.

She stared at the younger girl and Nofret stared back, fear filling her eyes as she saw Meryt's reaction. The package contained an amulet, a charm for protection from the gods. It was an *udjat* eye, the symbol of the great god Horus who had fought and defeated his evil brother Seth. Horus had lost an eye in the battle, but it had been restored by Thoth, the ibis-headed god of scribes. Ever since, the *udjat* eye had been a powerful symbol of sacrifice and healing.

But this was no ordinary *udjat* amulet. It was made of pure gold, inlaid with precious lapis lazuli and glass. A priceless object … the sort used by embalmers to protect the body of a high official or even a king, inserted in among the swathes of linen that were wrapped around the body.

Meryt went cold. She felt as though the light of the sun had left them; the shadow of Re's disapproval chilled her heart. Embalmers' amulets were sanctified, destined for the land of the dead.

'The gods …' breathed Meryt. 'You are risking the wrath of the gods.'

Nofret's eyes widened in terror. She stared at Meryt-Re, speechless. Then, before Meryt could stop her, she turned and ran headlong down the path.

CHAPTER THREE

Meryt-Re followed Nofret down the path, her mind reeling. Why would anyone risk such a thing? It didn't make sense. She wondered if the loss of the amulet had been noted. It was just about possible that it had not, if it had already been placed among the linen wrappings around a body; but in any case, how could Nofret have accessed a wrapped body, and tampered with it unnoticed? The embalming of kings and officials was a meticulous process, with every stage recorded and every jewel accounted for by stern-faced scribes. But Nofret was only a servant girl …

Then Meryt recalled that Nofret had been heading *away* from the village the night before, as the sun was setting. She must have been going back, once the workers had left. Surely this was not a plan of her own making? Nofret seemed a wary, fearful creature, and had definitely become more so in the last few weeks. Someone had put her up to it, and the obvious culprit was her owner, Userkaf.

There still seemed little sense in such a risky

action. Amulets held great power – especially an *udjat* eye such as this – but it was surely beyond a man like Userkaf to make use of it. In any case, as she and Kenna had discussed only that morning, Userkaf was already popular and well connected. He was never short of offers of beer from his colleagues, and as a draughtsman, his skills were always in demand. He could command high prices for moonlighting for other villagers, for officials elsewhere, in fact for anyone who could afford to have their tomb decorated in the royal style. Userkaf lacked for nothing, and would surely not wish to bring the wrath of either the village or the gods upon his head. He got into enough trouble as it was with his riotous ways!

Meryt slipped back into the village and walked up the main street to her home. Nofret had long since vanished. She remembered with relief that Senmut and Baki were away working in the royal tombs, and that there would be relative peace in the household for a few days. The men were supposed to work an eight-day week with two days' break at the end, but frequently found excuses to make the week shorter, or to return on some kind of pretext halfway through. If Senmut was training Baki, they might actually stay away for as long as they had intended.

Tia was working away on the loom once more, while Nauna had returned and had taken Meryt's place with the flax and spindle. Their row of the day before appeared to have simmered down, and Tia smiled as Meryt entered.

'This will soon be big enough for a kilt,' she said, indicating the cloth on the loom. 'Then I'll be able to make Henut a winter dress.'

'Dress for me?' piped up Henut, who was in the process of smearing charcoal all over her podgy body. 'A pretty one?'

'Yes, a pretty one,' Tia smiled at her.

Such an everyday scene made Meryt feel more at ease, as though the strange events of the last two days were somehow unreal. 'I'll take over, if you like,' she said to Nauna. 'You can take a break.'

Nauna nodded, and got to her feet. 'Don't tangle the thread,' she said gruffly, handing the spindle to Meryt.

'Of course not,' Meryt replied politely, used to Nauna's ungraciousness. The fact was that Nauna's eyesight was not as sharp as it had once been, and if anyone tangled the thread, she did – but it didn't do to point out such things. Nauna's wrath was best left unkindled.

Meryt sat cross-legged and lost herself in the work, letting thoughts of recent events wash over her. She thought again of her dream, and her encounter with Ramose ... she relived the memory of his chubby body and his gasp of surprise as she ran into him. She wondered if she should tell Tia, but then decided against it. She would stick to her resolve, and wait for further guidance. She bent over the spindle.

The evening was drawing in when Meryt heard the sound of wailing go up, somewhere in the south-west of the village. She sat upright and listened. There was no mistaking it: the piercing cry of a mother and her friends and family as death visited a household. It was an all-too-familiar sound in Set Maat, but this time Meryt knew with certainty where it was coming from. It was as though a voice spoke clearly in her head: *Tanefru's newborn has died.*

She put down the spindle and hurried out of the house, making her way to Dedi's home. As she drew near, it became clear that she was right. A crowd of women had gathered around the house next door, and from inside came the shrieking and moaning of the newly bereaved. Dedi and her mother, Wab, would be somewhere among them, Meryt was sure.

She spotted Dedi just inside Tanefru's house, and went to her side. Together they joined in the chorus of stricken wailing that filled the house and the street outside. Meryt clutched the amulet around her neck and wept. It was easy to find tears for another villager's loss, for everyone had experienced similar pain at some stage. Meryt wept for her parents, the neighbour's stillborn whose death she had foreseen, and her own predicament as much as for Tanefru's tragedy.

Darkness came and the wailing slackened off. It would rise again, formally, once the child was wrapped and taken to the family tomb for burial; then, if they had the money, Tanefru's family might even employ professional mourners to give a resounding farewell. But for now, the sorrowing friends and neighbours went to their respective families to see to their needs, and to eat.

Meryt and Dedi went back to Dedi's home and sat in the front room. Dedi went and fetched a lamp from the courtyard, and the two girls sat in silence.

'You were right,' said Dedi, after a while. 'The gods required the newborn's life.'

Meryt nodded, uncertain what to say.

'You see these things,' said Dedi, in a low voice, staring at her friend. 'Are you not afraid of such a gift? Does it not come from Sekhmet?'

Meryt shook her head vehemently. The idea that people might come to see her as different because of a few casual words filled her with fear. 'Believe me, Dedi, I am just like anyone else. When I need help I turn to our goddess Ahmes Nefertari, or to Hathor. I wish no one any harm.'

Dedi smiled gently. 'I believe you,' she said. 'I know you well enough. But others may not always be so ready to understand. You must be careful what you say.'

The wick sputtered in the oil, and Meryt watched in silence as Dedi tweaked it with a pair of copper tongs. Dedi sighed.

'The truth is I sometimes wish you could see more. There is trouble up at the tombs. My brother Ahmose took a consignment of lamp wicks over there today, and says that Father is having problems with the men. They are becoming restless and rebellious.'

'Why?' asked Meryt. 'I have heard nothing of the sort from my uncle.'

'There's no reason why you should. Sennedjem's gang has no problems, as far as I know,' said Dedi. 'Only Father's men are unhappy.'

Meryt was surprised. If the workmen were unhappy, it was usually to do with their conditions or pay – factors that affected both gangs. She could see no reason why Nebnufer should be having more problems than Sennedjem. They were both reasonable foremen and treated their men fairly. Nebnufer was perhaps a little sterner than his counterpart – her uncle Senmut, who worked under Sennedjem, sometimes said that he respected the greater discipline of Nebnufer's gang.

'Strange,' said Meryt. 'Perhaps there's a dispute between some of the men. That can make it difficult to work together.' She thought of Tia and Nauna, always squabbling in the courtyard.

Dedi shook her head. 'It's not that. Ahmose says that Father is having difficulty keeping control. He has somehow lost the men's respect.'

Meryt was shocked. 'But it is not for them to question him!' she exclaimed. 'He was appointed by the vizier. The gods are with him.'

'Perhaps,' said Dedi. 'But sometimes the will of the men is stronger.'

She stood, and fetched another lamp from an alcove. Meryt watched her graceful movements as she lit the wick, unsure what to say. As in affairs of marriage and love, Dedi knew much more than she did about the hierarchies of the workmen and the business of building the tombs. Her own uncle was a man who went to work dutifully and did as he was told; he spoke little of the life he led away from home, so most of what Meryt knew she had learnt from the street, or her friends.

'Will you eat with us, Meryt?' Dedi asked, placing the lamp on the floor.

Meryt shook her head, and stood. 'Thank you. I'll head back home.'

The household was quiet when Meryt returned. The two children were sleeping in the back room, and there was no sign of Tia or Nauna. Meryt padded softly through to the courtyard and saw that everyone had already eaten. The pot of leftovers from the day before had gone. She heard voices, and realised that Tia and Nauna were on the roof.

Meryt fetched a leek from the store and broke off some bread from a loaf. As she did so, she realised that the two women upstairs were quarrelling. She crept closer to the stairway, and listened.

'She left the spinning unfinished,' she heard Nauna say. 'She's a lazy good-for-nothing. The sooner she marries, the better.'

Meryt held her breath. They were arguing about *her*.

'She has been spinning for most of the day,' she heard Tia protest. 'She is always willing to help. She is still young.'

'I was a wife at her age,' Nauna retorted, her voice bitter and angry. 'I had given birth to Senmut. She has been a burden on the household for too long. And Heria is only too anxious to see her son married.'

'Heria!' Tia's voice cracked with scorn. 'Yes, she wants to see Ramose married. But it is a sad state of affairs when a man cannot make up his own mind about such a matter.'

Pressed up against the wall, Meryt didn't notice one of the cats enter the courtyard. It jumped on to a stool, clattering a copper pot that was resting against it.

The voices upstairs fell silent.

'I'll go and see what it was,' Meryt heard Tia say, after a pause.

Meryt fled to the back room, and crept under a cover next to Henut. As Tia peered in, she pretended to breathe deeply, and Tia went back to the roof. Meryt threw off the cover and lay silently, thinking. So it was true that Nauna as well as Senmut wished to get rid of her. The words about Heria were more difficult to understand. Ramose was her oldest son. She must surely be proud of him; and surely it was not in her power to make him marry against his will?

For the next few days, Meryt felt as though time were suspended. She dreaded the return of Senmut from the tombs, for then she might be forced to give an answer about Ramose. Her sleep was dreamless and she despaired of receiving a clearer message from the goddess, and puzzled constantly over the one message she was sure she had been given. Its obscurity infuriated her.

The night of the men's return came all too quickly – and with it, a flurry of energy that had everyone out in the streets. The men had come back in a state of high excitement and the village soon filled with the babble of voices.

'The *kenbet* is meeting!' cried a voice, as Meryt sat on the rooftop, trying to see what was going on. Quickly, she ran downstairs. Senmut and Baki had just arrived home, and were being questioned by Tia and Nauna. The *kenbet* was the village council, which met once a week to decide on matters of dispute.

'There is trouble in the other gang,' Senmut explained. 'The men are saying that Nebnufer has been pushing them too hard and that the quality of the work is suffering as a result.' He shrugged. 'Nebnufer's gang has always been the more disciplined. I don't know why it has become a problem now.'

'But why is the *kenbet* meeting?' said Meryt. 'Can't the matter wait until the usual time?'

Senmut looked at his niece vaguely, and shrugged. 'The foremen always want to nip any dispute in the bud. Let them meet. I shall not be going. I'm hungry. I hope there is plenty of food in the courtyard.'

Meryt thought of Dedi, and her concern for her father. Council meetings were open events that anyone could attend, and she wanted to go – if she could get away. She caught Tia's eye, and indicated the doorway. Tia gave her a little smile, which Meryt took to be a sign of consent. She slipped away before Baki could realise she was going and cause trouble.

She made her way up the main street to the northern end of the village, where the council meetings were held outside the gate, in the shadow of the village shrines. A crowd had already gathered, awaiting the arrival of the council members, murmuring and gossiping in excitement. Council meetings were always a source of intrigue in the village, for they dealt with all the minor crimes and disputes that cropped up – but a dispute that actually involved a council member was a special treat, and the villagers were coming out in their droves.

There was a hush as the foreman Sennedjem appeared, and made his way through the crowd to the big square of mats laid out for the council to sit on. He was a tall, good-humoured man, generally very well liked; his judgement was respected both in the tombs and back in the village – even if, as Senmut was always pointing out, his approach sometimes lacked discipline.

Sennedjem was quickly followed by Paser, the chief scribe at the tombs, Montu, a police inspector, a draughtsman named Amenakht and Hori, the village scribe who lived close to Meryt. The council members varied, but they nearly always included at least one of the foremen and a senior scribe; recently, Nebnufer and Sennedjem had been sitting on the council together. So it seemed especially strange to see the five men gather with one of their number missing, and the crowd grew quiet as they settled down on the reed mats.

The hush became even deeper as Nebnufer himself appeared, accompanied by his wife, Wab. He moved forward with his head held high and his step dignified, nodding to friends with a small, grave smile as he passed by. Wab held on to his arm, her beautiful features calm and serene. If either Nebnufer or his wife were concerned about the council proceedings, they were very determined not to show it.

Meryt craned her neck where she stood to see if Dedi had come along to support her father. She saw that she had: she and her two older brothers were following a respectful distance behind. Meryt squeezed forward to be closer to her friend, and managed to catch her attention. Dedi gave a wan, fearful smile, and Meryt could see that she was close to tears.

Nebnufer left Wab at the edge of the mats and joined his fellow council members – but instead of sitting in the centre next to Sennedjem, as he usually did, he sat to one side, on his own. There, he gazed out at the crowd gathered around him, his expression frank and open. He had the air of a man with nothing to hide, and nothing to be ashamed of.

There was a shout and the crowd broke into a curious chatter as Nebnufer's accusers appeared and pushed their way forward. They were three workmen

– a painter and two draughtsmen. One of the draughtsmen led the way, and was clearly the spokesman for the others – a confident, stocky figure. Meryt felt a thrill of apprehension, for this man was none other than Userkaf.

Userkaf raised his hand in greeting to the council. 'May the gods be with you – life, prosperity, health!' he boomed, in his loudest voice.

Sennedjem bowed his head in acknowledgement. 'In the name of the gods – life, prosperity, health,' he replied. 'You have come with a complaint. Let us not wait any longer. Speak, and tell us of your concerns.'

Userkaf stepped forward on to the centre of the square matting and drew himself up tall. He shot a glance at Hori, who had his papyrus brush ready to keep a record of the proceedings.

'Friends, and members of the council,' he began. 'We all know each other. We know what is required of us before the king and before our gods. We build resting places for our kings that will last them throughout eternity. It is a heavy burden of responsibility, but one that we all shoulder proudly.'

A murmur of agreement rippled through the crowd. Userkaf waited for this to subside, then continued. 'I bring to you the charge that foreman Nebnufer is failing us in this task. We work hard under his supervision and direction. We work harder than the men on the other gang, for no greater reward. We have never complained about this. But now, he is pushing us too hard. He cares more for his own advancement than he does for the quality of our work. He pushes us so that we are forced to rush and not give of our best. He wants our side of the tomb to be finished before that of Sennedjem, so that he may stand in glory – even if the resting place of our god the king is badly executed as a result.'

Meryt scrutinised the faces before her as she listened. Nebnufer remained calm and dignified, his expression unreadable. She looked at the council. The police inspector and the draughtsman were listening with avid interest, clearly lapping up every word. Hori the scribe cast mistrustful looks in Userkaf's direction and had dislike written clearly on his features. Sennedjem and Paser the scribe both looked uncomfortable, and at the mention of his name, Sennedjem shifted uneasily.

'I call upon the council to note our complaints, and to reprimand foreman Nebnufer,' finished Userkaf, bowing low before the members of the council.

A silence fell upon the crowd. It was evident to all that Userkaf had taken a big risk. Everyone knew that he was hot-headed and impulsive, but this took more than impulsiveness. Surely he would not make charges against his foreman publicly – with the backing of fellow workmen – unless there was some foundation to them? It was well known that Nebnufer and Sennedjem were good friends and respected each other, and that Sennedjem's son Neben-Maat would soon be marrying Dedi. The whole affair put Sennedjem in a difficult position.

Sennedjem stood. 'We have heard you, Userkaf,' he said. 'Now let us hear your colleagues.'

One after the other, the two other men stepped forward and stated that Userkaf's words were true. When they had finished, Sennedjem turned to Nebnufer.

'Brother Nebnufer,' he said. 'Is there anything you wish to say in your defence?'

A ripple of muted surprise ran through the crowd. Sennedjem would not use the term 'brother' lightly in such circumstances. Was he siding with his fellow foreman already? Nebnufer got to his feet, and took Userkaf's place in the centre of the square. His aura of power and dignity was impressive, and a hush fell once more.

'Friends,' said Nebnufer. 'I have worked in the tombs for many years. I was appointed as foreman by the vizier eleven years ago. In that time, I have learnt what men can do in the course of one day, what is fair to ask of them, and what is beyond their powers of strength and concentration.'

Meryt could see that his brow was furrowed, and that he was choosing his words with great care. Sennedjem was watching him intently, anxiety etched on his face. It would be difficult for Nebnufer to defend himself without making Sennedjem look sloppy, and it suddenly occurred to her that this was the whole idea. Of course! Userkaf could not have chosen a better way to sow seeds of unrest in the village. But why?

She listened as Nebnufer laid out his case. He stated that his working practices had never changed in eleven years; that he had the greatest respect for Sennedjem; and that he would continue to carry out the king's work with whatever strength and wisdom the gods accorded him.

It was clear and simple. There was no personal reference to Userkaf or his friends. Nebnufer sat down once more, and the council huddled together to discuss the matter. The crowd waited impatiently for their judgement, chattering among themselves. Meryt slipped forward further, and reached Dedi's side. She squeezed her friend's arm.

'It will be fine, Dedi,' she whispered. 'It's obvious what the council will think. Userkaf is wasting his time.'

Dedi regarded her with big, anxious eyes. 'Do you really think so, Meryt?' she asked. 'How can you be sure?'

Meryt smiled gently. 'It is simply a matter of justice,' she said. 'It's easy to see what Userkaf is trying to achieve. The council cannot find in his favour.'

Dedi shook her head. 'I don't see what you see, Meryt,' she said. 'But I hope you are right.'

They fell silent as Sennedjem stood once more. 'We have reached our conclusion,' he said. 'Userkaf, stand before us.'

Userkaf stepped forward, with the three other men gathered around him.

'We cannot accept the charges you have brought,'

said Sennedjem. A shout went up from the crowd – a mixed response of approval and surprise. It quietened quickly to allow Sennedjem to finish. 'Nebnufer is a wise and conscientious foreman. He demands the best of his men, and your best is what you must give. Do not rail against it, but be proud that you are working in the Great Place under one of the king's best servants.'

Now, the crowd erupted in a babble of voices, and Sennedjem had to shout his final words. 'Go quietly to your homes. And may the gods be with you ...'

 CHAPTER FOUR

Dedi grabbed hold of Meryt's arm in excitement. 'You were right!' she cried.

She flung her arms around her friend's neck, and Meryt laughed, glad that the fate of Dedi's family was safe for the time being. Dedi kissed her cheek, then turned to look for her father, who was now surrounded by happy well-wishers. Meryt hung back to watch as Nebnufer made his way forward through the crowd with his sons close behind and Wab at his side once more.

As the people dispersed, Meryt followed slowly. Darkness was falling and the glow from lighted lamps could be seen inside the houses she passed. She didn't want to go home until she had to, so she took the turning that led to Kenna's house. At every street corner there were clusters of men deep in discussion about the council meeting and Meryt avoided them, hopping from shadow to shadow as she had done as a child. But from the snippets that she overheard, it was clear that Userkaf's accusation had caused a great stir.

'Meryt!'

Kenna's voice behind her made her jump, and Meryt spun around. 'I was coming to find you,' she said. 'Were you at the meeting? I didn't see you.'

Kenna grinned. 'Would I miss a spectacle like that?' he responded cheerfully as they approached his house. His father and some of his brothers were gathered outside with three or four neighbours, all stroking their chins and shaking their heads at the scandalous meeting.

'Come. We'll go up on to the roof,' said Kenna. 'I'll get a lamp and some beer.'

Meryt slipped past the men and into the house. There was no one in the front room, but a gaggle of women sat in the middle room and Meryt braced herself. Kenna's family was one of the largest in the village – three of his five brothers and all four sisters lived in the little house with his parents, as well as two widowed aunts, their young children and a grandmother. The women loved to gossip, and they stared at Meryt curiously as she walked past with her cheeks burning. It was dawning on her that Dedi might not be the only one to have drawn conclusions about her friendship with the fourth son of the family. She and Kenna were both of marriageable age; in the eyes of most people, such an association could have only one conclusion.

The light in the courtyard was dim, and Meryt was glad of a few moments in shadow. She watched Kenna preparing the wick and lighting it from the bread oven while her embarrassment faded. When the lamp was burning brightly, he handed it to her and picked up a flagon of beer, a strainer and two cups. Then he beckoned, and they made their way up the steps to the rooftop. There, they could hear the murmur of voices from the street below, and it was evident that Userkaf was still the main topic of conversation.

'He was lucky the council did not respond more harshly,' commented Meryt, as they settled themselves on the reed matting.

'Yes. Father says he is tough to work for,' agreed Kenna.

Meryt frowned. 'I meant Userkaf,' she said.

Kenna stared at her, surprised. 'Userkaf?'

Meryt nodded, studying her fingernails as Kenna strained the beer into the cups. 'I think he is lucky the council did not punish him for making such an accusation. Nebnufer hasn't done anything different from usual,' she said. 'He has always pushed the men quite hard, hasn't he?'

'Judging by Father's endless complaints, I'd say so,' said Kenna humorously, handing her a cup.

Meryt smiled, but her mood was serious. 'The men are bound to grumble,' she commented, thinking of her uncle. 'Working in the tombs isn't easy for either gang.'

'True,' said Kenna. 'So what are you getting at?'

Meryt took a sip of the beer. It was fresh, and still had a pleasant, bubbling tang as she rolled it over her tongue. 'I think Userkaf is up to something,' she said. 'I don't think he has anything real to complain about. He is trying to make trouble.' She paused, wondering whether to mention Nofret's amulet, then decided against it. The power of such objects was not to be trifled with, and she would not want to unleash something that she could not control.

'I can't see why,' said Kenna. 'Surely he's just lazy. He was hoping that Nebnufer would be forced to make life easier for his gang.'

It seemed so simple, and for an instant Meryt latched on to Kenna's view with a lighter heart. But then she thought of the foreman Nebnufer walking solemnly through the crowd, his wife at his side, and how he had sat apart from his fellow council members. A different outcome would have rocked the whole village.

'Think about what might have happened,' she said. 'If the council had judged in Userkaf's favour, Nebnufer's authority would be greatly diminished among his men. A rift would have been sown between the two foremen. And that would have been the least of it. In the long run, who knows where it would lead? It could be disastrous for Nebnufer's family – all of them.' She thought of her friend's engagement to Neben-Maat. 'Even Dedi.'

'Dedi?' A smile flashed across Kenna's face at the mention of her name, and Meryt looked at him sharply.

'Yes, Dedi,' she repeated, watching Kenna closely

in the flickering light of the lamp. 'She is engaged to Neben-Maat. If Sennedjem and Nebnufer were pushed apart, such a marriage might not take place.'

A strange, soft look had come across Kenna's features, and Meryt stared at him in disbelief. Surely Kenna had not fallen for her friend's charms along with everyone else?

Kenna gazed into his beer cup. 'I would not want any harm to come to Dedi,' he murmured, almost as though Meryt were not there.

Meryt felt a strange, unfamiliar twist of pain. 'Well, Userkaf might yet make sure of it,' she snapped, springing to her feet.

Kenna looked up at her in astonishment as tears pricked at the back of her eyes. 'What's wrong?' he demanded. 'What did I say?'

Meryt glared down at him, full of dismay and rage. 'Nothing,' she managed to respond. 'I'm going home.'

By the time she had reached the first street corner, Meryt regretted behaving so impulsively. Kenna must have wondered what had come over her. She felt wretched and ashamed, but too proud to go back. It wasn't wise to roam the streets alone after darkness, and Tia would be worrying about her. She would have to go home.

The groups of gossiping men had begun to disperse. Meryt walked slowly, dragging her feet. Why on earth had she reacted to Kenna like that? What if he did admire Dedi's beauty? It would be strange if he did not. There was no harm in it. Meryt kicked herself time and again, but could still not bring herself to turn back. The matter would have to be resolved some other time.

She reached home, and stepped quietly through the front door. Tia and Nauna were in the middle room, plucking feathers from two plump ducks in the lamplight. Meryt stared in surprise. Senmut must have done some trading during the council meeting. Of course – they were for Baki's ritual feast. Two ducks! There would be plenty of rich eating in the next few days – and plenty of work for the women of the household too.

Tia smiled up at Meryt as she stood in the doorway. 'Did you go to the meeting?' she asked.

Meryt nodded, ignoring Nauna's disapproving frown. She squatted down next to Tia. 'Userkaf is stirring up trouble in Nebnufer's gang,' she said. 'But the council saw through him easily enough. Can I help?'

Tia gave Meryt a knowing smile and nodded discreetly in the direction of Nauna's duck. Meryt saw what she meant immediately. Thanks to the older woman's failing eyesight, tufts of feathers still remained untouched.

'Take this one to the courtyard,' said Tia, handing Meryt her own bare-skinned duck. 'Nauna, I'll finish yours off. Meryt will clear away the feathers.'

Meryt took the duck and padded through the house. The sound of Senmut's snores greeted her from the back room, the usual effect of a flagon of beer after a week at the tombs. In the shadows, Meryt saw that Baki was asleep too. Relieved, she carried on into the courtyard and placed the duck in a copper pot, out of reach of the cats.

When she had taken the second duck from Tia's skilful fingers, Meryt stuffed the mound of feathers into a linen sack and carried it up to the roof. She rescued her ostracon from the corner and lay down, propping the sack behind her head. The smell of the duck feathers permeated it but it was soft and comfortable. Curling up on her side, Meryt thought once more of Kenna's expression as he spoke of Dedi. How lucky her friend was to be rich and beautiful, admired by so many of the men in the village. No one had ever thought of her in that way, she was sure. Except Ramose, perhaps, but that idea was not a pleasant one. With an ache in her heart, she managed to fall asleep.

There was little chance to escape from home for the next two days. The whole household became a hive of activity as preparations were made for Baki's ritual feast. Meryt gathered that her cousin would undergo his ritual with five other boys of a similar age in the forecourt of the chapel of Amen-Re, and that Senmut had offered his home as a place of celebration for the men of all five families in the evening.

Meryt knew that the boys themselves would be in

no fit state for feasting. Circumcision was an extremely painful ritual and their wounds would take time to heal. Apart from Baki, they would all go home to be looked after by their mothers or other womenfolk, and as such, the event would be a very male affair.

On the morning of the ritual itself, Meryt was left in charge of baking bread and cakes while Tia and Nauna prepared vegetables in the back room. Henut and Mose hung around the courtyard, getting in the way of both Meryt and Nes, the Nubian servant girl who had been brought in to grind a new batch of grain.

Baki wandered around the house with a cocky smile on his face, occasionally joining his younger brother and sister as they played around Meryt's feet. 'You will have to wait on me at the feast tonight,' he said to Meryt, grabbing a chunk of freshly baked bread. 'I'll be a man. You'll have to do as I say.'

'I'm waiting on the guests. Tia will look after you,' Meryt told him, unwilling to be drawn into an argument. She took a bowl of freshly ground wheat from Nes and added a little salt and honey.

'I'll be at the feast too. I won't need looking after,' boasted Baki. 'Father's gone to buy wine. He says I can drink as much as I please after the ritual. I won't feel any pain.'

Meryt shrugged. She knew that there were also ointments that would reduce the pain a little, but nothing could take it away entirely. 'If you say so.'

'Do you doubt me?' Baki demanded. He ripped his bread apart and took a bite.

Meryt looked at him. How could he be so arrogant? 'Take care that you don't anger the gods,' she warned him. 'They may give you greater pain than you're expecting.'

'You would say that,' replied Baki. 'And I suppose you'll make sure they do, with one of your curses.'

'Baki!' Meryt glared at her cousin. She knew he was taunting her, but the words were too painful to ignore. 'I do not curse *anyone*, do you hear me? You should mind what you say. You know as well as I do that words of power shouldn't be trifled with.'

Baki laughed gleefully. '"Words of power shouldn't be trifled with",' he mimicked, then stuck out his tongue. 'Save your lessons for your new husband, Meryt. I'm sure Ramose will lap them up.'

Meryt felt cut to the core. Quickly, she glanced around at Henut, Mose and Nes the servant girl. Henut was happily feeding scraps of bread to the goat. Nes was bent over the corn, still grinding methodically. But Mose was listening, his eyes wide as he took in every word. She felt so angry with Baki that she wanted to strike him.

Before she had the chance, they heard Senmut's voice calling Baki.

'Ah! There you are.' Senmut appeared in the doorway, a cheerful smile on his face. 'Are you ready for your ritual, Baki? We have to go in a minute.' He

handed Meryt a flagon of wine. 'Keep that somewhere cool and give me four of the best loaves. We
shall make offerings to Ptah and Amen-Re before the
ceremony.'

Meryt did as he said, handing two each to Senmut
and Baki. Tia appeared next to Senmut, her face
drawn and anxious. She embraced her oldest son,
and gave his black side-lock a final caress. Meryt
could see the fear in her eyes, and felt a wave of sympathy for her aunt in spite of her anger with Baki.

'Take this,' she heard Tia whisper, pressing an
object into Baki's hand. 'I have pronounced many
spells over it. May it protect you and deliver you
from suffering.'

Baki opened his hand, and Meryt caught a
glimpse of what lay on his palm. It was Tia's
favourite amulet, an *udjat* eye of Horus made of
faience, glazed a deep cobalt blue.

The household immediately seemed more peaceful
once the men had gone. Meryt made a big batch of
flat loaves, placing the shaped lumps of dough on
the outside surface of the little domed oven. They
were the easiest kind of loaf to make, for when they
were cooked, they simply dropped to the floor. The
emmer wheat cakes were trickier. They had to be
cooked on the inside of the oven and watched carefully, and Meryt was pleased when they came out
round and golden.

Tia brought in a big bowl of onions, garlic, leeks,

peas and beans, and began gutting the ducks. The mothers of the other five boys arrived one by one, bringing gifts to add to the feast. As Tia sat with Mose, making a note of them all on an ostracon, Meryt took the opportunity to escape to the roof.

In the still heat of the early afternoon, sound travelled easily across the village. Meryt leant against the wall and looked out over the rooftops, listening to the bleating of a neighbour's goat. The murmur of voices drifted up from the streets and courtyards, interspersed with spurts of laughter. Now that the working week had ended, the murmuring seemed deeper as more male voices joined in.

She turned at the sound of footsteps. It was Mose, standing uncertainly at the top of the stairway. Meryt held out her arm and the eight-year-old came to stand next to her.

'Have you finished writing down all the presents?' Meryt asked him.

Mose nodded. 'Tuya brought two more ducks. The others brought bread and vegetables.'

'We won't go hungry then, will we?'

Mose smiled briefly, but he seemed preoccupied. Meryt thought of her exchange with Baki, and felt a stab of fear.

'Is something troubling you, Mose?' she forced herself to ask.

Mose dug his finger into a little hole he had made in the mud brick. Meryt watched him, seeing from his furrowed brow and pursed lips that his mind was

73

working furiously. At last, he looked up. 'When you get married, will you still come and see us?' he asked.

It was like a punch in the stomach. Meryt stared at her little cousin speechlessly for a moment. 'Who says I'm getting married?' she whispered eventually.

Mose's face brightened. 'You mean you're not?'

'I don't want to, no.'

'But Baki said …'

'Don't listen to Baki. He was teasing me.' Meryt felt desperate. If everyone assumed she was going to marry Ramose – even the children – there would be little chance of getting out of it.

Mose's calm eyes gazed at her. She could tell he wasn't convinced, but his next words surprised her all the same. 'You shouldn't have to marry if you don't want to,' he said.

Meryt touched his arm. These days, little escaped the eight-year-old, and she felt glad that he understood. But the pressure was mounting. Senmut would demand a decision before long.

When Baki returned, it was not on foot but in Senmut's muscular arms. The neighbouring women had left to greet their own menfolk, and Meryt was sitting with Nauna preparing fruit. She watched from the courtyard as her uncle carried her cousin inside and laid him down in the back room. Baki was whimpering, his shorn head making his dark eyes seem all the wider as he stared up at Senmut and Tia through his pain. Meryt thought of his boasts earlier that day, and shook her head grimly.

Tia knelt beside him and held his hands. 'May Isis protect you – life, prosperity, health,' Meryt heard her whisper. 'May your suffering be taken from you. Peshedu, have mercy on my son.'

Senmut left her to it and walked through to the courtyard. He seemed in good spirits, and smiled expansively. 'How are the preparations going?' he asked. 'The guests will be arriving soon. Are you ready to serve, Meryt?'

Meryt shook her head, and scrambled to her feet. 'No, Uncle. I'll get ready now.'

It was a role she hated. Senmut could not afford to buy any servants or to hire them for an evening's revelry. Of course there was Nes, but she was employed by the government only to grind the grain. So whenever Senmut had friends around, he expected his niece to play the part of a hired hand.

Meryt went through to the middle room and opened a wooden casket. She took out a mirror of highly polished bronze, a little pot of khol and another of red ochre, and a string of cowrie shells. Quickly, she slipped off her linen dress and packed it into the casket. She was slinging the cowrie string around her hips when Senmut came into the room.

'I'll need my best kilt and wig,' he said. 'Tia's busy with Baki. Bring them to me when you're ready – I'll be on the roof.'

Meryt nodded, and reached for the khol pot. With

a little brush, she gave her eyes a thick black outline, trying not to smudge the edges. Then she dabbed some of the red ochre on to her cheeks and reached into the casket once more for a beaded necklace. Last of all, she reached for her wig – a cheap one made of date-palm fibre that she hated, because it made her itch.

In another casket lay Senmut's finest kilt, made of pure white linen and painstakingly ironed into many beautiful pleats by Tia. Next to it lay his wig. Meryt grabbed them both and headed on to the roof, sucking in her cheeks as the cool evening breeze chilled her bare skin.

'Thank you, Meryt,' said Senmut as she handed him the garments. His mood was still cheerful, and Meryt hoped it would remain that way.

'Do you need anything else?' she asked.

He shook his head. 'No. Go and help Nauna now.' He paused, and smiled. 'You'll make a good wife, Meryt.'

Meryt stared at him, her throat dry. But Senmut was already wrapping the beautiful kilt around his loins, humming a tune. Before he could say anything else, she turned and ran quickly down the stairs.

The evening drew in swiftly. As the ducks roasted on a fire, Senmut's guests arrived and settled themselves in the middle room. Nauna remained in the courtyard while Meryt ferried to and fro, first serving wine, then dishes piled high with meat and vegetables.

Whenever she passed through the back room, Meryt spared a moment for Tia, who scarcely moved from her son's side. Baki made a poor patient, as Meryt had suspected he might. He writhed on the bed, groaning continuously and making bad-tempered demands for more wine. Tia gave him small swigs, and bathed his forehead with a cool, soothing ointment. Meryt passed her aunt small platefuls of food and begged her to eat, but Tia would not be tempted. She seemed lost in the world of her son's pain and could think of nothing else.

The workmen were unused to drinking wine. On a daily basis they drank beer, and the stronger brew soon began to go to their heads. With each journey through to the middle room, Meryt was greeted with louder gales of laughter; and as their eyes lapped up the sight of her growing body, it became harder to keep her smile in its place. She consoled herself with the tastiest morsels of duck, crisped up on the fire and seasoned with salt, popping them into her mouth surreptitiously as she carried the serving plates through.

At last the men stumbled off into the night. Meryt rescued her dress from the casket and joined Mose and Henut where they lay on the roof, out of the men's way. Henut was already sound asleep, duck fat smeared around her mouth and a peaceful expression on her face.

'Everyone's gone. You can go down now, if you want,' Meryt whispered to Mose. 'There's lots more food too, if you're hungry.'

Mose shook his head. 'I've had enough.' He sat up and looked anxiously at Meryt. 'Will Baki be all right? Mama seems so worried about him.'

'Of course he will. He'll be his usual self in a few days.' Meryt's heart went out to the sensitive eight-year-old, who knew only too well that he would suffer the same fate in a few years' time. All the same, he was right to observe that Tia seemed more worried than she should be. 'Mama's worried because Baki is her first child, that's all,' she added. 'Make the most of the peace and quiet. He'll be teasing you again in no time.'

Mose lay back down again, reassured. Meryt fetched a sheet and her precious ostracon before lying down beside him. She gazed at the image of the goddess Hathor, her frustration welling up inside as she mulled over the day's events. Soon Baki would be back on his feet and Senmut would turn all his attention to getting rid of her. Why was nothing becoming clearer? She thought again of her dream – the image of Ramose disappearing over the mountain with her father, Peshedu ...

Peshedu. How Meryt wished she had known him – both him and her mother, Simut. Simut had been so young when she died, a shimmering shadow of a girl. Sometimes Meryt wondered if she would suffer the same fate, if she ever tried to give birth. She had heard it said that such things could be passed from mother to daughter. But it was too frightening a thought to dwell on for long.

Her image of Peshedu was stronger. Tia spoke of him so often that Meryt had a clear picture of him in her mind – a lean, muscular man, not tall, but with a firm jaw and humorous eyes. There was also the bust of him in the front room niche, which Tia had commissioned on his death. It had been made by one of his friends, a fellow-sculptor, who had lovingly recreated his features when he had been struck down by the disease that stole so many men of the village in their prime.

Meryt re-examined her dream from every angle. Looking through the window to see her father … The hot desert wind, whipping around his linen kilt … The appearance of Ramose, travelling back from the kings' tombs … none of it made any sense. Somehow, it seemed as though Peshedu held the answer, but how could that be?

There was only one solution: she would have to ask him personally. Not in the front room, where he had never lived, but in the tomb itself, where his embalmed body lay together with those of his ancestors.

Meryt-Re drifted restlessly into sleep and woke at dawn. The village was already coming to life in the streets around, but Mose and Henut were still sound asleep. Meryt rose quietly and crept down the stairs. In the dim light, she selected a ripe pomegranate and an untouched loaf of bread from the leftovers of the feast, and picked up the wooden kindling sticks with which the family kindled fire. She put them in a little reed basket and added a handful of dry straw. Then she slipped through the house to the front room, where she collected her packet of incense and the burner.

Baki was at last asleep, with Tia on the floor beside him. She had fallen asleep where she sat, kneeling by the side of the bed with her head resting on her arms. Meryt tiptoed past Senmut and Nauna, both snoring in the middle room, and out into the street.

Although it was the last day of the weekend, many of the villagers were already awake, taking advantage of the cool light of dawn. As Meryt headed south, workmen on donkeys trotted past her on their way to tend fields in the valley, servant girls walked sleepily towards her to start their monotonous job of grinding the grain, and the more diligent women were sweeping the street outside their houses.

Suddenly, Meryt stopped. Just up ahead of her, the wiry figure of Nofret appeared from a side alley. Her head was bowed and she turned south towards the gate without seeing Meryt. With a little skip, Meryt hurried after her to catch up.

She touched the servant girl on the shoulder. 'Nofret.'

Nofret spun around, her eyes wide with fear.

'It's only me,' said Meryt gently. 'I wish you no harm. May I talk to you?'

The servant girl recoiled from her, her shoulders tense.

'Please,' said Meryt. 'You can trust me, I promise.'

Nofret said nothing, but fell in beside Meryt as she carried on walking towards the village gate. Once they had passed through it, Meryt stopped.

'Where are you going?' she asked. 'To the embalmers' workshops?'

Nofret nodded.

'Which way? Over the mountain?' Meryt indicated the route through the eastern cemetery where the two girls had met before. This time, Nofret shook her head.

'You don't need to go that way because today you have nothing to hide.' Meryt's words were more a statement than a question. The servant girl nodded, and bowed her head.

Meryt studied her. She knew that the burden of secrecy was a heavy one, and sensed that Nofret might be ready to unload it. 'Come with me,' she said gently. 'Dawn has only just broken. You have plenty of time. I am going to make an offering at my father's tomb.'

Nofret looked anxious. 'I can't …' she began.

'Not for long,' Meryt reassured her. 'It will be quiet in the chapel courtyard. Come.'

The servant girl hesitated. But then, as Meryt started up the path that led to the western tombs, she began to follow.

Meryt walked west towards the cliffs, where the villagers' tombs formed a large, sprawling cemetery across the lower slopes, their little pyramid-topped

81

chapels dotting the limestone hillside. Unlike the disused eastern cemetery, this one was well maintained,
for each tomb was assigned to a living family. She
took a little path that led south-west, then stepped
into one of the chapel courtyards.

Nofret paused at the entrance.

'It's safe here,' Meryt told her. She felt a pang of
sadness. 'Hardly anyone visits. Most of my relatives
are dead.'

Nofret sidled into the courtyard and joined Meryt
where she was crouching down in the first patch of
morning sunlight. The two girls faced east, soaking
up the warmth.

'At least you have some relatives,' said Nofret
quietly.

Meryt looked at her, the meaning of her words
sinking in. Nofret was a servant girl, bought by
Userkaf for a quantity of grain. It was a harsh fate.
Girls with families did not become servants to be
bought and sold like animals. 'Do you know what
happened to yours?' she asked.

Nofret nodded. 'My father was caught thieving.
He was beaten savagely and sent to work in the
stone quarries, far to the south. I don't suppose he
lived long. After that, my mother was forced to
become a servant. We were separated when I was
five. I had a younger brother too. I don't know what
happened to him.'

She said all this so calmly that Meryt was astonished, and she blurted out the first thing that came

into her head. 'Your father went through all that – and yet you are stealing yourself!'

'Don't say that.' Nofret's voice was sharp.

Meryt frowned. What did the servant girl expect her to say? Thieving from the royal embalmers' workshops was madness. 'Look,' she said. 'I saw the amulet with my own eyes. You cannot deny it, Nofret. Is it your master, Userkaf, who demands that you steal?'

Nofret shook her head vigorously. 'No! No …'

'You would do better to admit the truth,' Meryt pressed her. 'How many more have you stolen?'

'What is it to you?' cried the servant girl, her eyes flashing defensively. She scrambled to her feet. 'You can prove nothing. And in any case, you will soon be stuck with Ramose for a husband and the curse of Sekhmet on your head. Why should you care?'

Meryt leapt to her feet and faced her. '*What* did you say?' she demanded. She was taller than Nofret and towered over her, shaking with rage. 'Who told you this?'

Nofret backed away a few steps, her eyes filling with fear once more. Meryt moved quickly and barred her path. '*Who?* If you don't tell me I shall come with you to the embalmers' workshops and tell them what I have seen.'

Nofret's shoulders dropped in defeat. She shrugged. 'It's no great secret. Nes told me,' she said. 'Do you think that servants never talk among themselves?'

Meryt let out her breath slowly, remembering

Baki's taunts of the day before. The Nubian servant Nes had been sitting there quietly all the time, grinding the grain, taking everything in. It was a sobering lesson.

Folding her arms, she looked at Nofret coolly. 'And you think I wield the power of Sekhmet,' she said, a slight threat in her voice. 'Perhaps it is time you showed the gods greater respect. Your father's fate was mild compared to what they can bring upon you.'

She expected the servant girl to quail before her, but now, Nofret's attitude seemed to have shifted. She narrowed her eyes and gave a little smile. 'You wouldn't dare curse me,' she said, inching around Meryt towards the exit.

Meryt snorted, and let her pass. 'I hardly need to,' she retorted. 'You are doing enough for the gods to curse you of their own accord!'

As Nofret bounded down towards the main path, Meryt sat down in the patch of sunlight to think. The servant girl baffled her. On the one hand, she was the weak, timid creature she had always been. But on the other, she had a streak of something else – something fearless, sly, and full of defiance. It was strange. She had said that she was not stealing for her master, Userkaf, which was only natural; she would be terrified of admitting such a thing. But to deny it with such craftiness did not add up. Could it be that the servant girl wanted to harness the power of the amulets for her own purposes?

It was impossible to work out. Meryt sighed, and thought of her other discovery: that gossip about herself and Ramose was spreading through the village like wildfire, at least among the servants. It wouldn't be long before everyone knew. The thought of her friend Kenna flashed into Meryt's mind and her heart filled with anguish. How would he respond? Would he be sorry to lose his childhood friend or happy to see her married off? If only she could prevent the whole thing ...

Well, she had to try. She picked up the basket containing her offering and stepped towards the chapel of her father's tomb.

CHAPTER FIVE

The chapel was a lovely little place, its mud-brick dome decorated inside with pictures of Meryt's great-grandfather greeting the gods and tending a vineyard in the Next World. As well as a house, each worker in the Great Place was also allocated a tomb, and as long as men apprenticed their sons those tombs remained within a family. Now, Peshedu's line had ended, for Tia and Meryt didn't count. Without an apprentice to hand it on to, his tomb would soon go to someone else. Tia would eventually lie along-side Senmut, and Meryt ... well, there was no saying what would happen to her.

But for now, Peshedu lay undisturbed somewhere beneath the chapel, the tomb entrance sealed and hidden so that no one could break into it. Meryt stepped reverently to the chapel threshold and looked inside.

She gasped. There, on the chapel altar, lay a fresh offering. Figs, a fresh lettuce and two loaves. Meryt sniffed the air, which still held the faint smell of incense, and stepped inside. As far as she knew, the only person who made regular offerings to Peshedu was Tia. But Meryt was sure her aunt had not visited the tomb in the last two days – Tia had been totally absorbed by Baki's ritual! And besides, the loaves were not as she or Tia made them. Meryt's heart began to beat faster.

She held out a trembling hand and picked up the lettuce. Its leaves were still crisp. She put it down and gently pressed one of the loaves. Her finger left a deep imprint in the soft bread. Whoever had been here had visited in the last few hours – probably late the night before.

Meryt took a deep breath. Such offerings were not made lightly. There were few villagers who could afford to give away much of the food they ate. So there was someone who had enough of a connection to her father to give him some of their freshest goods … and Meryt had no idea who.

She searched her mind for an answer, but drew a blank. It was a total mystery. Eventually, she moved the offering carefully to one side and reached into her basket. She fetched out the pomegranate and the loaf and placed them on the altar. She prepared the incense in the burner, then placed the straw in a heap and quickly produced sparks with the kindling sticks. From her little straw fire, she lit the incense.

'Peshedu, blessed spirit of Re – life, prosperity, health,' she began, swinging the incense. 'Hear your daughter's prayer. These are troubled times. I may be forced to marry the stonecutter Ramose against my will. I have asked for help from the goddess Hathor but she has sent me only one dream. In this dream, you guide Ramose away from me towards the Great Place. Father, what does this mean?'

She fell silent for a moment and stared at her offering, imagining her father enjoying the ripe pomegranate in the Next World. Then she spoke again.

'Peshedu, blessed spirit of Re – life, prosperity, health. Tia says you plague the family and that she has no peace from you. Father, why should this be? I believe you were a good man, and I have been a good daughter since you left us for the sacred barque of Re. I have served Senmut and Tia well and done their bidding. Please answer my prayer.'

As she prayed, the rays of the sun reached the chapel door and inched towards the altar. Meryt stared at the patterns formed by the smoke dancing in the sunlight, then gazed at the stranger's offering – the lettuce, the figs and the two fresh loaves. 'And who has been here before me?' she murmured, as the last of the incense burnt out.

By the time Meryt left the chapel, the whole of the western cemetery was bathed in morning sunlight. She walked down to the village slowly, swinging her reed basket, watching the comings and goings from the southern gate. As she reached the road, one of Kenna's brothers came out of the village on his father's donkey. He trotted past her with a smile and a wave, calling that he was off to do a little moonlighting in an official's tomb.

Meryt waved after him, then turned back to the gate. She didn't see the woman in front of her.

'Careful!' the woman cried out as Meryt jogged her basket. It fell, its contents spilling on to the road.

'Oh! I'm sorry –' Meryt hurriedly crouched beside the woman to help her pick up everything. She stared at what lay on the ground. Plants of all sorts, flowerheads and seeds. Lotus blossoms and the root of the mandrake. Pungent fenugreek and hemp, thorny twists of acacia, and many others that Meryt did not recognise. The woman must have been down in the valley gathering all this since before the break of dawn … Meryt looked at her face. It was Teti, the *rekhet*, the Knowing One.

Meryt felt her stomach twist in fear. Teti's powers of divination and magic were well known in the village, and she did not want to anger her. 'I'm so sorry,' she repeated.

Teti was picking up each stem and blossom tenderly, brushing off the coating of white limestone dust. But many were bruised, and seeds lay scattered all around. She shook her head. 'Don't worry,' she said. 'I can always collect more.'

'Let me help you,' blurted Meryt.

Teti looked at her, a little smile playing on her lips. Shyly, Meryt met her gaze. She had never been this close to the Knowing One before, and she was surprised at how young and gentle she seemed. Her face was oval and pretty; her eyes smiled as though she laughed a lot.

'I doubt you know how,' said Teti. 'Can you tell one leaf from another?'

Meryt looked at the profusion before her. 'I know some,' she said. 'I know the celery and the acacia and the lotus. I could learn.'

Teti seemed amused. 'Very well,' she said. 'Do you know where I live?'

Meryt nodded. 'Just outside the village wall on the north side.'

'Tomorrow or the day after?'

Meryt thought for a moment. The men would return to work in the tombs the next day. Until they had gone, she would do better to show willing around the house.

'The day after,' she replied. 'I suppose you leave before dawn.'

Teti nodded. 'The morning dew has powers of its own,' she said, with a smile. 'But only those who rise early can harness it. What's your name?'

'Meryt-Re.' Meryt returned her smile, feeling glad. She placed a delicate lotus blossom on the top of Teti's basket, remembering Dedi's words only a few days before. *You sound like Teti*, she had said. Standing here with the *rekhet* in front of her, the words seemed somehow less frightening.

'Thank you, Meryt-Re,' said Teti. 'I'll look forward to it.'

Nauna's voice greeted Meryt when she was still four houses' distance from home.

'About time too! Where do you think you've been?'

Senmut's mother was standing in the street with a broom, keeping an eye on local goings-on. Meryt quickened her step, breaking into a jog. It wasn't worth explaining things to Nauna. She gave the older woman a respectful nod and slipped past her into the house.

The middle room was empty save for the remnants of the feast, which were strewn across the floor, and the air stank of stale wine and beer. In the back room, Baki still lay on the bed, his eyes bright with pain.

'The wine is finished,' Tia was telling him. 'I'm sorry, Baki. The men drank it all.' She spotted Meryt in the doorway, and gave a wan smile. 'I will send Meryt to Harmose for another ointment.'

Meryt stepped forward. 'Do you want me to go now?' she asked. 'I could go before clearing up.'

Nauna appeared behind her. 'Any excuse to avoid work!' she grumbled.

'Nauna, Baki is in pain,' said Tia sharply.

The older woman sniffed. 'Senmut was much braver,' she muttered. 'I didn't have to waste grain on ointments and wine. He took the pain like a man.'

'I am a man,' came Baki's voice from the bed. 'Little you know about it, Nauna.'

'Enough, Baki,' said Tia firmly. 'Don't speak to your grandmother like that. Meryt will go to the doctor.'

'Shall I take grain from the cellar?' asked Meryt.

Tia nodded. 'Or a leftover loaf or two, if there are any.'

91

Meryt went into the courtyard and replaced the kindling sticks. Henut and Mose were milking the goat, Henut holding a bowl while Mose squeezed the udders expertly. Meryt had a quick look around. There were four loaves left, and she put two into her linen bag as Henut smiled up at her.

'Dada has a headache,' the little girl told her. 'We're mustn't make any noise.'

Meryt thought of the previous night's revelries, and guessed that Senmut had staggered on to the roof once the sun had risen to get more sleep. 'Never mind. You can help me in the middle room when I get back. I won't be long.'

She headed out to the street once more, this time walking north to the doctor's house. Her job was soon done. Harmose accepted the loaves and told her to apply a mixture of honey and goose fat to Baki's wound.

'Wrap it up with lint,' he told her. 'He'll be fine in a few days.'

'Is that all?' asked Meryt.

'Yes, yes,' said Harmose brusquely. 'Why, what else do you expect for two loaves?'

Meryt hesitated. 'I thought there might be a charm. A spell,' she suggested.

Harmose wiped his forehead impatiently. 'There's no evil to cast out of a wound like that. It was made by the priests,' he said. 'What good do you think a spell would do? Apply the honey and fat as I've told you.'

Meryt stood at the doctor's door uncertainly. She

did not want to return home empty-handed. 'We have no goose fat,' she said.

'Oh, by Sobek and Mut! Wait here.'

Meryt did as he said, her dislike of the man mounting with each passing moment. At last he reappeared with a small jar half-full of fat.

'Bring the jar back when the fat is finished,' he snapped. 'I'm a doctor, not the king's fool.'

It was a disagreeable morning. Baki wailed as Tia did the doctor's bidding, and Nauna grumbled constantly as though it were she who had the headache. When Senmut at last came down from the roof, he growled at the children and demanded food that had been finished off the night before. As the heat of the day drove everyone into the shade to rest, Meryt escaped, and ran to Dedi's house.

'Meryt!' her friend greeted her in a low voice. 'Come in. Father is asleep with my brothers on the roof, but we can sit in the courtyard.'

The two girls padded through the house, past the womenfolk, who were dozing in the middle room, and out into the yard at the back. Half of it was shaded with reed roofing, and the girls squatted down to chat.

'How are you? Did Baki endure his ritual well?' asked Dedi.

'Well enough,' replied Meryt, with a grimace. 'But I doubt being a man will improve him much.'

'Oh, you never know,' said Dedi. 'A few months of

hard work in the tombs will do him good – although he'll be one of Sennedjem's men. He won't be working under Father's strict regime, will he?'

Meryt looked at her friend, trying to gauge her expression. It was the first time she had ever heard Dedi refer to Nebnufer's firm hand in the tombs. Userkaf's accusation must have had an impact, despite the council's findings. 'I doubt there is really so much difference between the two foremen,' she said in a reassuring tone.

Dedi laughed. 'I was only joking,' she said. 'I agree. There has been much discussion of it over the last few days, and Sennedjem came to eat with us last night. He and Father are still firm friends.'

Meryt felt relieved. The two foremen were clearly sticking together, and her friend seemed to think the matter was closed. She decided not to mention her misgivings about Userkaf. It could do no good, for she did not know what the troublesome draughtsman's aims might be. 'So did Neben-Maat come to dinner too?' she asked.

Dedi flushed. 'Yes,' she said, with a coy smile. 'Sennedjem is happy for the marriage to go ahead. I shall be Neben's wife before the harvest.'

'That's wonderful! What will you be …'

Meryt's question was drowned as someone banged on the front door, and the two girls looked at each other in surprise.

Dedi frowned. 'I wonder who that can be? Most people are asleep.'

The banging continued. 'Nebnufer!' called a voice. 'Wake up. There is news!'

The face of Ahmose, one of Dedi's brothers, appeared at the top of the steps. 'Who is it, Dedi?'

'No idea,' she replied. 'Should I go and see?'

There was more hammering on the door. 'Yes, hurry up!' Ahmose told her. 'I'll wake Father.'

Meryt waited while Dedi went to open the door. Within seconds, a workman from Nebnufer's gang was rushing through the house and up the courtyard steps. Dedi trailed after him, looking bewildered. She beckoned to Meryt and they followed the man up on to the roof.

'It's Userkaf again!' cried the man. 'Nebnufer, you must do something!'

Nebnufer was sitting with his legs covered in a linen sheet, and his sons on either side. 'Calm yourself,' he said. 'I cannot do anything until I understand what you are saying.'

'Userkaf is not satisfied with the findings of the council. He is going to consult the oracle. This is what I have heard.'

'Where did you hear it?'

The man looked uncertain. He hesitated, and Meryt realised he was afraid. 'I ... I just heard it on the street,' he said. 'I came to tell you right away.'

Nebnufer rose to his feet. 'Thank you, Ipuy,' he said. He placed a fatherly hand on the man's shoulder. 'We shall see. Things rumoured on the street do not always come to pass.'

'But …' Ipuy began, shuffling his feet.

Meryt saw conflict on his face and wondered what he was hiding. Nebnufer must have seen the same thing, for he smiled gently. 'Are you sure this is only a rumour?' he asked.

'Yes … yes,' the workman assured him. 'I overheard it. That's all.'

'Well, it will not be long before we find out,' said Nebnufer. 'The oracle speaks this evening. I shall continue to rest until then. Go peacefully, Ipuy, and may the gods be with you.'

'Aren't you going to do anything?' Ipuy demanded.

Nebnufer looked at him sternly. 'The gods are just, Ipuy,' he said. 'Amenhotep is my guide just as he is yours. Let the oracle speak. I shall not prevent it.'

The workman left. Nebnufer and his sons were silent, and Dedi led Meryt back down the steps away from them. Dedi's beautiful face was still, the happy smiles gone. The two girls were sitting down in the courtyard as Dedi's mother, Wab, appeared in the doorway.

'What happened, Dedi?' Wab asked. 'What did Ipuy want?'

'It was about Userkaf,' Dedi told her.

Wab hurried up the steps to the roof, and Dedi sighed. 'I thought it was all over,' she said, her voice trembling slightly. 'I don't understand why Userkaf is causing so much trouble. What if …'

She trailed off, but Meryt could guess her friend's mind. *What if we are forced to call off the marriage?* She reached and touched Dedi's arm.

'Don't worry,' she said. 'Your father is right. The oracle is just. Everything will be fine and Userkaf will be shamed.'

'But he seems so determined,' said Dedi. 'What is he trying to achieve?'

Meryt shrugged. She did not know the answer any more than Dedi did. She thought of Nofret and the amulets but, as she had done with Kenna, she kept the information to herself. No good could come of speaking about it. Let the thefts rest on Nofret's head alone.

'He will achieve nothing,' she said firmly. 'Just wait and see.'

Dedi smiled briefly. 'I hope you are right. Will you come to the parade of the oracle with me? Mother and Father will be preoccupied. You make me feel safe, Meryt.'

Meryt was surprised. 'Will Neben-Maat not go with you?'

'How can I ask him?' Dedi's eyes filled with tears. 'I dare not make things difficult for Sennedjem and his family.'

'But ... you are engaged to him. He should support you,' Meryt protested.

Dedi shrugged. 'Father says it is better to keep our troubles to ourselves,' she said.

'He is a proud man.'

'Yes.' Dedi's eyes appealed to Meryt again. 'So will you come with me?'

'Well, of course I will, if you're sure.' Meryt rose to her feet. 'I have to go now, but I'll call for you later.'

Meryt-Re walked back down the main street. The heat of the sun was now less intense, and people were beginning to bustle around once more. Suddenly, a familiar figure appeared from a side alley, and Meryt stopped, her heart thumping hard. It was Kenna. The memory of her hurried exit a few nights before flooded back, and she felt overcome with embarrassment and shame.

'Meryt!' Kenna called to her.

Meryt averted her gaze, and kept on walking.

'Don't be like that. Talk to me.' Kenna strode to her side and touched her arm.

Meryt's cheeks were hot. She stopped, but stared at her feet.

'Whatever I said to upset you, I'm sorry,' said Kenna. 'I couldn't understand why you left so suddenly. I have never known you to behave like that.' His voice was warm and he seemed genuinely puzzled.

Meryt hesitated. She desperately wanted to restore the friendship to normal, whatever his feelings for Dedi. She looked up. 'I'm the one who should be sorry,' she said. 'I was being foolish. I meant to come back, but somehow it was too late.'

'So there is nothing wrong?' Kenna's eyes searched her face.

'Nothing,' said Meryt. She changed the subject hastily. 'I saw your brother this morning, on your father's donkey. He said he was going moonlighting.'

'Yes. There is work to be done in the Place of Beauty.' Kenna shrugged. His brothers' workload had never really interested him, for he could not share in it. He fell in alongside Meryt as she continued along the street. 'How is Baki? Do you have to stay at home later on?' he asked.

Meryt thought of the oracle, and hesitated, unsure whether to mention it. 'Baki's fine,' she said. 'Why?'

'There is news,' replied Kenna. 'Userkaf is going to consult the oracle about Nebnufer.'

Meryt was taken aback. 'So it's already common knowledge!' she exclaimed.

'Oh, I wouldn't say that. Someone mentioned it to Father this morning,' said Kenna. 'He's on Nebnufer's gang, so he was bound to hear about it. Will you come with me to see what happens?'

'I have agreed to go with Dedi,' replied Meryt, and looked away, not wanting to see Kenna's response. Perhaps his face would light up, just as it had done before.

'We could all go together,' he suggested.

Meryt said nothing, but something tightened inside her. She did not want to spend the evening witnessing Kenna's admiration for her friend, but what could she do? She had told him that nothing was wrong.

'Couldn't we?' Kenna persisted. 'It would be fun.'

Meryt shrugged. 'All right,' she agreed grudgingly. She shot him a glance. 'But I doubt Dedi will see it as fun.'

Kenna looked instantly ashamed at his thought-lessness. 'No, of course not,' he said. 'Well, we are her friends. I shall be glad to offer her my support.'

Despite her jealousy, Meryt had to agree. 'I think she may need it,' she said.

The household was quiet when Meryt returned home. Senmut had gone out, and Baki was asleep. Tia and Nauna were sitting in the courtyard with the children, weaving – or pretending to weave, for it did not take Meryt long to work out that Tia was exhausted.

'Did you manage to get any sleep?' she asked.

Tia shook her head. 'Baki was restless. I couldn't leave him.'

Nauna tutted. 'You have more than one child to care for,' she chided her daughter-in-law. 'Remember the unborn one and take care you do not lose it.'

For once, Meryt agreed with Nauna, and she squatted down next to her aunt and held her hand. 'Do you think you could sleep now? I will take your place at the loom.'

Tia looked at her gratefully, and as she hauled herself to her feet, Meryt saw that her belly was growing daily. There were not so many months left before she gave birth. Three, perhaps. Four at the most. She allowed Tia to lean on her arm and guided her inside to the middle room.

Meryt spread out a reed mat and Tia flopped down on to it. 'Heria came to visit,' she murmured, looking up at Meryt with weary eyes.

'Heria!' As far as Meryt was concerned, there was only one reason for Heria to visit, and that was to obtain an answer to her son's proposal of marriage.

'Don't worry,' said Tia softly. 'Senmut wasn't here. I told her you hadn't decided yet.'

'And what did she say?'

Tia smiled. 'She said they could wait a little longer,' she said, and closed her eyes.

Meryt heaved a sigh of relief, and left her aunt to sleep. So there was still time. She thought of her offering to Peshedu and silently repeated her prayer as she went back to the courtyard. As she settled down to work at the loom, Nauna made her excuses and went up to the roof, and Meryt relaxed. For once, being at home was peaceful; Mose sat nearby, scribbling all the lessons he had learnt on a pile of ostraca, while Henut played her favourite game of teasing the cats. Meryt worked steadily through the afternoon until Baki awoke and shouted out from his bed, demanding beer. She took him a cupful just as Kenna called from the street.

'Shhh, Kenna! Tia is sleeping,' Meryt called back, in a low voice. 'I'll be with you in a minute.'

'Where are you going?' demanded Baki.

'None of your business,' Meryt responded curtly.

Baki's eyes flashed. 'Things are going to change around here, Meryt,' he said. 'I'll soon make it my business to know where you go.'

Meryt felt a frisson of fear, but kept her features

101

still. 'I'd like to see you try.'

'Just you wait,' muttered Baki.

Meryt glared at her cousin. It was strange, seeing him without the side-lock of youth that she was so used to. His whole head was now a dome of tiny bristles, which somehow suited him, but the fact was that she had reason to fear what it represented. Baki was no longer a boy; and with both men of the house against her, things could indeed 'change around here'.

She dumped a flagon of beer by the side of his bed, then quickly tidied up the weaving in the courtyard before hurrying through the house to find Kenna.

The street was already busy, for the weekly parade of the oracle – like the council meetings – brought everyone out in droves. The statue of the god Amenhotep I was carried on the shoulders of four priests, stopping to answer the questions of the villagers as it went along. It was easy to tell the god's opinion, for when he said yes, he caused the priests to move forward; when he said no, they moved backwards. Meryt had never dared ask the god a question, for what if he gave an answer she did not want to hear – in front of all the other villagers? But watching others do so was one of her favourite pastimes, all the same.

Dedi was waiting for them in the doorway of her home. News of Userkaf's plans had definitely spread, for a few villagers were hanging around nearby, waiting to see if Nebnufer would emerge.

'Let's get up to the shrine,' said Dedi, joining her two friends on the street. 'I hate it when everyone stares.'

Kenna smiled sympathetically, and Meryt watched him, biting her lip. Now that she had become aware of it, she couldn't believe that she hadn't noticed his attraction to Dedi before. It was written over his whole body – the way he bent towards her, the way he smiled, the way he listened to what she said. As they walked up the street, Meryt fell behind, battling with herself. *Kenna would never act on it*, she scolded herself. *Dedi is engaged to Neben-Maat*. But however often she repeated it, the niggling ache inside her stayed the same.

The parade of the oracle set out from the shrine of Amenhotep and Ahmes Nefertari, which was nestled among the other gods' chapels to the north-west of the village. From there, it moved down to the village gate and along the main street before returning the same way. The villagers ran in front and behind, singing hymns of praise and offering flowers, while anyone with a question ran into the path of the oracle and fell to their knees to ask it.

A priest was already standing at the entrance to the shrine. He was barely recognisable as one of the workmen on Sennedjem's gang, a carpenter who built the scaffolding in the tombs. As part of a rigorous purification, the carpenter had completely shaved his head and his body – even his eyebrows – and stood silently at the gates, surveying the crowd that was slowly gathering.

Meryt, Kenna and Dedi squatted in the shadow of a nearby chapel. Dedi was quiet and played with a bracelet nervously, pushing it up and down her slender arm and casting sidelong glances at the shrine. Soon, the area was full of people, all waiting for the oracle to emerge.

'Is your father going to come out?' Kenna asked her.

Dedi nodded. 'He and my mother together, as they did for the council meeting.'

There was a hush as the carpenter priest raised his hand, then an excited murmur as the four priests came into sight with the statue of the god balanced on a litter held high on their shoulders.

'Behold our god Amenhotep – life, prosperity, health!' cried the carpenter priest, now raising both his arms. 'Come, people of Set Maat, and bring him your concerns, for he rules justly over us.'

The statue moved forward slowly, the faces of the priests still and solemn. There was a flurry of movement as the first petitioner ran forward and prostrated himself before the oracle. The priests came to a halt.

'My lord Amenhotep – life, prosperity, health!' cried the man. 'My cattle have fallen sick. Will they die?'

The crowd became silent, and the statue seemed to tremble for a moment. Then the priests stepped forward all at once, and everyone cheered, while a group of singers started a hymn. The man bowed in gratitude and scurried back into the crowd.

A woman was next, stepping forward to kneel with great dignity before the statue. 'I have only daughters,' she said in a clear voice. 'We need a son. Will I bear one soon, my lord?'

The statue shuddered, and the throng held its breath. Then, slowly, the priests stepped backwards – one step, then two, then a third. Everyone murmured and gasped, staring at the woman to gauge her reaction. She held on to her dignity well, rising slowly to her feet and turning away with her head bent.

The oracle moved on. Meryt, Dedi and Kenna followed close behind, joining in with one of the hymns, as more villagers came forward with their queries. There was still no sign of Userkaf, and Meryt began to hope that it had all been a vicious rumour after all. The parade reached the village gate and began to process down the main street.

Suddenly, a shout went up, and Meryt craned her neck. Kenna was taller, and she leant on his arm. 'Can you see anything?' she asked.

'It's Nebnufer,' he replied. 'Dedi, your father is standing at the end of your alley. But I still can't see Userkaf.'

'Perhaps fear has kept him away,' said Meryt in a low voice, squeezing her friend's arm.

But she spoke too soon. The oracle had come to a halt and the crowd fell quiet. By moving to the edge of the parade, the three friends were able to see

Userkaf, elbowing his way forward to stand in front of the priests.

The arrogant draughtsman did not prostrate himself. He stood with his head high so that everyone could see him.

'Lord Amenhotep of the village,' he boomed. 'Life, prosperity, health! Answer my question. Is Nebnufer our foreman working his men too hard?'

The throng of villagers was now completely silent. A puppy began to bark and was silenced immediately. Everyone's eyes rested on the priests and their sacred litter. For a moment, they seemed to sway forwards, and a ripple of excitement rose from the crowd. But the feet of the priests stayed still. Then slowly, surely, the litter swayed back, and the feet of the priests moved with it.

'No!' The crowd shouted in unison, and then a riotous jabber of voices broke out. People pressed forward and the leading priest warned everyone back. 'Respect Amenhotep our Lord! Let him continue his journey through the village!'

Meryt stared at Userkaf, who was still standing in the way of the oracle. She watched the emotions flit across his face in fascination. This was not a man who was easily thwarted. She saw him turn to face Nebnufer with a grimace – but not a grimace of disappointment, or of defeat. It was the expression of a man who would not stop here. His features were full of purpose, and the purest rage.

 CHAPTER SIX

The rest of the parade was conducted with much singing and dancing. The crowd followed the oracle to the bottom of the street and back again, clapping their hands and chanting prayers. Meryt barely noticed the man who walked along at the edge of the crowd, close to where she and her friends were dancing.

It was Dedi who noticed. 'Meryt!' she exclaimed. 'Look!'

Meryt peered through the mass of swaying bodies. There, plodding along with a placid smile on his face, was Ramose. She went cold. Her immediate instinct was to run away.

'Dedi, I must leave. Now.'

Dedi grinned at her, oblivious to Meryt's agony. 'Don't be ridiculous. He's made a proposal of marriage. You should say hello, at least – he is not going to eat you.'

'I can't. I just can't. I have to go,' Meryt protested, turning her back on the stonecutter before he could spot her.

Their exchange attracted Kenna's attention. 'What's going on?' he asked.

Meryt glared at Dedi and shook her head, begging her friend with her eyes to give nothing away. 'I have to go back to the house, that's all,' she said. 'Tia needs me to care for Baki.'

Kenna looked surprised. 'But the parade is almost over. She can wait a little longer, surely? You didn't mention it before.'

Meryt glanced from one friend to the other, feeling desperate and torn. She did not want to leave them together to enjoy themselves without her. At the same time she could not bear for Ramose to come over and announce his intentions before Kenna. Suddenly, she spotted Dedi's handsome fiancé Neben-Maat, and felt a surge of relief.

'Look, Dedi. It's Neben-Maat. He's looking for you, I'm sure.'

Dedi spun around, her face alight with happiness. At the same time, Meryt saw Kenna's smile fade, and her heart contracted. Somehow, life was proving very unfair. 'Goodbye, Kenna,' she said.

He tore his eyes away from Dedi, who was reaching up to kiss Neben's cheek. 'Oh … see you soon, Meryt,' he said vaguely, as Meryt turned and left the parade to go back down the street.

Meryt retired to the roof early that night. She curled up under a sheet and turned her back to the staircase, so that anyone who came up would know not to disturb her. It had been a long day, and her mind would not rest. As she churned everything over, Meryt pushed away the thought of Kenna and tried to ponder Userkaf instead. What would the draughtsman do next? What did he want? Perhaps it was true that he had nothing to do with the stolen amulets, for his aims seemed to be of a much more personal kind – disruption among the men, and division between the foremen.

But her mind soon drifted to Dedi, and her happiness with Neben-Maat. Would he and his family stand by her, if Userkaf succeeded in his aims? If they did not, Dedi might be forced to look elsewhere for a husband. *What if she chooses Kenna?* whispered a voice in Meryt's mind, and she sat up abruptly to rub her eyes and stare out into the darkness. She shook herself. *Don't be absurd*, she told herself sternly. Dedi's marriage was still safe, and in any case, she would never pick their friend as a husband – Kenna had no status or wealth to offer her.

Meryt lay back down again and tried to sleep. But now it was the problem of her own marriage that plagued her, and the memory of Ramose returned, ambling along with the parade like a docile pet donkey. *Peshedu, Hathor, please answer me!* Meryt mouthed silently into the night, then remembered her ostracon, and got up again to fetch it from its hiding place.

With the little flake of limestone tucked safely under her head she managed to sleep at last, but only fitfully at first, flitting in and out of dreams. At first they were random images, little more. She saw Teti's face, smiling up at her, and her plants strewn on the street. She saw Nofret's stolen amulet. She saw Dedi and Neben-Maat, running down the street with their arms around each other, laughing and singing in happiness.

She sank into deeper sleep for a few brief hours, then surfaced again to dream brighter, harder dreams. The colours were sharper and the story drew her along, pulling and pushing her so that she twitched and shivered where she lay. She was with her cousin Baki. They were walking in the valley, heading back to Set Maat from the market. They had been to buy a duck and some extra vegetables. Baki was tormenting her, pulling her hair, pushing her into the irrigation channels so that her linen dress was soon spattered with mud. They approached the road that led to the great temple within the Fields of Djame. They could see the massive mud-brick walls surrounding the beautiful stone temple that lay within ... and still Baki carried on taunting her until she could bear it no longer.

She was about to strike out. She was raising her arm. Her cousin was cowering away from her – but before her blow could land, there was a flurry of fur and snapping yellow teeth. A dog was after them, one of the mangy feral creatures that skulked at the edge of the desert. Forgetting their disputes, they ran.

The road seemed endless. The dog was ferocious, giving out deep snarling growls as it bounded after them. Meryt could feel flecks of its slaver on her back and smell the stench of its breath. She thought her heart would stop with fear, for dogs were her worst enemies and she could not bear to be near them.

Suddenly the dog had gone and Baki was in front of her, laughing and holding up his hand.

'It bit me,' he was saying. 'Look, see how it bleeds. The dog bit me ...'

Meryt woke up in terror. She flung off the sheet and looked around with wild eyes, expecting the creature to jump from the shadows. There was nothing there, and as her sight adjusted to the familiar shapes of the rooftop, she let out a long, slow breath.

With a sure, unerring instinct, Meryt knew that the dream meant something. It was not a random collection of images, drawn from the scenes of the day. She relived the terror of the dog's breath on her back and the sight of the gaping wound in Baki's hand.

Surely this had nothing to do with Ramose! She pressed her fingers to her temples, thinking it through. No. There was nothing ... Nothing to link it to the stonecutter, or to her father, or to the previous dream that had come to her.

It must be to do with Baki. She lay back down again, staring up at the eastern sky where the first light of dawn was growing. Her cousin lay in the room below, no doubt sleeping peacefully; it was the third day since his ritual and his pain must be less by now, but Meryt was filled with foreboding. After a few minutes, the sky was lighter, and she could stay still no longer. She got up and crept down the stairs to stand in the doorway of the back room.

Baki lay on his back on the bed. Tia had at last been persuaded that he could be left to sleep alone, and she was with the rest of the family in the middle room. In the dim light, Meryt could see that her cousin's eyelids were flickering. He muttered something, shifting his head to one side, and she tiptoed closer.

It was difficult to tell for sure, but Meryt thought his breath was shallower than it should be. There were two spots of high colour on each of his brown cheeks. With a trembling hand, Meryt reached and touched her cousin's forehead. It was damp and clammy.

Baki stirred, and Meryt retreated hastily to the door. On seeing her, the goat clambered to its feet in the courtyard and started bleating for food. Meryt fed it some wilted lettuce leaves to keep it quiet, then peeped around the door again. Her cousin slept on.

Meryt returned to the roof to wait for daylight, her heart full of fear. What was happening to Baki? Had she in some way caused it? She pondered her recent thoughts and actions, terrified that she had brought evil into the house despite herself. She knew she had never wished it. She might hate Baki at times, she might fear for her own future, but her love for Tia and the children was too strong for her to ever deliberately cause them grief.

As the first rays of sunlight hit the western cliffs, Meryt crept downstairs once more. Baki was awake. Tia had arisen too, and she was changing the mixture of honey and fat that had to be applied to his wound.

'Ow! Don't – let me do it –' Baki protested, his face drawn in pain.

Meryt watched him as he dipped his fingers in the pot of honey that Tia held out for him. He seemed lively enough; perhaps there was nothing wrong, after all. But as Baki touched his cut, he flinched.

'The redness has spread,' he commented anxiously. 'Mama, it hurts.'

'More than yesterday?'

'Yes. Look, it is oozing too.'

'That is only the badness coming out,' Tia reassured him, though her voice was worried. 'Does it hurt too much to apply the dressing?'

Baki gritted his teeth. 'No, I can do it,' he muttered, wiping on the honey and reaching for the goose fat. When he had finished, he lay back so that Tia could wrap the wound in lint, and saw Meryt standing in the doorway.

'What are you staring at?' he snapped.

'I am concerned for you, that's all,' replied Meryt. She took in the brightness of his eyes and the spots of colour that still stood out on his cheeks, and hesitated, wondering whether to voice her fears. 'Your cheeks look hot.'

Tia looked at her quickly. 'Meryt, what do you mean?'

Meryt swallowed, then shrugged as Senmut appeared from the middle room, yawning and stretching.

'Are you well, Baki?' he asked, as he walked through to the courtyard.

'Yes, Father,' Baki replied. 'But I still have pain.'

Senmut poured out some water into a bowl and splashed his face and neck. 'The pain will fade,' he said, reaching for a linen towel. 'You'll be joining me in the tombs next week, you wait and see. Meryt, fetch me a clean loincloth, will you?'

Meryt did as he said. She would be glad when Senmut had left for work, out of the way. With any luck he would be gone for the full eight days and Baki would be well by the time he returned.

But once Senmut had set off with a group of other workmen for the tombs, Tia took her to one side. 'What was it you were saying about Baki?' she asked in a low voice.

Meryt took in her aunt's drawn, tired features, the deep fear that sat in her eyes, and the dark circles that lay under them. There was no point in making things worse for her, especially as she knew nothing for sure. 'Don't worry. I was just being sympathetic,' she said, with a smile. 'That was all.'

There was a knock at the door, and Tia went to answer it. Meryt was relieved, as she knew that her aunt would not have time to enquire further. Because

114

it was the start of the week, the king's servants would arrive one after the other – fishermen with fish, gardeners with vegetables, and the laundrymen to collect the dirty linen.

Tia checked each delivery meticulously and made a careful note of all the linen while Meryt and Nauna baked a fresh batch of bread. The monthly wages of grain were not due for another week and they rationed the flour carefully, for Senmut had exhausted most of their stores to pay for Baki's feast. Baki himself lay idle, drifting in and out of sleep as the women bustled around him. Meryt glanced at him occasionally, unable to dispel the fear that her dream had evoked. She willed the memory of it to fade, but it remained vivid, plaguing her with anxiety whenever she thought about it.

She was sweeping out the house in the early afternoon when there was a knock on the door, and Kenna's face appeared. 'Working hard as usual,' he commented, coming into the front room. 'Can you take a break?'

Meryt propped her broom against the wall and they walked though the house. Tia was sitting with Baki, and the children were helping Nauna in the courtyard, so Meryt led her friend up to the roof.

Kenna came straight to the point. 'Is something wrong?' he asked bluntly. 'You don't seem yourself at the moment. You left in a hurry last night – one minute you were there, and then you'd gone. That's the second time you've done that recently.'

Meryt looked away. *You only had eyes for Dedi*, she wanted to say, but she knew it wasn't quite fair. The sight of Ramose had driven her away too. 'You're imagining it,' she stuttered. 'I told you, I had to come back to care for Baki.'

'I know you too well, Meryt,' responded Kenna, looking at her closely. 'Something is troubling you, I'm sure of it.'

Meryt played with the edge of the reed matting, feeling cornered. Part of her was full of envy as she remembered Kenna's eyes gazing at Dedi, mingled with dread at the thought of Ramose. Another part was glad that Kenna cared enough to persist with his questioning – he was, and always had been, a friend she could rely on.

'I have been happier,' she admitted. 'These are difficult times.'

'Difficult? In what way?' asked Kenna.

Meryt hunted for something to say. 'I am worried for Nebnufer,' she said. 'There is trouble brewing in the village.'

Kenna snorted. 'What of it?' he asked dismissively. 'This is not your concern, Meryt. Though as it happens I have some news on that score.'

'What?'

'People are saying that Userkaf only dared to consult the oracle because he is blessed by the gods.'

Meryt gasped. 'Blessed by the ...!' Her mouth dropped open. 'But that's crazy.' She thought quickly, unable to believe that people were so gullible. 'If the gods cared so much for him, Amenhotep would have found in his favour,' she pointed out.

'Perhaps. But he behaves like a man of power, and he has done well for himself recently. Everything he does seems to bring him greater wealth and influence, whatever the oracle might have said.'

There was a faint edge of awe to Kenna's voice, and Meryt drew her breath in sharply. 'Do *you* think the gods are with him?' she asked.

Kenna shrugged. 'I don't know what I think,' he said. 'I wish no harm to come to Nebnufer, of course. Especially for Dedi's sake. But when a man begins to smell of success, it's important to respect him. He has some of the gods on his side, at least – and they must be powerful ones.'

With a jolt of fear, Meryt saw that Kenna's words were true. Her thoughts flashed to Nofret's amulets and she shivered. Perhaps it was their magic that he was harnessing, after all – perhaps their power could turn people in his favour. It was frightening. Meryt wished she had never encountered the servant girl on the hilltop. Such knowledge was a dangerous thing.

'Meryt?' Kenna looked at her questioningly, then lay down sideways on the matting, leaning his head against his wrist. As he did so, he disturbed her linen pillow and the ostracon of Hathor was nudged from underneath it. He stared at it curiously. 'What's this?' he asked, picking it up.

Meryt snatched at it. 'Don't touch that.'

But Kenna was too quick. He rolled out of her way, holding the ostracon at arm's length. 'So it's yours,' he said, sitting up. 'You are consulting the goddess Hathor.'

It was mortifying. 'Give it back!' demanded Meryt, reaching for it again. It was no use. Kenna's arms were longer, and she was not going to make things worse by fighting for it.

'Hathor,' said Kenna, looking at her strangely. 'The goddess of love. Is there something you haven't told me, Meryt?'

Meryt buried her face in her hands. She could hide the secret no longer. In any case, what was the point? He would hear it soon enough from the servants, or on the streets. 'I have received a proposal of marriage,' she mumbled.

'Marriage! Who from?'

'Ramose. Son of Heria and Paneb.' She forced herself to look at her friend and found that Kenna was frowning.

'Is this why you are upset?' he asked uncertainly. 'I don't know Ramose well, but he seems decent enough. This should be a good thing, surely.'

'A good thing!' Meryt felt anguished. 'I don't want to marry him, Kenna.'

Kenna held Meryt's ostracon in his hands and fingered it gently. It was difficult to tell what he was thinking. 'Why not?' he asked.

Meryt was speechless. She held out her hand for

the ostracon. Kenna handed it over, searching her face, but she could still find nothing to say. She was tucking the flake of limestone safely back under the linen pillow when they heard footsteps coming up the stairway. It was Tia, and her face was grave.

'Is something wrong?' asked Meryt, instinctively knowing what the answer would be.

'I need a messenger to go to Senmut,' said Tia. 'Would you go for me, Kenna?'

'Why?' demanded Meryt. 'What's happened?'

'It's Baki,' said her aunt, in a frightened voice. 'He ... he is not well. His wound swells and grows redder and he is beginning to moan in pain.'

Kenna rose to his feet. 'Of course I'll go,' he said. 'What should I say?'

'That he must come back at once,' said Tia, her face pale. 'Tell him that Baki needs him.'

'I will take Father's donkey and bring him back on it,' said Kenna. 'Is there anything else I can do?'

Tia shook her head. 'No. It is good of you to go.' She smiled briefly. 'Meryt, I need you to help me.'

The three went back down the stairs. Kenna set off immediately, running off down the street to collect his father's donkey. It took more than an hour to reach the Great Place on foot, but with the help of the sure-footed animal Senmut would be back before sunset.

As Meryt and Tia returned to Baki's bedside he leapt up, his eyes wild, and ran into the courtyard.

'Give me wine!' he shouted, crashing among the

beer flagons and flinging the empty ones to one side. 'Why is there no wine?'

Little Henut took fright at the sight of her desperate brother and began to howl. One of the flagons glanced the goat's back legs and it bleated pitifully, while Nauna threw her hands in the air and began her usual tirade at the terrible state of her son's family. Only Mose made no noise, melting into the background and running lightly on to the roof to escape.

Meryt ran and grasped Baki by the elbow. 'Baki, there is no more wine. You must rest. You will only make yourself worse.'

He bellowed and tried to throw her off but he was weaker than usual, and Meryt was determined. With Tia helping on his other side, they managed to control him and hold him still until his breathing grew calmer.

'Baki, you must lie down,' said Tia in a trembling voice. 'I will dress your wound again to give you some relief.'

Baki spat on the ground. Meryt could feel the heat surging through his body and her heart quaked with fear. But then the fight went out of him and he allowed them to lead him back inside. Meryt squatted in the courtyard, comforting Henut, while Tia tended his wound. Mose stayed on the roof out of the way, but Henut continued to whimper, her little world shaken by Baki's outburst. Meryt stroked her hair until Tia called for her once more.

Tia beckoned Meryt to the front room. 'Baki is

calmer now,' she whispered. 'I must go to Peshedu's tomb. It is not enough to make an offering here. I must go and speak to my brother in his own chapel.'

'Tia, this has nothing to do with my father, surely!' Meryt stared at her aunt in disbelief. 'Why would he wish harm to Baki?'

Tia's eyes pleaded with her. 'Please, Meryt, just do as I ask. Take care of Baki while I'm gone. Nauna is useless, she has no sympathy for him. I won't be long.' She reached into a casket for some incense and a burner. 'Would you fetch me a loaf and some dates from the courtyard?' she asked over her shoulder.

As she did so, Meryt remembered the mysterious offering that she had found in the chapel the morning before. 'Someone else has been offering to Peshedu,' she told her aunt, handing her the loaf. 'I went there myself yesterday.'

Tia looked startled. 'How strange! Are you sure?'

'At first I thought it must be you,' said Meryt. 'But it was not our bread lying there.'

'No, no. It wasn't me.' Tia shoved the loaf and dates hurriedly into a bag. 'Well, I must go. I want to be back for when Senmut arrives.' With a brief, worried smile, she kissed Meryt on the cheek and was gone.

Meryt wandered back through the house. The job of looking after Baki was not one she particularly relished, and she was relieved that his eyes were closed as she walked past. She slipped into the courtyard and sat down with her back leaning against the wall of the house – out of sight of her cousin, but close enough to hear his movements.

Nauna and the children were on the roof, and all was quiet for a while. Meryt listened to Baki shifting around on the bed, and watched the goat chewing peacefully in the shade. She thought of Kenna, riding up over the mountain to fetch Senmut, and her cheeks flamed when she remembered what he had said about Ramose. How could he call it 'a good thing', even if ... even if ... She struggled with her thoughts, unwilling to admit what was really in her mind. In the end she could not block it out. How could he say such a thing, even if he didn't want Meryt himself?

Meryt hugged her knees in frustration. It was all Dedi's fault. Until her friend had put the idea in her head, she had never thought of Kenna as anything other than a friend. But as soon as Dedi had said *such friends can become lovers*, she hadn't been able to get it out of her mind. Now it was there, plaguing her, while Kenna pined not for her but for Dedi. And Ramose? Meryt's heart filled with rage at the dim-witted stonecutter who had not even had the gumption to propose to her in person.

'Mama!' Baki cried out from his bed, and Meryt scrambled to her feet. Baki was sitting up, staring around him, and when he saw Meryt he yelled again. 'Mama! I want some wine!'

'Tia's not here,' Meryt told him. 'And there isn't any wine. I will fetch you some beer.'

She hurried into the courtyard and picked out a fresh flagon of beer, a cup and a strainer. Baki continued to call out. Meryt felt frightened at the harshness of his cries, and clutched the amulet around her neck before returning to her cousin's bedside. There, she averted her gaze from the glazed, feverish look in his eyes and concentrated on straining the beer. Then, to her relief, she heard footsteps. She guessed that Tia had returned, and looked up with a smile at the doorway.

It was not Tia. It was Senmut, still covered in the white gypsum plaster that was the mark of his trade. Meryt's smile faded and she handed the cup of beer to Baki. Senmut marched to his son's bedside and tilted his chin up, studying his face, then placed a hand on his forehead. 'Where is Tia?' he demanded.

'She'll be back in a minute,' Meryt told him. 'She hasn't gone far. She left me to look after Baki.'

'Father, I want wine,' said Baki, his voice hoarse. 'Meryt won't give it to me.'

'There isn't any!' protested Meryt.

'You won't give it to me,' her cousin persisted. His breathing was now shallow and irregular and beads of sweat stood out on his forehead.

Meryt just had time to see the dismay on Senmut's face as it dawned on him that Baki really had fallen sick. Then he turned on her, his expression threatening. 'I don't want you caring for my son,' he told her.

'But Tia asked …' Meryt stuttered.

Senmut's eyes flashed. 'You heard what I said.

123

Keep away from him, do you hear?'

Meryt's mouth dropped open. Then she backed away. 'Yes, Uncle.'

'Then go.'

The expression on Senmut's face was thunderous, and Meryt didn't need to be told twice. She turned and ran from the house, heading for the eastern hill-top overlooking the River Nile. When she reached the summit, gasping and out of breath, she flung herself down on a rock and thumped the ground in frustration. It seemed as though the whole world were conspiring against her – the whole world, or perhaps the gods. But why? What on earth had she done?

After a while, she calmed down and gazed out over the view, fingering her father's scarab amulet. There was no way she could go home, not right away. She knew from experience that Senmut's anger would take some time to cool, and while Baki was still unwell it would be best to keep a low profile. She decided to wait for nightfall and creep in for shelter once everyone else was asleep. Meanwhile, she needed to think.

These were indeed difficult times, and Senmut's reaction to her made little sense. Did he really think she was a danger to Baki? Surely he could not believe that! But then she remembered her dream, and the seed of doubt that had been there ever since she'd woken up began to grow. She thought of Tia, making her offering to Peshedu, and frowned. Could it be that both herself and her father were cursed by the gods? Perhaps Senmut was right to say that nothing good would ever come of her.

When at last the sun had set and all she could see were the twinkling lamps in people's houses, Meryt crept back down the hillside and through the village. When she reached her home, she stood outside the front door and listened. There was a murmuring of voices from the back room and the courtyard, but there was no one in the middle room. As quietly as she could, she stepped inside and opened a large wooden casket. Fumbling in the darkness, she felt around until she found an old linen cloak. She closed the casket softly, wrapped the cloak around her shoulders and tiptoed back into the front room to lie down.

It wasn't easy to fall asleep. Meryt was hungry. She dreaded Senmut walking through and finding her, though for the moment she could hear that he was busy arguing with Tia. She guessed that Tia was reasoning with him on her behalf; at least, she hoped so. Tia was her only ally in the household, other than the children. She curled into a ball, comforted by the fact that she was going to help Teti in a few hours' time. Thinking of the *rekhet*'s warm smile made her feel better, and she gradually drifted off to sleep.

She woke a few hours later. The household was quiet. In the darkness of the front room, it was harder to tell whether dawn was on its way, so she threw off the cloak and went to the front door. Out on the

125

street, she saw the faintest glimmer of light to the east, and felt relieved that the night was almost over. The people of Set Maat were early risers, but even so the streets were still deserted as Meryt headed north. She jumped nervously as a guard dog yapped at her, and broke into a jog until she reached the gate.

Teti lived in a little house outside the village wall. Meryt knew that her husband had been a scribe, one of the men who registered the attendance of the men at the tombs and oversaw their supply of equipment. But, like so many people of the village, he had died young. Teti had no children and had lost their house, which had been handed on to another workman. But scribes were well paid, and Teti's inheritance had allowed her to build her own home just outside the village walls. There were several such houses, and Meryt was unsure which one belonged to the *rekhet*. So she sat on the path that led to the valley to wait.

The sky was only just growing pink when she heard footsteps, and saw the *rekhet* approaching with a smile on her lips.

'Ah, here you are,' said Teti. 'Thank you for coming.'

'Oh! Thank you for letting me,' said Meryt, scrambling to her feet. 'It's the least I can do. I'm so sorry I jogged your basket.'

Teti's smile broadened. 'These things happen for a reason,' she said. 'Shall we get going?'

They walked at a brisk pace down towards the river valley. Meryt noticed that Teti's eyes were trained on the ground, scanning the path and the rocks around, and that nothing escaped her notice. Sometimes she bent down to scoop up a pebble or even small pieces of dung, wrapping them carefully in linen and popping them in her basket. They passed between the grand mortuary temples and soon reached the area of irrigation, where suddenly there was rich, black earth and the new crop was pushing up its lush, strong shoots.

But Teti was not interested in the farmland that morning. She led Meryt down towards the river along winding pathways where wild plants and rushes grew.

'Look! The dew,' she said, reaching out to a big, bold plant and gently pulling its leaves towards her. With her other hand, she fished out a little bottle and curved the edges of a leaf towards its rim. Meryt watched as the droplets of dew were captured one by one. Teti smiled at her. 'I use so much. I'm always running out,' she said.

They moved on, and Teti pointed out the plants she needed to gather – wild dill and hemp, different sedges and wormwood. Meryt warmed to her task and was soon absorbed in the hunt, picking flowers for her own enjoyment as well as the plants for Teti. There were date palms along the riverbank too, and their fruit lay scattered here and there. Meryt's stomach rumbled and she remembered that she had not eaten the night before. She gathered some of the dates and ate them hungrily.

Suddenly, Teti gave a shout. 'Meryt! Come back!'

'What is it?' Meryt looked up. She had wandered away on her own, and was now very close to the water's edge. Teti was beckoning her urgently, and out of the corner of her eye, Meryt saw a sudden ripple on the surface of the river.

'This way!' shouted Teti.

It was a crocodile. Meryt caught a glimpse of its slitted snake-like eyes before its snout broke the surface. She yelped in fear, then ran, scratching her legs on the sharp edges of reeds and tearing her linen dress. She reached Teti but could not stop. Her terror had taken over. Suddenly, she was back in her dream with Baki, running away from the maddened dog with all her strength. Her legs pumped on and on.

She ran until she reached an open field where she collapsed in the mud, her lungs sore and wheezing. It was several minutes before Teti appeared, her face full of concern.

'Meryt! Are you all right?'

Meryt nodded, still unable to speak, as Teti knelt beside her and stroked her arm.

'You did well to run so hard,' said Teti. 'You should not have strayed so close to the water.'

Meryt struggled to get her breath back. 'I know,' she gulped. Everyone knew of the dangers that lurked in the Nile, and children were taught not to dabble in the shallows in areas where the crocodiles were plentiful.

Her breathing grew steadier, and Teti gazed into

her eyes. 'You did well to run so hard,' the *rekhet* repeated. 'But the crocodile would not have pursued you. It likes to take its prey by surprise. So it was not fear of being caught that drove you on like that. It was something else, wasn't it?'

Meryt felt mesmerised by Teti's soft brown eyes, which seemed to see beyond the surface, deep into her mind. 'Yes,' she whispered.

'Can you tell me about it?' Teti asked gently.

Meryt hesitated. 'It was a dream,' she said.

'You were being chased?'

'Yes. By a dog.' Meryt shivered.

'And were you alone in this dream?'

Again, Meryt hesitated, fearful of what might happen if she were honest. She knew that Teti's powers included divination, similar to the powers of the oracle. People went to her if they were afraid to go through the usual channels. Meryt had the feeling that Teti could give an interpretation of her dream, if she chose ... but she was not sure that she wanted to hear it.

'You don't have to tell me.' Teti's voice was soft and reassuring.

'I was with my cousin Baki,' Meryt blurted.

'And did the dog bite you?'

Meryt took a deep breath, and shook her head.

'It bit your cousin Baki,' guessed Teti.

Meryt raised her eyes to those of the *rekhet*, biting her lip, and nodded. 'Do you know what it means?' she whispered. 'I am so afraid. He has fallen sick.'

Teti squeezed Meryt's arm. 'I am not surprised. This is not a matter to be taken lightly.' The *rekhet*'s face grew serious. 'Your cousin has been touched by magic.'

Meryt stared down at the mud on her linen dress, her heart pounding. 'Will he live?' she managed to ask.

Teti reached for Meryt's hand, and pulled her to her feet. 'That too will depend on magic,' she said.

 CHAPTER SEVEN

Meryt and Teti continued to gather plants until the sun was bright, glistening on the river and warming their skin. Meryt desperately wanted to question the *rekhet* further, but as the sun's heat increased, Teti's movements became quick and purposeful, moving rapidly from one plant to another, and she did not like to interrupt her.

'We must get back,' said Teti. 'The plants will soon wither in the sun.'

They walked quickly towards Set Maat, meeting field labourers and temple priests along the way, but it was not until they climbed the final stretch of path that Meryt found the courage to speak. 'Teti,' she said, 'what is the magic that has touched my cousin Baki?'

'I don't know,' said Teti simply. 'What I have told you comes from the wisdom of the *Dream Book*. I can't tell you anything else without knowing the details.'

'I fear for him,' said Meryt. 'Would you help me?'

Teti smiled. 'Of course,' she said. 'But now is not the time. I have many things to attend to. Come back later, or tomorrow. Can you do that?'

Meryt nodded, relief flooding through her. 'Thank you.'

'And thank you for your help,' said Teti. 'You have learnt something, I hope.'

'Oh! Plenty,' Meryt exclaimed. 'I shall remember the crocodiles in future.'

Teti laughed merrily, and winched her basket higher on to her hip. They had reached the fork that led to her group of houses, and she set off down it leaving Meryt on the main track. 'Take care, Meryt,' she called, waving as she walked out of sight.

Meryt wondered what to do next. Under normal circumstances, she would go home to help Tia with the chores. But circumstances were not exactly normal. Senmut would still be there, so it would be better to stay away for as long as possible. She wanted to be sure that his wrath had abated, or at least that she had something to offer Baki, by the time she showed her face again.

She considered a visit to Kenna or Dedi but decided against it. She still felt a little raw from Kenna's words about Ramose, and too proud to burden Dedi with her problems. After skirting around the northern village wall, she scrambled up the hill that overlooked the village. There was no cemetery and no track on this side, and she picked her way carefully, trying not to stub her toes on the sharp limestone rocks.

'I thought I might find you here,' said a voice as

she made the final few steps to the top.

Meryt looked up. 'Nofret!'

The servant girl was sitting where Meryt usually sat, on a flat slab polished smooth by generations of villagers who had enjoyed the same spot.

'I need to speak to you,' said Nofret.

Meryt remembered their last encounter, and felt instantly suspicious. 'Why?' she asked. 'Have you more gossip to report?'

Nofret shook her head. 'No,' she said. 'I want to ask for your help.'

Feeling wary, Meryt sat down near the servant girl and studied her face. Nofret's expression was humble, or seemed to be. 'What sort of help?'

Nofret reached for a bag that lay by her side. 'You know that I am in trouble,' she said in a low voice. 'You have seen one of the amulets and you know that I risk displeasing the gods.'

'Yes,' said Meryt. 'What you are doing is very foolish.'

'It is worse than you think,' whispered Nofret. She opened the bag, and Meryt grew curious. 'The amulets have great power. The man who requires them may do the village harm and may hurt me even more.'

'Userkaf?' asked Meryt.

'No, no, not Userkaf. He has nothing to do with all this.' Nofret said the words quickly, and Meryt frowned, watching in silence as the servant girl reached inside the bag.

'I need protection,' Nofret carried on. She fetched out a fine linen shawl, a pretty beaded collar and a copper bangle. 'I need protection from the gods and I need protection from the man who wants the amulets.'

Meryt gazed at the objects laid in front of her. 'And what have these got to do with it?' she asked, bewildered.

Nofret smiled nervously. 'They are for you,' she said. 'You know that I have heard you have the power of Sekhmet, who brings destruction and illness. Nes says so, and others too. But Sekhmet offers protection as well, does she not?'

Meryt's mouth dropped open. It was so astonishing a proposal that she wasn't sure she had understood correctly. 'You are asking me to protect you?'

The servant girl nodded, and Meryt stared at her. Surely Nofret did not believe that she held any real power? In fact, she doubted that anyone did, deep down – including her uncle Senmut. The villagers were fond of gossip and all too ready to leap on a story, whether they really believed it or not; especially if it suited their own purposes.

'I can't. I have no power. This is just a rumour,' she said eventually. 'There is no truth in it.'

The servant girl pursed her lips. 'Such rumours always come from somewhere.'

'Well, this one didn't come from me,' said Meryt. 'It came from the wagging of neighbours' tongues.'

'I don't think so. Nes says you are different. She works in your house and she says she can sense it.'

Meryt felt a tingle run up and down her spine. She thought of Baki, lying on his sick bed. She thought of her dream, and the words of Teti: *your cousin has been touched by magic*. Her mouth felt dry, and she swallowed as Nofret pushed the shawl and bangle towards her, then picked up the beaded collar and held it against her own neck.

'See how lovely it is,' said the servant girl. 'The beads are mostly faience and glass, but there are a few of carnelian too. It would suit you.'

Meryt saw how the beads glinted in the morning sun, their colours bright and enticing. There were three strands fastened to a large red scarab in the centre. It was lovely. A sudden vision flashed through her head – sitting on the roof with Kenna admiring the collar around her own neck – but then, as Nofret offered it to her, she snapped to her senses. 'Do you really think the protection of the gods can be bought in this way?' she exclaimed. 'What are you thinking of?'

The servant girl's smile wavered for a moment, but then she shrugged. 'We make offerings to the gods all the time,' she said. 'They are payments, as far as I can see.'

It was a strange way of looking at things, but Meryt could see that it was true, in a way. And yet ... surely this was different? She didn't know what to think. Tentatively, she reached out and touched the shawl. It was of the finest quality, soft to the touch and purest white. Beautiful – the sort of thing that Dedi would wear; the sort of thing that only the wealthiest women wore …

And Nofret was a mere servant girl. Meryt looked up sharply. 'Where did you get these things?' she demanded. 'Who gave them to you?'

Nofret's face dropped, but then quickly clouded with anger. 'They are all I have,' she exclaimed. 'All I have ever had. My mother gave me the shawl when we parted. My father left me the collar. I earned the bracelet with my own hands.'

Meryt shook her head. 'I don't believe you,' she said.

'You've got to believe me!' insisted the servant girl, her eyes bright with determination. 'I am afraid, Meryt. Why else would I give you everything I have to protect me?'

Because I know you stole the amulets, thought Meryt, but said nothing. She sat back on her haunches and picked up the bracelet. This was not a fine object, like the shawl and the collar. It was a simple piece of copper – three strands woven together and clumsily soldered at the join. Could it be possible that Nofret was telling the truth? She could have earned a bracelet like this; it was barely a *deben*'s worth. And if the other two items were all her inheritance, she must be truly desperate.

She thought of the stolen amulets. Meryt did not want to have anything to do with their theft, and these gifts looked remarkably like a bribe – a bribe to buy her silence, not her protection. She would be foolish to accept them. But the servant girl was taking huge risks and was obviously in danger, all the same. Was this some kind of test? She remembered what Teti had said, only that morning – *These things happen for a reason.*

With a deep breath, she reached her decision. 'I don't want your precious goods, Nofret,' she said. 'I am not a goddess. You cannot make offerings to me.'

Frustration spread across the servant girl's features. She was about to protest, but Meryt held up her hand. 'It doesn't mean I won't help you,' she carried on, watching Nofret carefully. 'I will see what I can do – but only if you tell me the name of the man you are serving.'

Her heart quaked as she said the words, for she knew she was playing with fire – or worse. It was madness to meddle with the gods like this, but it was too late now. She had plunged in, and would have to carry the thing through.

Nofret's black eyes sparked angrily. 'I can't tell you that,' she said.

'Then I can't help you,' Meryt responded.

The servant girl snatched up the shawl and collar. Her pleading expression had gone. She glared at Meryt, then stuffed the items back into her bag.

Meryt shrugged. 'Perhaps you don't want protection as much as you thought,' she said. She watched as Nofret reached for the copper bangle, her lower lip wobbling, and Meryt suddenly realised that the servant girl was on the verge of tears. 'Of course, I will keep all your secrets,' she added casually.

Nofret looked up, the light of hope springing back into her eyes. 'If I tell you, you must swear,' she said. 'You must swear not to speak to anyone.'

Meryt nodded. 'I swear.'

'By all the gods and your ancestors.'

It was a heavy oath, and Meryt hesitated, clutching her protective amulet. Then recklessness gripped her, and she nodded again. 'By all the gods and my ancestors.'

Nofret leant forward. 'The man is Kha, the painter,' she whispered. 'He is a friend of Userkaf's and visits his house. He said that if I did not do what he asked, he would speak ill of me to Userkaf and that I would be beaten – or ... or worse.'

Her eyes looked big and haunted in her narrow face, and for the first time, Meryt felt some sympathy for the scrawny servant girl. She would hardly be the first servant to be abused by the men of the village. 'And what he wanted was ...' she prompted.

'The amulets.'

'Nothing more?' pressed Meryt, knowing that favours could take many forms; servant girls often gave birth to children that had no father to call by name.

'No.' Nofret's expression was wry. 'Isn't it bad enough that he makes me steal for him?'

Meryt sighed. 'Yes. Yes, of course it is.' She

138

shrugged. 'Well, your secret is safe with me.'

The servant girl flashed her a relieved smile, and rose to her feet. 'Thank you, Meryt,' she said. 'I am very grateful. May the gods be with you.'

Meryt watched as Nofret scurried down to the eastern cemetery and disappeared between the dilapidated tombs. Now that the other girl had gone, she could scarcely believe what had happened – or what she had agreed to. She went over what she had said in her mind, terrified that she had acted with disrespect towards the gods.

The main thing was that she had denied having any powers. And she had sworn not to speak of the amulets, or reveal the name of the painter, Kha. An oath of secrecy – there was no harm in this. Surely there was no harm in this! There was nothing for the gods to be angry about.

Nofret thinks you have powers, whispered a voice in her head. *By saying you would help her, you allowed her to think you have powers.*

'Nonsense,' she muttered to herself. 'Nofret is a thief who wants my silence. That is all.'

But the other girl's haunted features swam before her and she shook her head. Whatever her own problems might be, she was glad she was not a servant girl.

She got up and began to walk down the hillside towards the village. It was still only late morning, so she crossed the road by the village gate and climbed the hill on the other side, up into the western cemetery. The sun was growing warm as she wandered slowly towards her father's tomb.

In Peshedu's chapel, the offerings still lay on the altar – the mystery lettuce now dry and shrivelled alongside the unfamiliar loaves of bread, and her own offering next to the loaf placed there by Tia. Meryt stood before them and murmured a prayer to Peshedu. 'Peshedu, blessed spirit of Re, protect your daughter from the powers of evil. Keep the power of sacred amulets from harming me. Restore Baki to health so that I might live peacefully in Senmut's house. And deliver me from marriage to Ramose.'

It seemed a lot to ask from a blessed spirit of Re. The dead had their own concerns, and Meryt's heart felt heavy. She wandered back into the chapel courtyard to sit down in the sun and lean back against the courtyard wall. As ever, it was a comfort to feel the presence of Re as he made his passage across the sky, and his golden rays soon made her sleepy. Tired from having risen so early, she began to drift off.

She had no idea how long she slept. It was the sound of footsteps that awoke her, jerking her out of a deep slumber. She passed a hand across her face, disoriented, then leapt up to see who was there.

The chapel was empty. But someone had been there only a few minutes earlier, for the smell of incense hung heavy in the air and a fresh offering had been placed on the altar. Meryt stared at it. Figs – and more of the unfamiliar bread, laid neatly next to Tia's loaf. She turned and ran out of the chapel to peer down the pathway.

The figure of a woman was walking briskly towards the village gate. Meryt narrowed her eyes and shielded them from the sun, trying to work out who it was. It was not Tia, that was sure. Then, just as she was about to disappear from view, the woman turned to wave at one of the village guards, and Meryt saw her face.

It was Heria, the mother of Ramose.

Dumbfounded, Meryt went back through the courtyard and into the chapel. If it were not for the smell of incense that still hung in the air and the fresh offering that lay on the altar, she would almost have thought she'd imagined it. But the figs were plump and ripe, and the loaves were freshly baked. There had been no one else on the pathway, and in any case the tombs of both Paneb and Heria's own families were further round to the north of the cemetery.

So Heria was making offerings to Peshedu. Why? Why? After all that had happened over the last few weeks, Meryt felt a sudden rush of rage. She leapt at the altar, snatched up Heria's loaves and flung them out into the courtyard with all her strength.

'How dare you! How *dare* you!' she cried, shaking with fury, and reached for a fig. She hurled it after the loaves and it landed on the rocky ground with a little thud, its skin splitting open to reveal the rich red flesh within. It looked like a raw, gaping wound, and at the sight of it Meryt's rage disappeared as quickly as it had erupted. She raised a hand to her mouth in terror at what she had done and walked slowly outside.

'I'm so sorry,' she murmured, picking up the broken fruit, and tenderly brushing off the white dust that now coated it. She carried it reverently back into the chapel and laid it on the altar once more, then did the same with the loaves of bread. Kneeling down, she began to rock slowly to and fro, tears streaming down her face. 'Forgive me, forgive me,' she wept. 'I didn't mean to do it. Father, forgive me. The fig is not so badly damaged and I would bring you another if I could. Please forgive me.'

At last she grew quiet again and sat still, trying to work out what Heria's visits might mean. There was no family connection that Meryt was aware of. Tia and Senmut had little to do with Heria and Paneb – or at least until recently. The proposal from Ramose had changed things a little, but as Meryt thought about it, the more the whole situation seemed strange. She had never known Ramose well. Men of the village were usually much more forward with their courtships, and many couples became lovers before living together in marriage. But Ramose had barely spoken to Meryt in the past, and his proposal had come via Senmut.

There was one obvious explanation for this. *He only wants to marry me because he can't get anyone else*, Meryt thought to herself resentfully. And she was supposed to feel grateful because she was an orphan who was lucky to be living in the village at all.

But that didn't make sense of the other things that had happened: Heria's visit to their house, Heria's offerings to Peshedu ... Ramose might be a dull-witted son, but surely most mothers were not involved so deeply in their sons' affairs? Tia had said as much to Nauna on the roof when Meryt had overheard them talking. And even if it were for the sake of her son's marriage, making offerings to a girl's dead father was taking things a little far.

Gazing at the food upon the altar, Meryt suddenly felt the gnawing pangs of hunger. Apart from the dates that she had found along the riverside, she had eaten nothing that day, and very little the day before. The smell of the ripe fig reached her nostrils and her mouth watered. A fig and some fresh bread ... But she had damaged the offering enough already. Whatever its purpose, she would not desecrate it further. She pushed away the temptation and scrambled to her feet.

Meryt made her way towards the western gate. She decided to visit Kenna. Her cheeks flushed at the thought of speaking to him again, but he was still her friend; he was bound to find her something to eat.

To her disappointment, he wasn't in.

'He is taking food to his brother in the Place of Beauty,' his mother told her. She and Kenna's aunts stared at her curiously, and Meryt retreated hastily to the street.

Her stomach rumbled, and she wondered whether

to visit Dedi instead. But somehow, the idea of telling her friend that she was hungry was too humiliating. She wandered through the village, uncertain what to do.

She stood at the north gate, then walked out of the village. A group of men were lying in the shade not far off, taking their midday break. They had been employed to dig a great pit in the hope of hitting water, which would make life in the village easier; but they had found none after months of digging. Rumour had it they would soon be told to give up. Averting her gaze from their grins, Meryt turned around and soon found herself at the start of the little track that led to Teti's house under the north-western cliffs. She stopped. She barely knew the *rekhet*. Could she really return so soon? She had said 'come back later', hadn't she? Well, it was later now – not much later, but she had nowhere else to go.

Plucking up her courage, Meryt stepped down the path and sized up the little row of houses. It was difficult to guess which one belonged to Teti, and she peered at the whitewashed walls trying to pick up clues. A young boy of about four emerged from one, and smiled up at her innocently. Meryt smiled back and crouched down to his level.

'Do you know which house is Teti's?' she asked him.

The boy grinned at her and pointed to one of the houses. Meryt thanked him, then approached the house and knocked gently on the door. Now that she was here, she felt doubly nervous. Perhaps Teti was asleep, and would not take kindly to being woken. Perhaps the *rekhet* had not expected her to return until at least the evening …

But Teti's face, when it appeared, was warm and welcoming. 'Meryt! What brings you back so quickly? Come in.'

Meryt followed her through the cool mud-brick rooms, casting quick glances around as they went. The whole house was filled with the scent of incense, herbs and aromatic flowers, and there were pots and bowls in every nook and cranny. Teti led her through to the courtyard at the back and turned around.

'Is everything well with you, Meryt? I didn't expect you until the sun had lost its heat.'

The *rekhet*'s voice was searching, and Meryt shrugged awkwardly. 'There are problems at home,' she admitted. 'I'm sorry I couldn't wait until later.' Her eyes strayed to some loaves of bread that lay in the corner, and her stomach grumbled loudly.

'Why, you are hungry, Meryt! Sit down. I will bring you something to eat.'

Meryt smiled weakly and sat where Teti had indicated, on an area of neat reed matting in the shade. The *rekhet* said nothing more. She stoked up her oven and disappeared into her cellar for a moment, re-emerging with a pot half-full of food that Meryt guessed was a leftover stew of some kind. She eyed it hungrily as Teti placed it on top of the oven and gave it a stir.

'Can I help?' she offered.

Teti smiled and shook her head. 'It won't take long,' she said, reaching down into the mouth of the cellar. She brought out a cucumber and a bunch of coriander. After dicing the cucumber, she placed it in a little bowl, then began to chop the coriander. Her fingers worked quickly, and Meryt watched her deft movements with pleasure. 'I didn't expect you to give me a meal,' she said awkwardly. 'Thank you, Teti.'

'Life is full of the unexpected. We'll talk once you've eaten,' the *rekhet* replied, placing the salad by Meryt's side. She stood and spooned some of the stew into a bowl. It was made mainly of fava beans and lentils, heavily flavoured with onions and garlic, and Meryt accepted it gratefully. She tore a chunk of bread from the loaf that Teti offered her and began to eat.

It seemed as though nothing had ever tasted so delicious. The stew was infused with other, more subtle flavours, and Teti's bread was unusually soft. Meryt savoured each mouthful until she finally wiped her bowl clean.

'More?' Teti's eyes were smiling as she reached for Meryt's bowl.

'Just a little,' said Meryt guiltily. 'I'm sorry …'

'Don't worry. Eat,' Teti ordered her, returning the bowl with another generous spoonful of the stew. 'I'm glad to see someone enjoying my cooking so much.'

Meryt grinned, her heart warmed by both the food and the welcome. When she at last laid down the bowl, she felt as though a burden had already been lifted from her shoulders – though she could not say exactly why that should be.

'Now,' said Teti, sitting down beside her. 'You are going to tell me what has happened that has left you hungry and with no one to turn to. Does your cousin Baki have something to do with this, by any chance?'

Meryt nodded. 'My uncle is angry with me,' she said. 'He sent me out of the house.'

'And why did he do that? Because Baki is sick?'

'It wasn't my fault,' Meryt blurted anxiously.

Teti smiled. 'I didn't assume it was. Just tell me what happened.'

Meryt bowed her head, wondering where to start. She took a deep breath. 'Last year, I foresaw that a neighbour's child would be still-born,' she said. 'There has been trouble ever since. Nes the grain-grinder and all the neighbours like to gossip. People talk of Sekhmet …'

She looked up to see how Teti was reacting, and saw that she was listening intently.

'My cousin Baki likes to torment me,' Meryt carried on. 'He has always hated me and this stupid rumour has played right into his hands. He poisons my uncle against me whenever he gets the chance, saying that I curse him and place the hand of Sekhmet upon him. Now my uncle fears and hates me too.'

147

She stopped, slightly out of breath. She had never voiced this openly before.

'And how do you feel about Baki?' asked Teti softly.

Meryt swallowed. She couldn't deny the truth. 'The dream – I didn't … I've never …' she began, her lip trembling. Then she took a deep breath. 'I have come to hate him in return,' she blurted. 'But I have never wished him harm.'

Teti nodded and smiled knowingly, then stood up. 'There is something I want to show you,' she said. 'Wait here.'

Meryt wiped her hands on her dress. They were sweating and she could feel her pulse ringing in her ears. Why had she admitted so much? She kicked herself. No good could come of unleashing her feelings in this way. If you named something, you gave it life; by naming so much hatred, who could say what powers might be unleashed? She thought of Nofret and the amulets and felt as though she were walking on deep banks of Nile mud, slippery and treacherous, into which she might fall, and at any time be devoured by the crocodiles …

She looked up as Teti returned with a roll of papyrus manuscripts under her arm, and frowned in bewilderment. 'I can't read very much,' she said. 'I haven't had any schooling. I just know what my cousin Mose has taught me.'

'Don't worry,' said Teti. 'You could learn, if you wanted to. For now I shall read what you cannot read yourself.' She settled down on the mats and began to unfurl the papyri. 'These belonged to my ancestor Ken-her-khepeshef,' she said. 'He was a scribe, and a man of great learning. I have inherited his library and it has taught me a great deal'.

Meryt watched, feeling nervous, as the *rekhet* picked out one particular papyrus. What was Teti going to say about Baki? She hadn't commented yet. Perhaps the script contained curses for those who hated their cousins – or worse.

'This is the *Dream Book*,' Teti told her. 'You are a dreamer, Meryt. It is a gift. You must learn to harness it, and use it for good.'

'But everyone has dreams,' protested Meryt.

Teti cocked her head on one side. 'Not in this way,' she said. 'There is more to it for you.'

'What do you mean? I have only told you about one dream. How can you possibly know?' cried Meryt, growing frightened. 'I didn't want to dream about Baki!'

'No, of course not,' said Teti. 'At the moment, it is your dreams that have power over you. But I see that you can reverse this, so that you have power over them and interpret them, if you choose.'

Meryt stared at her. She didn't understand. 'Can't anyone do this?' she whispered.

Teti shook her head. 'No, Meryt. They can't. People have dreams that they take to other people for interpretation. Some people have access to the *Dream Book*. But few people dream on behalf of others, or have the awareness that I can see in you.' She opened out the *Dream Book* papyrus and ran down the text with her finger. 'Here,' she said. 'This is the list of unlucky dreams: *If a man sees himself in a dream being bitten by a dog – bad. He has been touched by magic.*'

Meryt squinted at the papyrus. She had heard of the *Dream Book* before but she had never seen a copy, and it would not have been much good to her even if she had. Her cousin Mose had only taught her simple heiroglyphs – how to spell the names of some of the gods, and how to spell her own name – and this papyrus was not written in heiroglyphs at all. It was written in the flowing text of scribes and she couldn't read a word of it.

She swallowed. 'I didn't see myself in the dream,' she said. 'Or at least, it wasn't me that was bitten.'

'Exactly,' said Teti. 'You saw your cousin, and now he has fallen sick.'

Meryt got up, her heart full of fear. 'It wasn't my doing,' she cried out.

Teti looked up at her, her face serious. 'You cannot run away from this, Meryt,' she said. 'It is part of you. Everything will be fine as long as you learn to understand it.'

'No!' Meryt didn't want to hear it. She backed away.

Teti shook her head regretfully and began to roll up the papyrus. For the first time since their meeting on the path, Meryt felt afraid of Teti. She knew little about this woman. Dedi's family had turned to her occasionally, but Senmut and Tia preferred to ask for advice from the gods, or the oracle as a last resort. She edged away from her towards the door.

Teti got to her feet and stared down into Meryt's eyes. She suddenly seemed taller, more imposing, and Meryt began to tremble.

'You want to go,' said Teti.

Speechless, Meryt nodded.

The *rekhet* shrugged. 'Very well. Go.'

Teti's eyes burnt into her and Meryt couldn't bear it. Without another word, she turned and ran through the house and didn't stop until she reached the village gate.

When she approached the main street she stopped to catch her breath, and walked slowly towards her home. Perhaps Baki would be getting better, she thought desperately. If he was on the mend, the whole issue would go away, and she would be able to make her peace with Senmut. Life could go on as normal. Maybe, if Baki recovered, her uncle wouldn't mind if she refused Ramose ...

She had to know what was happening. *Please, oh please let everything be better*, she muttered to herself. With more purpose in her stride, she walked the last stretch to the house, and peered through the front door. There was no one in the front room, and she stepped in soundlessly to listen. The first sounds to greet her were Nauna's voice, chiding Henut, and the bleating of the goat. Meryt held her breath, and tiptoed towards the middle room.

She could hear Tia, murmuring in a low voice. She was soothing someone … soothing Baki. And now, Meryt could hear the sound she dreaded. A low moan, followed by shallow, rasping breaths. Her cousin was still sick. In fact, judging by his struggling lungs, he had got worse.

Footsteps pattered down the courtyard steps, and Meryt darted for the door. But then she heard Mose's voice, sharp and clear. 'Mama, you have been sitting there all day. Are you never going to rest?'

Tia's reply was fainter, but just loud enough for Meryt to hear. 'I must care for Baki until your father gets back. I can't leave him, my sweet. I'll be fine.'

So Senmut was out! What lucky timing. Her heart lifting, Meryt stepped into the middle room and called out softly. 'Tia!'

Tia appeared at the door at once, her face alight with relief. 'Meryt! There you are. I've been so worried about you. I sent Mose out to look for you …' Tears sprang to her eyes and she wrapped Meryt in a warm welcoming hug. 'Where have you been?'

'Senmut sent me out,' said Meryt. 'But I crept back in to sleep.'

'Did you? Oh, I'm glad.' Tia engulfed her in another hug, then began to sob. 'I'm so afraid, Meryt. Baki is very sick. His skin is on fire and he barely knows what he is saying. He sweats so much …'

'Isn't Nauna helping you?' asked Meryt.

'Nauna does nothing.' It was Mose who answered,

his young face tight and angry.

Tia sniffed and wiped her face. 'Come through. I need to sit by Baki.'

Meryt hesitated, then followed her aunt into the back room. There, she squatted down with Mose on the floor while Tia wiped her sick son's forehead with a cloth. Baki tossed and muttered, his eyes half-open but glazed and unseeing.

'What will happen if I stay? Is Senmut still angry with me?' asked Meryt.

'I have told him this is not your fault,' Tia replied. 'And I've told him I need your help, especially as I grow larger. I don't know if he listened to me. He is beside himself with worry – it's as though no one else exists. Even his unborn child is of no account to him.'

Meryt bowed her head silently. She badly wanted to help her aunt. But she could see that hoping Baki would be better was just wishful thinking, and she was afraid of the part she might have played in his sickness. She stood up. 'Perhaps it's best if I go,' she said.

'Please don't,' said Tia. 'We can work things out with Senmut. I'll talk to him again …' Her voice trailed off as her eyes moved to the doorway.

Meryt looked around quickly. Senmut was standing there, his arms folded. As silence fell on the room, he moved to Baki's bedside and examined his son.

'He is worse,' he muttered. 'There is no doubt

about it. He is worse.' He spun round and pointed at Meryt. 'How long has she been here?'

Tia stared at him in dismay. 'Senmut, Meryt has been here only a few minutes. Baki has been the same for several hours now. I need her help.'

Fury whipped across Senmut's features. 'Look at my son! See how he is suffering – and you dare to talk of keeping this girl in my house!'

'It's not Meryt's fault,' protested Tia. 'How can you think so, Senmut? She has never harmed anyone.'

'She has brought the curse of Sekhmet upon us and you say she has done no harm! My mother can give you all the help you need.' Senmut turned to tower over Meryt, his face twisted and menacing.

Meryt scrambled out of his way and made for the door. 'I'm going,' she said.

'Yes, you are going!' Senmut's eyes flashed. 'And I tell you now, Meryt-Re, that if you ever set foot in this house again I shall beat you and call down the wrath of all the gods upon you.'

'Senmut!' Tia sounded horrified.

For the second time in only a short hour, Meryt found herself running away, fleeing blindly down the street.

 CHAPTER EIGHT

Meryt ran to the southern gate, through the eastern cemetery and up the hillside to her favourite spot. Her heart and lungs were bursting, not only with exhaustion but from anguish and disbelief. She flopped down on the polished rock and buried her head in her arms.

He doesn't mean it, she told herself. *He can't possibly mean it.* Meryt had lived with Senmut and Tia for as long as she could remember and she knew no other home. She could not believe that Senmut would end it all so completely, in a moment of anger. Surely this couldn't be true.

And yet, when she thought of the fury in her uncle's eyes and the tightened fists held clenched by his sides, she realised that the situation was indeed a reality. Her uncle had forbidden her to return and she would have to abide by that – for the time being, at least. She sat very still, staring out towards the Nile, as the implications began to dawn on her. She would have to find somewhere to go. She might even have to leave the village. But if she did not belong in

Set Maat, where did she belong? It was the only life she had ever known. The lush river valley stretching out below her seemed like a yawning void. Life there was very different to that of the rocky desert village she had always known, where government servants brought the families all they needed. Down in the valley, peasants toiled under the hot sun to grow their crops, and wages were not guaranteed. She could always become a servant girl, of course ...

The mere thought of it filled her with horror. In desperation, she began to think through the options. There was Kenna's household, but she quickly dismissed it. It would be unbearable living among those gossiping women. She would get no peace from them. And in any case, the house was already so crowded; it was unlikely that Kenna's father would agree to keep her in the first place. The other alternative was Dedi. Meryt's heart sank at the idea of admitting her predicament. Dedi's mother was sharp-eyed and sharp-tongued, and nothing fooled her. It would not be long before she discovered the real reason for Meryt's presence – if, again, she agreed to take her in.

The only other person that Meryt could think of was Teti, but she felt a shiver of fear at the idea of returning to the house of the *rekhet*. In any case, she could not ask for shelter from a woman she barely knew. There had to be somewhere else.

She mulled over the options for more than an hour. In the end, she decided that however difficult it might be, she would have to swallow her pride and go to Dedi. Dedi's family might take her in for a few days, at least; in the meantime, she thought hopefully, something might change.

She walked down to the village slowly, deciding what she would say. The last thing she wanted to do was cause any alarm. Dedi's family had had enough to contend with over the last few days, and she did not want to add to their anxieties.

When at last she knocked on the door, Dedi greeted her warmly. 'Meryt! I haven't seen you since the oracle. Where have you been?'

Meryt smiled and shrugged. 'Things have been happening at home.'

'What kind of things? Come up to the roof and tell me all about it.'

Dedi's breezy tone was reassuring, and Meryt began to relax a little. She accepted a cup of pomegranate juice and followed her friend's graceful form up the courtyard steps.

'Neben has just left,' Dedi told her. 'He has made all sorts of plans for our house. He has just commissioned a new set of furniture from one of Father's carpenters.'

Meryt felt a pang of envy. How wonderful it must be to speak happily of one's future home! But then she reminded herself that nothing in life was ever certain. Even Dedi's future had looked precarious over the last couple of weeks. She smiled, and sipped her juice.

'I think he is making a special effort,' Dedi carried on. 'He wants to reassure me that all will be well, and that Userkaf hasn't changed anything.'

'That's good,' agreed Meryt. 'I'm glad for you, Dedi.' She knew her voice sounded flat, but she couldn't help it.

Dedi scrutinised her. 'You seem tired,' she said. 'Tell me what's happening at home.'

Meryt toyed with her cup. 'It's Baki,' she said. 'His circumcision did not go well. His wound has gone bad and he has developed a fever.'

'Oh no!' Dedi's eyes widened in concern. 'Have you consulted Harmose?'

'Yes, of course. Though to be honest, he has not been much use.' She hesitated, trying to stop herself from blurting out the full story. 'The house is in chaos. Senmut has come back from the tombs to care for him. He says it would be better if I stayed somewhere else until Baki recovers.'

'But how is that going to help?' Dedi exclaimed. 'You do so many of the chores for Tia.'

Meryt shrugged. 'I know, but ...' She hunted for the right words to explain the situation. 'I have never seen my uncle like this. He is desperate with worry and I don't think he knows what he says. Anyway, I have agreed to stay away for a while, if I can.'

Dedi stared at her. 'Where will you go?'

This was harder than Meryt had anticipated. 'I would like to stay in the village,' she said, trying to keep her tone light, 'so that I can help if I'm needed. But ...'

'You should stay here,' Dedi interrupted. 'I will speak to Mother. There won't be a problem. You can sleep with me.'

The relief felt like a cascade of stones tumbling down the mountain, and Meryt's eyes filled with tears of gratitude. 'Are you sure? I will do anything to help – the weaving or the grinding or making beer ...'

'Hush,' said Dedi. 'Leave it with me. Don't worry, Meryt. You have been a good friend to me.' She smiled, and reached out to touch Meryt's shoulder. 'Father is returning from the tombs tomorrow for the festival of Meretseger. He has decided to throw a party for some of his men. You can help us organise that.'

While Dedi went downstairs to talk to her mother, Meryt lay in the shade to wait. The relief was enormous – but now that Dedi had offered to take her in, she also felt burdened with guilt. The memory of Baki's sweat-drenched face swam before her eyes and she felt panic rising. Perhaps Senmut was right to have banished her. She thought of Teti's words. *You cannot run away from this, Meryt ... It is part of you.* Perhaps she really did bring misfortune upon those around her. Was anyone safe? Or did she only bring harm if she thought ill of someone? What if she brought calamity to her friend's house?

She closed her eyes and took deep breaths until

the fear subsided, then sat up and hugged her knees, rocking gently as she tried to calm down. If Wab agreed that she could stay, of course she would accept. But this would only be a temporary solution. She would have to think of something soon – she would either have to find a way of placating Senmut, or find somewhere permanent to live. With her heart sinking, she suddenly realised that the usual way forward was to marry.

Ramose … perhaps, if she went to her uncle and told him she would accept his proposal, Senmut would accept her as part of the family again. But then, she thought in despair, what would be the point? She would live with the bumbling stonecutter in any case, and not in her uncle's home.

The image of Baki's feverish face flashed before her eyes again and she shivered. Even if she somehow made her peace with Senmut it would not help her cousin's plight. She could not escape what Teti had told her. Baki's fate depended on magic. However much she hoped for it, he was not going to recover overnight.

'Meryt.'

Wab's voice greeted her, and Meryt stood up hurriedly. She had always been in awe of Dedi's mother. Like her daughter, she was full of grace and beauty, but she had a stern air of authority about her that made Meryt quail inside. She bowed her head shyly.

'Dedi says that you wish to stay with us for a few days,' Wab continued. Meryt was aware of her steady gaze upon her, and shifted uncomfortably. 'I am sorry to hear that there is illness in the house.'

'I will do all I can to help, if you are good enough to allow me to stay,' Meryt said, raising her eyes to the older woman's.

Wab seemed to be sizing her up carefully. 'I am surprised that your aunt does not have greater need of you,' she said. She sounded suspicious. 'She is heavy with child. This is not the time to be sending away what help she has!'

'No,' agreed Meryt, her voice trembling slightly. 'To tell you the truth, Tia would rather I stayed. It is my uncle who has asked me to leave.'

'Yes. So Dedi told me.' Wab's tone was unconvinced. For a moment, Meryt thought that she was going to question further, or send her away. But then she shrugged. 'Well, as it happens, an extra pair of hands will come in useful this week. And Dedi will be pleased to have you here.'

Meryt looked at her friend, who was grinning in excitement. She smiled nervously, then turned back to Wab. 'Thank you very much,' she said. 'I am very grateful. And I will work hard for you, I promise.'

Wab raised her perfect eyebrows. 'I will expect it,' she said.

'Mother wants us to make the perfume cones,' Dedi put in enthusiastically. 'The servants will make all the bread and beer, but we can prepare the flower garlands for the guests.'

'Yes,' agreed Wab. 'And there will be other work

too, if you have time.'

In spite of her situation, Meryt's smile widened. Making perfume cones and flower garlands was not exactly the most unpleasant of tasks. Her time of exile might even be an enjoyable one.

Dedi slipped her arm around her mother's waist. 'You won't make us work too hard, will you, Mother?' she asked playfully.

Wab's stern features relaxed a little. 'Hard enough. But I am not your father,' she responded, a smile twitching her lips.

Dedi laughed merrily, and Meryt recoiled in surprise. How could this family take Userkaf's accusations so lightly? Did they not see what he was like? Yes, the council and the oracle had found against him, but he would surely spring back with something new. That much was obvious! Meryt opened her mouth to speak, then changed her mind. It was too great a risk – she could not afford to jeopardise her lodgings so soon.

Wab went back down the steps, and Dedi reached for Meryt's arm, squeezing it in delight. 'It's going to be so good having you here,' she said. 'We don't need to make the cones until tomorrow. They will lose their shape if they're made too soon. But we can choose a nice girdle for you to wear around your hips.'

Meryt's mouth dropped open. 'But I won't be actually going to the party, will I?' she asked.

'Of course you will,' laughed Dedi. 'We all will. In

fact I was wondering if you would like to play the lyre.'

'Play the … what, at the party?'

'Where else, silly! You play it much better than I do. If you play the lyre and I play the sistrum, we will only need to hire a harpist and some dancers. Father will be pleased – the party is costing him enough as it is.'

Meryt felt almost winded. She loved playing Dedi's lyre, but she had never played it in public. It would be an enormous privilege to play at Nebnufer's party. She swelled with pride and happiness – and then, just as quickly, the weight of her situation dawned on her again, and her heart sank. How could she play the lyre happily at a party when Baki lay sick – and she had no home to call her own?

'What is it?' asked Dedi anxiously. 'You don't need to worry about it, Meryt. You're just as talented as the musicians we usually hire. You have time to practise. You'll manage easily.'

'It's not that.' Meryt chewed her lip, then managed to smile. 'I would love to play the lyre. Thank you, Dedi.'

'So what is it?' Dedi was persistent.

Meryt realised that she could carry on no longer. It was crazy, thinking that she could just hide in her friend's house, away from the life that had crumbled around her. The fact was that she knew what Baki needed. Senmut might not take her back whatever happened, but she would never forgive herself if she did not at least do her best to save his oldest son. She took a deep breath and looked her friend in the eye. 'Dedi, do you trust me?'

Dedi looked taken aback. 'Of course I do. Why?'

'There is something I have to do. I can't rest until I've done it.'

'What sort of thing?'

Meryt searched her friend's face pleadingly. 'I can't tell you. Not yet. Will you trust me enough to let me go for a few hours?'

Astonishment flooded Dedi's features. 'Meryt, you're not a prisoner! We are not going to make you stay in the house against your will. You are a guest.'

She seemed almost offended, but Meryt was too anxious to care. 'Thank you, Dedi,' she said quickly. 'I'll be back as soon as I can. Then I will do everything you want me to, I promise.' And before Dedi could reply, she turned and ran lightly down the staircase.

The sun was disappearing behind the Peak of the West as Meryt emerged from Dedi's house. She gazed up at the darkening western cliff for a moment and mouthed a silent prayer to Meretseger, the goddess who lived there. Meretseger was a brooding goddess with none of the loving kindness of Hathor, and perhaps it was fitting to turn to her at a time such as this.

She hurried in the fading light to the edge of the village and slipped out through the northern gate, then up the pathway that led to Teti's house. Feeling breathless with nerves, she knocked on the *rekhet*'s door.

It was a while before there was an answer. When Teti appeared, her eyes looked big and wide, almost trance-like, and for once she did not smile.

'Meryt,' she said in a low voice. 'I'm glad you have come. I am helping someone at the moment. Go up to the roof and wait for me there.'

She ushered Meryt through her house, and Meryt saw three huddled figures in the front room – women who covered their faces as she passed. The room smelt strongly of incense and other herbs, and the atmosphere was heavy and depressed. Meryt felt a chill run through her. She wondered what was happening, but knew instinctively that death was hovering close by. Teti took her as far as the courtyard, then pointed silently at the staircase. Meryt nodded, and the *rekhet* disappeared back into the house.

There were no lights up on the roof. Meryt sat and looked out to the Peak of the West, watching its silhouette gradually blend in with the night sky. The desert air was growing cooler every evening, and she wished she had brought something to wrap around her shoulders. Her memory flitted to Nofret, and the beautiful linen shawl she had offered. Meryt dismissed the thought hurriedly. She already owned a shawl; the problem was that all her belongings, such as they were, lay in Senmut's house. She had access to nothing, not even her ostracon of the goddess

Hathor. She rubbed her arms and legs, and waited.

'I'm sorry to keep you so long.' Teti's voice greeted her, and she turned to see the *rekhet* appear at the top of the steps, carrying a lamp. She stood looking over to where Meryt was sitting, her face still solemn in the flickering orange light.

Meryt stood up, her heart beating faster. 'Would it be better if I came back another time?' she asked, almost hopefully.

'No, no. You can come downstairs now.' Teti turned and went down again and, summoning all her courage, Meryt followed her.

In the front room, Teti busied herself with clearing away the remains of the incense she had burnt, and made the room bright with several lamps. She disappeared for a moment, then returned with a handful of fresh herbs that she wafted around the room, muttering to herself.

'There. The air is lighter now,' she said, when she had finished. To her astonishment, Meryt realised it was true. Teti smiled, and sat down next to her. 'I am glad you are here, Meryt.'

Meryt smiled nervously. 'I want to know how to save Baki,' she blurted. 'He is very sick and it is all my fault. I have to face up to it, as you said.'

Teti looked at her quickly. 'Did I say it was your fault? I don't think so.'

'But you said …'

'That you have a gift with dreams.'

Meryt was puzzled. 'Yes, but I dreamt about Baki

and you told me he has been touched by magic.'

Teti shook her head. 'You have misunderstood. Seeing something does not mean that you caused it. These are two different things. The dream may be yours, but the magic has nothing to do with you.'

Meryt sat in silence, allowing Teti's words to sink in. At last she raised her head. 'But can we still save him?'

'We can try. But first, you must tell me all that has happened with him in recent weeks.'

Meryt's heart leapt into her mouth. To tell the whole story might mean mentioning Ramose and Heria. Perhaps this was where her prayers had led her – perhaps it was Teti who could give her the words of the goddess. And at the prospect of being told that she must marry the stonecutter, her courage failed her. 'Just about Baki? Or other things?' she stuttered.

'Just about Baki,' Teti reassured her. 'Why, what else might there be?'

'N ... nothing,' said Meryt. She hesitated. 'But there are other things that affect the whole family.' She regarded the *rekhet* fearfully.

'Let's start with Baki,' said Teti calmly.

Nodding in relief, Meryt went over what she had said that morning: her own entry into the family at the age of two, the rivalry that had always existed between herself and her cousin, and how Senmut always favoured his oldest son.

'Baki has been training as a plasterer for two years

now,' she explained. 'Senmut has assurances from Sennedjem that he will be taken on by the gang. But it has brought out the worst in Baki. He seems to have no respect for others or for the gods. He speaks lightly of curses and thinks that nothing can touch him. He went into his ritual with a smile on his face, for he did not believe that he would suffer pain. I warned him that he should be careful but he laughed at me. And now he has fallen sick.'

Teti listened carefully. 'And how has he been treated?'

'My aunt has made offerings. I dare say my uncle has too. And I went to Harmose, the doctor.'

'What did he give you?'

'He told us to apply honey and goose fat. We had no goose fat, so Harmose gave us a pot of his own.'

Teti snorted. 'Old and rancid, no doubt.'

'I don't know. It was only a small pot and Tia soon finished it.'

'Well, that is as much as you can expect from Harmose. He is not the best of his profession. His father took much greater care over his patients. It's time the government appointed someone new, but who is to say so? All the men still swear by him.' Teti sighed. 'This story tells me little, I'm afraid. It is possible that Baki has brought the evil upon himself, for the gods can sometimes be harsh. I can weave a spell to bind the magic, and make a fresh balm to apply to his wound. After that … we shall have to wait and see.'

Meryt took this in. 'But … what about my dream?' she asked tentatively, not sure that she wanted to hear the answer.

Teti smiled. 'It is as I told you,' she said. 'You have dreams that other people do not. And you have taken the first steps to making use of your gift. And now, we must begin to weave our spell, if your cousin is to be saved. Wait here.'

The *rekhet* got up and left the room, but soon returned with a strip of linen and a *nefret* flower, one of the riverside plants that they had picked only that morning. She lay them at Meryt's feet, then opened a casket that lay in one corner and brought out incense and a burner.

'The flower will bring healing. We will bind it into the cloth with a knot,' explained Teti. 'We will make seven knots in all. The other six will bind the ailment and banish it from Baki's body.'

Meryt nodded, and sat quietly as Teti filled the incense burner, lit it and began to chant in a low voice, swaying gently to and fro. First she began with a list of names, calling them out in a rapid, rhythmic murmur. Then she reached for the linen and tied the first knot.

'Ailment of Baki, I call you by your most secret name and I bind you. The magic that has called you is broken. You will lose your power over Baki, son of Senmut and Tia.'

The lamplight flickered and smoked as Teti swayed more forcefully, her eyes closed and sweat breaking out on her forehead. Meryt watched her in awe, sliding away from her slightly for fear of what such magic might do. Teti twisted the linen in her hands and tied another knot, repeating the spell in a slightly louder voice, then another, until six knots were tied and the incantation chanted over each. By the time the six knots were tied, she was breathing heavily and Meryt was scarcely breathing at all, her back pressed against the wall of the room.

Teti opened her eyes, which now looked glazed and heavy. She picked up the *nefret* flower and made a final knot, encasing the delicate plant inside it. 'Ailment of Baki!' she cried. 'I call you by all your names and by your most secret name of all. In the name of all the gods I break the magic that holds you to Baki and I bind your power. You will allow the *nefret* flower to do its work.'

Silence fell, and Meryt allowed herself to breathe again as Teti gently caressed the knotted linen. When all was still and the incense had burnt out, the *rekhet* looked up and smiled. 'The spell is cast,' she said. 'I will make the balm for his wound in the morning, with fresh dew. Meanwhile you can take this and place it under his head. It would be better if the incantation were spoken at the same time, but this is probably the best we can do for now.'

'Senmut may not let me in,' said Meryt timidly. 'What should I do if he refuses?'

Teti handed her the linen charm and held on to her hand for a moment. 'You will find a way,' she said, looking deep into Meryt's eyes. 'Come back for the balm tomorrow.'

Full of hope and determination, Meryt went straight to her home, clutching the piece of linen close to her chest. She paused outside the front door, then raised her hand to the red wood. Tears sprang to her eyes as she did so. Here she was, standing at the door of her own home, afraid to enter – and about to knock as though she were just a stranger. Steeling herself, she rapped out a quick tattoo then stood back in the shadows to wait, praying that it would not be Senmut who answered.

It was Tia who came to the door. She looked out on to the street anxiously, her face pale in the moonlight.

'Tia!' Meryt whispered. 'It's me.'

She stepped forward, but Tia recoiled in fear. 'Meryt! Senmut ...'

'What's going on?' Senmut's voice called from inside the house.

'It's nothing,' she called, then turned to Meryt with a finger to her lips. 'You must go,' she whispered urgently. 'If Senmut finds you here ...'

She did not have time to finish her sentence. Senmut himself appeared, looking tired and irritable. 'Tia, come inside. Who wants us at this hour?'

Meryt swallowed. Summoning all her courage, she stood before her uncle, offering the charm.

'Teti the Knowing One has sent a charm for Baki,' she told him, her voice trembling. 'It is to break the

171

magic that hangs over him.'

Senmut stared at her. For a second, Meryt's heart filled with hope. Perhaps he would accept her, after all. But then he reached forward and snatched the knotted linen from her and flung it to the ground. With a furious glance at Meryt, he spat at it, then stepped forward and ground it into the baked mud of the street.

'That is what I think of your charm,' he snarled at her. 'Do you think I would allow such a thing to touch my son? You found good company in Teti. That woman is a good-for-nothing. She has the Evil Eye.'

And with that, he stormed back into the house. Tia hesitated, her face streaked with tears. Meryt thought she might stay to speak for longer, but Senmut was calling her and neighbours were beginning to peer out on to the street. She hugged Meryt quickly.

'I have to go,' she whispered. 'Where are you staying?'

'At Dedi's house,' Meryt replied, as Tia extricated herself.

'That's good,' said her aunt. 'They will care for you well.' She stepped back into the house and smiled wanly.

'But, Tia …' Meryt began.

It was no good. Tia had already retreated into the house, closing the door behind her. Meryt reached down and picked up the linen charm. The knots were still intact, and she brushed off the dust gently, her fingers trembling. *May the gods forgive him*, she murmured, fear gripping her heart. But she did not know which gods to address, or what their response might be. Clutching the charm tightly in her fist, she wandered towards Dedi's house, feeling empty, lost and confused.

It was Wab who opened the door. She stared at Meryt for a moment, then opened the door wider to let her in. 'It's late,' she said abruptly.

Meryt hung her head and said nothing. Wab tutted and ushered her through to one of the back rooms, where Dedi already lay under covers on the floor. She peeped out as Meryt appeared.

'Meryt! Where have you been? I've made up a bed for you.' She sat up, indicating the reed matting next to her, on which further covers were laid. 'Have you been out with Kenna?'

Meryt shook her head. All she wanted to do was crawl under the covers and fall asleep. She had failed Teti. She had failed Baki. And now, judging by the reception from Wab, she was being a nuisance to her friend's family too. She sat down heavily and slipped the linen charm under the matting.

'There's something wrong.' Dedi's voice was sharp. 'Meryt, where have you been?'

'I asked you to trust me,' Meryt mumbled.

'What was it that you were carrying when you came in?'

Meryt let her shoulders sag. So Dedi had seen the charm, anyway. She gave up. 'A charm,' she said dully. 'Teti gave it to me. It was to help Baki's recovery but Senmut would not allow me to give it to him.'

'Why ever not?' exclaimed Dedi.

Meryt looked at her. She knew that Dedi's family did not think badly of Teti. Perhaps there could be some support for her here, after all. 'He says Teti has the Evil Eye.'

'That's nonsense.' Dedi looked indignant. 'Teti is the most gentle person in the village.'

'Do you really think so?'

'Yes.' Dedi's eyes flashed. 'It is always the men who say things like that. I am sorry, Meryt. That's where you went, isn't it – to Teti?'

Meryt nodded.

'Well, I'm glad,' declared Dedi. 'You have done a good thing for your family.'

Meryt tried to smile. 'Thank you,' she said quietly, and lifted the covers over her legs. She could not bring herself to explain further. Let Dedi think the best of her; she had said enough.

Meryt slept fitfully in the strange room. She was afraid of rolling over and waking Dedi. It was just another fear to add to the many that ran through her mind, and she was tense and jittery by the morning. Dedi, on the other hand, slept soundly and was energetic from the instant she awoke.

From then on, Meryt scarcely had a minute to herself. Her friend was full of enthusiasm for the tasks of the day, the first of which was preparing the perfume cones. It was easy enough to do. Wab had ordered a vat of tallow from suppliers in the valley, which was to be softened with linseed oil and infused with the essence of frankincense and myrrh before being shaped into little cones. Every guest would be handed one as they arrived to fix to the top of their wig. There, they would gradually melt and release their sweet, heavy scent over the course of the evening.

Dedi and Meryt sat side by side, moulding the little mounds of fat and placing them on wooden boards. Dedi was happy and relaxed, humming a tune as she worked, and Meryt envied her. She sat in silence, worrying about the linen charm and about returning to Teti for the balm. What if Baki died before she was able to get them to him? And what if Senmut never allowed it?

When a servant brought bread and fruit for them to eat, she found she could barely touch anything. She nibbled on a piece of bread, wondering how to get away. But today was the day of the party and Wab was never far off, ordering her servants around and checking on everyone's progress. Meryt remembered that she would be playing the lyre that evening, and her stomach churned nervously.

'I'll get the lyre out once we've finished this,' said Dedi, as though reading her thoughts. 'We can practise for a while until the flowers are delivered. The servants will help us make the garlands – we won't have time to make them all ourselves.'

Meryt nodded, resigned to the inevitable. She would not be able to return to Teti's that day. The charm had been spat and trampled upon. *You will find a way*, Teti had said; but it was becoming all too clear that she would not.

'You look beautiful,' said Dedi, dabbing a little more red ochre on to Meryt's cheeks. 'You should wear green around your eyes more often.'

Meryt peered at herself in Dedi's polished bronze mirror. Her own wig, with its coarse date-palm strands, did little to flatter her. But Dedi and Wab had a spare wig that Wab had said she could wear. It was made of real human hair, shiny and smooth, that fell in an elegant line beyond her shoulders. To her surprise, Meryt felt a ripple of excitement. Perhaps, after all, the party would be fun, and she would be able to forget her troubles for a few hours. She smiled. 'Thank you, Dedi,' she said, and took a deep breath. 'I suppose the first guests will be arriving soon.'

Her friend nodded. 'Yes, we need to hurry. Mother wants us to greet them with the cones and the garlands at the door.'

She gave Meryt's make-up a final dab, then checked her own in the mirror. As ever, Dedi looked stunning. To distinguish her from the servants, she wore a dress of exceptionally fine linen – so fine it was almost transparent – which flowed around her body like the morning mist. She insisted that Meryt should also wear her spare linen gown, and lent her a collar of colourful beads to add to her own simple bangles. Along with the wig and the make-up, it made her feel special, and she followed her friend through the house with a lighter heart.

Nebnufer and Wab took up pride of position in the middle room of the house as guests began to troop in. The house was larger than most but it was still small, and Meryt realised that the invitations had been restricted to just a portion of Nebnufer's gang – mainly the draughtsmen, sculptors, painters and their wives. It was obvious why. This was no spontaneous party, but an attempt to placate the troublemakers.

When half the guests had arrived, Userkaf himself stepped through the door. Meryt slipped a garland around his neck, then one around the neck of his wife. The draughtsman barely noticed her, and so she studied him curiously. He was not handsome, but he had a strange, vibrant energy that made him seem very alive. His eyes were already darting around the house, sizing up what was on offer and who else had been invited. There was a murmur as he walked through to the middle room, and Meryt raised an eyebrow. There was no doubt that his arrival had caused a stir.

Dedi nudged her, and she realised that another guest was waiting for his garland. She picked one up – and stared at the man who stood before her. It was Kha, the painter. Nofret's tormenter. The man who demanded the sacred amulets for his own secret use ...

Kha lowered his head for her to slip the garland over it. 'Thank you,' he said politely, with a deep, warm smile.

Meryt tried not to stare at him, but she was surprised, all the same. He looked such a gentle man, one whose smile reached his eyes. He put a hand on his wife's waist and shepherded her forward, allowing her to lean on him a little. They seemed such a quiet, happy couple, and Meryt could scarcely tear her eyes away as they wandered through to join the throng. She took a deep breath, wondering what the evening would bring.

As servants began to offer drinks, Meryt and Dedi waited in the courtyard with the hired dancers. Their turn would come later; for now, a blind harpist was entertaining the guests on his own. The dancers were lively and full of chatter, sneaking drinks from the servants and sampling some of the food. Nebnufer had slaughtered a young pig from his little farm in the valley, and the smell of roasting pork filled the air.

Meryt sat with Dedi in one corner, watching the scene. 'You could go and join the feast,' she said to her friend.

Dedi smiled. 'I will join it later, with Neben-Maat,' she replied. 'For now I am happy to stay out here with you. Let my brothers do the hard work of talking to everyone. It will be more fun once the guests have drunk a few glasses of wine.'

Meryt felt grateful, for Dedi had gone out of her way to make her feel comfortable. She caressed the lyre on her knee, and when Wab at last beckoned them into the house, she realised she was looking forward to playing it.

The room was hot, and the heady perfume that everyone wore on their heads mingled with the smell of sweat and rich food. From the look on many people's faces and the raucous cheer that went up as they entered, Meryt guessed that the wine had been flowing freely. She glanced around quickly, trying to spot the people she knew. Userkaf had positioned himself opposite Nebnufer, and already had a bois-terous air. She looked for Kha. The painter sat in one corner with his wife, looking amused, but also slightly detached from the rest of the room. Meryt frowned in puzzlement. He was very different from the man she had imagined.

At a nod from Wab, Meryt began to play. The room fell quiet, and she was glad that she had started with the easiest tune. As the melody progressed, Dedi joined in with the sistrum, keeping up a regular rhythm, and the hired dancers swayed in time to the music. Soon, the room was alive with chatter once more, and Meryt relaxed. The party was fun. As she came to the end of the first tune, everyone clamoured for more, and she grinned. Her fingers flew as she plucked at the lyre, and time seemed to fly just as fast.

Eventually they took a break, and went out to the courtyard to breathe in the cool night air. Other people had gathered there too, escaping the confines of the middle room as the evening progressed.

'Can I get you something to drink?' said a voice, and Meryt turned round in surprise. It was Kha, and she looked at him warily. 'You must be thirsty, that's all,' he carried on. 'I was watching you. You are talented, you know.'

Meryt felt embarrassed. 'Thank you,' she mumbled. 'Water is all I need.'

'I will fetch some for you,' said the painter. 'Stay here.'

He was only gone a few minutes. He handed Meryt a cup, bowed politely, and disappeared. She gulped the water gratefully, feeling bemused. Could this really be the man that Nofret described?

'Meryt, we need to start again,' said Dedi at her shoulder. 'Neben has arrived. He wants to hear us play.'

Meryt followed her friend back into the main room. It bore little resemblance to the civilised gathering of a few hours before. People stood and sat where they pleased. One of the wives had drunk too much wine and was being comforted by others in a corner. Userkaf was telling a story, surrounded by a group of his friends. Meryt scanned the room for Kha, but he was nowhere to be seen, so she sat down and started to play once more.

This time there was no hush. The dancers gyrated

all around the room from one group to another. Nebnufer called out for more wine. Neben-Maat sat down next to Dedi and caressed her legs as she shook the sistrum. The room was full of shrieks and laughter and Meryt barely knew what she played.

And then one of the shrieks seemed louder. Meryt looked up in surprise, and her fingers ceased. Everyone turned to one corner, where a dancer stood in fury, her face now streaked with tears.

'He pinched me! He pinched me really *hard* –' She was clearly furious, and pointed a shaking finger at Userkaf.

'Come, come. A pinch is nothing. Let me soothe you,' laughed Userkaf, ignoring the glares of his wife.

'No!' The dancer shrieked again, and made a dash across the room.

Userkaf dived after her amidst a gale of laughter, and his group of friends cheered him on. But not everyone was amused. Ahmose, one of Dedi's brothers, stepped forward and barred the draughtsman's path.

'Let her go,' he said quietly. 'She is not for your pleasure. She has been hired by my father to dance.'

Instantly, Userkaf squared up to him. 'Not for my pleasure!'

'Leave it, Userkaf.' Ahmose's voice was firm.

Userkaf gave him a shove. 'Like father, like son!' he exclaimed, with a drunken leer. 'What d'you all think to that! *Not for my pleasure!*'

He shoved Ahmose again, and a shout went up around the room. Meryt looked around quickly. Nebnufer and Wab were not at their seats, but Neben-Maat rose and tried to steer Userkaf off.

But the draughtsman's blood was running high. He pushed Neben away and rallied his friends. 'We come to Nebnufer's party to be insulted by his sons!' he cried. 'Are we going to take such treatment?'

Those closest to him were spoiling for a fight. 'No!' they chorused, their eyes glittering, and Meryt scrambled to her feet in alarm. The situation was getting out of hand. Nebnufer's sons lined up and Userkaf threw a punch. In seconds, the men in the room were at each other – some throwing themselves into the action, others pulling them off, and the women screaming at them all around.

'*Stop at once!*' Nebnufer's voice resounded across the room, and the guests turned to face him – some guiltily, some furiously, and all in shock that the foreman could bellow so loud. 'I *will not* have my house turned into a common brawling place! Who started this?'

There was a pause. The guests looked around, some with flushed cheeks and defiance, others with shame. Dedi and Meryt stood side by side, their mouths open.

Then Dedi stepped forward. 'It was Userkaf, Father,' she said timidly, but her eyes flashed in anger all the same.

'Is this true?'

There was a murmur of agreement around the room.

Nebnufer turned to the draughtsman. 'Get out. You and all your friends. Get *out*!'

He spat out the words in rage, and there was no doubting that he meant it. Meryt thought she had never seen anyone speak with quite such power and anger. One by one, Userkaf's friends moved towards the door, their heads bowed in shame. Userkaf grabbed his wife's arm roughly and steered her towards the door.

There, before walking out, he turned around and pointed a finger at Nebnufer. 'Look at you,' he sneered. 'Standing there with all your little servants and your filthy roasted pig. You think you can tell me what to do, but I'll prove you wrong. You wait and see. One day I'll prove you wrong!'

And then he left, banging the door behind him.

CHAPTER NINE

There was a hush throughout the room once they had left. Nebnufer said nothing else. He stormed out and went up to the roof with Wab. His sons followed him. Meryt looked around. The servants were beginning to discreetly tidy up, so she joined in, glad of something to do. Dedi had disappeared, no doubt with Neben-Maat, and the last of the guests began to drift away.

Everything was piled into the courtyard to be cleaned in the morning, and the servants disappeared into the night. Meryt found a lamp and, wandering through the house, found that the little back room that she was sharing with Dedi was empty. She took off her borrowed fineries and looked around. To her relief, the linen charm was still where she had hidden it, tucked into a little crack in the mud-brick wall. She found her dress and a linen sheet and settled down in one corner, clutching the charm to her chest.

Meryt lay in the darkness with her eyes open, listening to the murmur of voices on the roof. By the sound of it, Nebnufer and his family were still embroiled in heated discussion. She thought over the events of the evening – the hot, sweaty room, the laughing guests, the drunkenness of Userkaf. And then she thought of the painter Kha, and the cup of water that he had brought for her. She shook her head. Her instincts told her that he was a good man. Nofret's story made little sense.

When at last sleep overcame her, she began to dream. First, there was a faint image of an object – something glinting in the sunlight. She felt drawn towards it, for it was an object of great beauty, and she wanted to hold it and touch it and own it for herself. Then, as she drew closer, she saw what it was. It was the stolen *udjat* amulet that she had seen on the hillside path – but it seemed brighter and bigger, the gold pulsating with radiance and the lapis lazuli a brilliant blue. She reached out to pick it up in great excitement. But as she touched it, she yelped and drew back in pain, for the amulet was hot – so hot that the tips of her fingers were burnt and she could only watch as the gold melted before her eyes, leaving the pieces of precious lapis lazuli scattered on the ground. She reached to pick them up one by one, but each one vanished as she touched it, leaving no trace.

It grew dark and she looked up in bewilderment. The moon was shining in the sky and a man was standing on the hilltop above the village, looking down at her. It was Kha, and his face was full of sorrow. All he wore was a ragged loincloth. As she gazed up at him, he opened his palm, and Meryt saw what he was holding. It was his painter's papyrus brush, but it was worn and tattered, a worthless object. Kha let it drop to the ground, shaking his head. Then he opened both his palms towards her, and she saw that he was holding nothing else.

The images began to blur, mingling with others in a confused jumble of colours and faces. But when Meryt awoke, the faint light of dawn was already filtering into the room, and the dream of Kha and the amulet was as clear as ever. With a sinking sense of dread, she knew that once again, her dreams had shown her more than she wished to know.

Meryt rose and found a little linen pouch in the courtyard. She placed the linen charm inside, then sat toying with it, her mind in turmoil. She knew she had to return to Teti's house to collect the balm for Baki, and the sooner the better – even if she had no idea how to deliver it. But she was terrified that the *rekhet* might begin to question her further. What if she asked about Meryt's dreams? She did not want to admit that there were more than the one she had described. Now, she had dreamt not only about Ramose, her father and her cousin, but about the matters which lay at the heart of the village affairs. Could she hide this from Teti, or would the *rekhet* see straight through her? If it was a gift, it was one she had not asked for.

But all the while, Baki lay sick in Senmut's house, and she could not refuse to help him. With great reluctance, Meryt padded out of the house and made her way in the early morning light to Teti's house.

'Meryt! I was expecting you yesterday,' said Teti at once, when she opened the door.

Meryt hung her head. 'I know,' she said, feeling wretched. 'I ... I had to help my friend's family. They have been good to me. I ...'

'Never mind.' The *rekhet*'s voice was urgent. 'Come in. I have the balm ready for you in the court-yard. You must not delay – your cousin's life hangs in the balance and may not last much longer.'

The words jolted through Meryt like the sting of a scorpion. 'How do you know?' she asked. She followed Teti inside.

'This is the way of his illness,' said Teti, over her shoulder. 'Though the spell will have done some good, at least.'

Meryt felt tongue-tied. She knew she should confess that Senmut had refused to accept the charm, but her courage failed her. As Teti handed her a little pot, she averted her eyes. 'Thank you,' she muttered, shoving the pot into her linen pouch. 'I will go to my home right away.'

Teti nodded. 'Hurry,' she said. A smile lit up her eyes, briefly. 'It is not yet too late.'

Meryt began to jog down the path, but once out of sight of Teti's house, she slowed to a walk. She had everything she needed to help her cousin, but the chances of her being allowed into the house were slim. She would have to think of some other way of reaching him; there was little point in trying to calm Senmut's rage. But however hard she thought, she could not think of one. She walked slower and slower, dragging her steps and staring at her feet, wishing that the problem would just go away.

She heard a donkey's quick little footsteps coming through the gate and looked up. It was Kenna. He reined in and dismounted, his face full of concern.

'Meryt! I've been looking for you. They tell me that you have left Senmut's house.'

'Yes.' Meryt didn't know what else to say.

'But why? What have you done?'

Meryt twisted the linen bag between her fingers, feeling miserable and ashamed. Kenna was so good and light-hearted; she could not bring herself to load him with her heavy burden. Besides, it might fill him with fear, and she did not want to lose his friendship.

'Baki is sick,' she said lamely. 'I am staying with Dedi for a few days, that's all.'

'Why should Baki's illness drive you from the house? It makes no sense,' said Kenna, in a matter-of-fact tone.

'Well, it's true, all the same.' Meryt hesitated. 'Don't worry, Kenna. I'm fine.'

She began to walk forwards once more, but Kenna put a hand on her arm. 'I am not entirely stupid,' he said quietly. 'I hear things just as much as everyone else in this village. I know what rumours go around and I know that you are in greater trouble than you say. Does our friendship count for nothing after all these years?'

Meryt felt tears forming and blinked them back. What good would it do to tell him the truth? There was nothing he could do to help her. Yes, he was her friend, but friends could not prevent unwanted dreams or unwanted marriages – and certainly not the shadow of death itself. He was better off not knowing, for then these things could not touch him.

'I know you are my friend, Kenna,' she managed to say. 'That is enough for me at the moment.'

'Enough for you!' Kenna's voice was anguished. 'Why will you not let me help you?'

Meryt looked at him calmly. 'What do you think you could do?'

'There must be something ...'

Their eyes met, and Meryt wished with all her heart that life was the way it had always been – that she and Kenna were on a carefree trip to the market, hunting for scarab beetles in the dust, or playing *senet* in the shade of his courtyard. But things had changed, and nothing could take her burden from her.

But then it struck her. There *was* something that Kenna could do. It was so obvious that she couldn't believe she hadn't thought of it before. 'Well ... perhaps there is,' she said slowly. 'It shouldn't be too difficult. You could fetch me my cousin Mose – without Senmut seeing him go.'

'Mose? But he is just a child.'

'He is less of a child than Baki,' said Meryt. 'If you do this, you will truly be helping me. But whatever you do, don't let Senmut see you. I will wait here, at the gate.'

'Is this all you will let me do?'

'You will be doing more than you know,' Meryt assured him.

Kenna traced a pattern in the dust with his stick, his face unhappy. Then he shrugged, and sighed. 'Well, if that is what you want, I'll do it.'

He vaulted lightly on to the donkey's back and turned back towards the village. With a sharp thwack of his stick, he pushed the creature into a canter and was off, his legs sticking out and his arms waving.

Meryt settled to wait in the shade of the village wall, watching the flow of traffic in and out. There were the usual comings and goings of the laundry-men and water-carriers, the gardeners and the bringers of wood. A pair of travelling traders approached on mules, and Meryt watched them, curious. Such people brought strange goods and strange tales. Most had travelled the length of the land and some even further, to lands she could not imagine, and told of unlikely places and even more unlikely beliefs.

The traders rode their mules sedately up to the Medjay guard at the gate. Meryt heard them being questioned, and discovered they had come from Per

Ramesses, far to the north, the city of the king's palaces. Meryt tried to imagine the splendour of it – the palaces, the gardens, the princesses and courtiers, all bedecked in the finest jewellery and gold – and wondered what the traders had come to offer and receive. She watched the guards let them pass, and caught sight of Kenna's donkey trotting through the village gate. And behind her friend, his arms around Kenna's waist, sat the little figure of Mose.

'I'm here!' Meryt called out to them. She got to her feet, her heart full of gladness at the sight of her cousin. She suddenly realised how much she had missed him, and her face split into a grin.

Kenna jumped off the donkey's back and helped Mose down to the ground. He looked so small and timid here, away from the family home, and Meryt drew a deep breath. She desperately did not want to get him into trouble, or do him any harm. She hoped she was doing the right thing.

'Shall I leave you?' asked Kenna. 'I could come back in a while, if you like. I was on my way to the coppersmith's forge when I met you. I could pick Mose up on the way back.'

Meryt hesitated, then nodded. 'Thank you, Kenna,' she said, smiling at Mose, who reached for her hand.

She led her cousin back into the shade as Kenna trotted off down the valley. When they were sitting comfortably with their backs against the cool mud-brick wall, she began to question him gently.

'Does Tia know you are here?' she asked.

Mose shook his head. 'Kenna climbed on to the roof and told me to meet him on the street. He said not to tell anyone. It was easy. Mama and Papa take no notice of what I do now they are caring for Baki.'

'Well, I'm glad you're here,' said Meryt. 'How is Baki? Is he any better?'

Mose studied his fingers. 'He is still very sick. Mama and Papa are afraid he will die,' he said softly.

Meryt took a deep breath. 'That is why I've brought you here. I have something that might help him.'

Mose frowned. 'What kind of thing?'

'It is a spell. And a balm for his wound. We must get them to him, somehow, but Uncle does not want me in the house. You might be Baki's only hope.'

Mose looked dubious. 'I don't see how that will help,' he said.

'This is serious, Mose. Baki might die,' Meryt said urgently. Surely he knew how Senmut felt about her? He had heard it all when she had visited. Mose might be young, but he had sense enough to realise what was going on.

'I know that.' Mose's face was calm.

'And you know that Uncle blames me.'

'Yes. But it isn't your fault.' Mose hugged his knees and rocked gently.

'Well … I hope it isn't. Not in the way he means,' agreed Meryt, not wishing to alarm him. She felt uneasy. At the very least, she had failed to deliver the charm, which in itself might prove fatal; and despite Teti's reassurances, she still felt a ripple of fear at what her hatred might have brought about.

But Mose's next words took her by surprise. 'Mama says it is her fault, not yours. She told me why Peshedu is always angry with her. It is because she did something bad, a long time ago. This is why Baki is sick.'

He spoke with great authority and Meryt was shocked. 'But whatever did she do to make Peshedu so angry?' she exclaimed.

'I don't know,' said Mose. 'She wouldn't tell me that.'

Meryt stared at him. Of course, Tia had always been bothered by Peshedu – and more so recently than ever before. It had always been difficult to understand. But if she had done something to anger him, what sort of thing would justify such a fate for Baki? 'And what does your father think?' she asked.

Mose pursed his lips. 'He is still blaming you. He doesn't believe what Mama says.'

'But you believe her.'

'Yes. Mama tells the truth.'

Meryt shook her head in bewilderment. There was no doubt that Mose believed what he was saying, but it made little sense to her. And meanwhile, Baki was drawing ever closer to the Next World.

'Listen,' she said, reaching for the linen bag beside her. 'Baki has been touched by magic. Whoever is to

193

blame, you must take what I have here.' She fished out the linen charm. 'This spell is strong enough to bind the magic, but we must get it to him quickly. Will you do this for me, Mose?'

Mose hesitated, then took the charm from her and examined it curiously. 'Mama is praying to Peshedu,' he said. 'But I will take this anyway.'

'Thank you, Mose. You must put it under his head, when Senmut is not watching,' Meryt instructed him. 'And here is a balm for his wound. Give it to Mama and tell her it comes from Teti. But whatever you do, don't tell Senmut.'

'I will try,' said Mose.

'Good boy.' Meryt gave him the bag containing the balm. 'And tell Tia – tell your mama – to come and visit me at Dedi's house, if she can. I need to speak to her.'

Mose nodded, and folded the top of the bag carefully. Then he stood, and looked down at Meryt with a mournful expression. 'I miss you, Meryt,' he said, in a small voice, reaching for her hand. 'Will you be coming back soon?'

Meryt swallowed the lump in her throat and tried to smile. 'I don't know, Mose. I really don't know.'

Mose hung his head, then shrugged and turned away. 'I don't want to wait for Kenna,' he said. 'He might be a long time at the coppersmith's. I'd rather walk.' And with that, he turned towards the village gate, the little linen bag dangling from his hand.

Meryt waited for her friend, thinking over what

Mose had told her. He was young, but he knew when adults were telling the truth and when they were fobbing him off. If Tia had told him she had done something to anger Peshedu, then it was probably true.

So what was the problem with Peshedu? Meryt's father seemed to be at the heart of many things. He had appeared in Meryt's dream with Ramose ... he was somehow connected to Heria ... and now Tia was saying that he had caused Baki's illness too, because of something she had done. But what?

Meryt had no idea, but a voice niggled away in her head and would not go away however hard she tried to ignore it. *Your dreams hold the answer*, whispered the voice. *You have to go back to Teti. Go and look at your dreams*.

It was maddening and frightening in equal measure, and Meryt sat fighting with herself, pulled first one way and then the other. When she finally spotted Kenna coming up the road on the donkey, she waved in relief.

'Where's Mose?' he asked, trotting up to her.

'He's gone home on his own,' Meryt told him. 'Thank you for fetching him, Kenna.'

'That's fine.' Kenna looked curious. 'I just wish I knew what was really going on.'

Meryt gave a little smile. 'And I wish I could tell you,' she responded. 'Maybe someday I will be able to.'

Kenna met her gaze. 'I hope so,' he said softly. He played with the donkey's floppy ears, and Meryt was filled with yearning – not just for the times when they had been free of troubles, but for a life in which Kenna might look after her and take all her troubles away …

But it was no use. Such a life could not exist. Kenna saw her as his childhood friend, no more. There was all the difference in the world between the looks he gave to Dedi, and the way he looked at her. She had to continue alone, and with this realisation, Meryt made up her mind about what she would do.

'Where are you going now?' asked Kenna. 'Do you want a ride with me back into the village?'

Meryt shook her head. 'I have to go and visit someone.'

'Visit someone?' Kenna looked puzzled. 'But we are outside the village.'

'It is Teti that I need to see,' admitted Meryt. Kenna's eyebrows shot up in surprise, and she regretted saying it at once. 'Look, I think she may be able to help me, that's all. Please don't ask why.'

'I wasn't going to judge,' protested Kenna. 'Teti is wiser than many in the village. My mother has turned to her before now.' He shook his head sorrowfully. 'But if you are turning to her, I know your problems are beyond me.'

'Yes.' There was little else she could say. It was true.

'Well … I hope you will come and find me soon, in happier times.' Kenna gave one of his lopsided grins, and Meryt smiled.

'Thank you, Kenna,' she said. 'I will.'

The smell of baking bread drifted from Teti's courtyard as Meryt approached her house. It was a comforting smell, and when Teti appeared with her hands coated in flour, Meryt smiled nervously.

The *rekhet* seemed to be in a good mood. 'Come in, come in,' she said gaily. 'I'm just kneading another batch of bread. Are you hungry?'

'No ... not really,' said Meryt, following her through to the courtyard. Her stomach felt like one big tangled knot; the last thing she felt like doing was eating.

'Are you sure? There's fresh bread, just out of the oven.' Teti squatted down by a big bowl and pummelled her dough.

Meryt spotted the pile of golden loaves, but still could not find an appetite. 'Maybe later,' she said politely.

Teti nodded. 'Did your cousin get the balm?' she asked.

'I hope so,' said Meryt honestly. 'I didn't give it to him directly.' She took a deep breath. 'Actually I was wondering if you could help me with my dreams.'

Teti looked up at Meryt with a warm smile, and lifted the dough out of the bowl. 'I'm glad,' she said. 'It is not as frightening as you think. Though I remember thinking so when I first discovered such things for myself.'

Meryt found her words reassuring, and watched as Teti ripped up the dough and shaped it into six round loaves. The *rekhet* checked the little oven and threw on more wood before sliding the loaves inside. 'There,' she said, rubbing the dough off her hands. 'I'll just wash, then we can begin.'

She tipped water over her hands and scrubbed them vigorously, then dried them and fetched the papyrus scroll that she had shown Meryt before.

'We will need this,' said Teti, 'but it is not enough on its own. There is much more to the understanding of dreams than the scribes can tell us.' She unravelled the scroll carefully. 'Do you want to start by reading this? For now I can read it to you, but you can learn to read it yourself too, if you wish.'

'Well – perhaps,' said Meryt, rather breathlessly. 'But there is a dream I would like to tell you first.'

'Another dream? Or the one in which Baki was bitten?'

'Another,' replied Meryt. 'I consulted the goddess Hathor recently and the dream I had was … was not what I was expecting.'

Teti looked curious. 'Go on,' she said.

Suddenly, the gates of her heart opened, and Meryt found herself pouring out the whole story – the proposal from Ramose, his mother Heria's offerings in her father's chapel, and the threats from Senmut. 'I begged for time,' she explained, 'and my uncle gave it to me. I made an offering to Hathor but when I dreamt, it was not only Ramose that I saw.'

'Describe the dream to me. Everything you can remember.'

Meryt frowned, trying to think of all the details. 'I was looking out of a window,' she began, 'and I saw my father, Peshedu, climbing up towards the Peak of the West. He met Ramose coming the other way, and Ramose turned to walk alongside him. Together they disappeared from view towards the Great Place.'

Then she went over it again, remembering more: the hot desert wind, the linen billowing around the men, and Teti questioned her over each point. 'You were looking out of a window,' said the *rekhet* thoughtfully. 'Well, the *Dream Book* has something to say about that. Let's find it, shall we?'

She pored over the scroll, running her finger down the columns for a moment. Then she stopped. 'It says here, *if a man sees himself in a dream, looking out of a window: Good. It means the hearing of his cry by his god.* The goddess heard your request, Meryt. There can be no doubt about that.'

Meryt stared at the script uncertainly. 'Are you sure that's good?' she asked.

Teti laughed. 'Of course it's good.'

So perhaps there was hope, after all! But then Meryt frowned. 'But I still don't know what it means,' she said. 'I don't understand what Peshedu has to do with Ramose.' She carried on with the story, describing what Mose had just told her about Tia.

Teti took it all in. 'You are blessed, Meryt-Re,' she said gently. 'Do not fear the gods, because they are with you, and so is your father.'

'But can it be true that he has brought about Baki's illness? Why would he do such a thing?' Meryt was still disturbed, despite the *rekhet*'s words of comfort.

'All these things will become clear,' said Teti. 'Peshedu has led Ramose away from you with the blessing of the goddess Hathor. Look at your dream. Feel your way through it. Can you not sense that this is so?'

'Well ... no,' said Meryt. 'I don't know what to think. I thought perhaps Peshedu was giving Ramose his blessing.'

'And so he might be,' agreed Teti. 'But not in relation to you.'

Meryt frowned. 'I don't see how you've worked that out.'

'You will learn,' said Teti, with a smile. 'In time, you will know which way a dream is leading. You must let your mind go. It will lead you to the truth if you allow it to.'

They lapsed into silence as Meryt thought it over. A cat appeared over the courtyard wall and Teti coaxed it towards them. It rubbed against her legs, purring loudly as she scratched it behind the ears.

Meryt reached out as the silky creature wandered over to her, begging for attention. 'I will try to understand, Teti,' she said, stroking its head. 'You are right. The dreams are not so frightening when you look at them closely.'

'No. I am glad you think so.'

The cat found a piece of bread crust on the floor and batted it with its paws, making them laugh, and Meryt suddenly realised she had managed to relax. It was peaceful here, on the outskirts of the village, and her fears were growing less. She watched the cat for a moment, then smiled. 'Do you think I could have a piece of bread now?' she asked.

'Of course.' Teti rose and fetched a fresh loaf, which she broke in half. 'Here you are,' she said, handing Meryt a chunk. 'I think we may be destined to eat bread together often, you and I, Meryt-Re.'

By the time Meryt got back to Dedi's house, it was as though the party had never happened. Each room had been cleaned from top to bottom by the servants and Meryt felt instantly guilty. Wab was marching around, stern-faced, giving orders for rooms to be swept when they were already clean, and Meryt wished she could shrink away unseen. But there was little chance of that.

'Dedi is waiting for you on the roof,' Wab snapped at her. 'You might tell us when you plan to go out and return.'

'I'm sorry, Mistress Wab,' said Meryt meekly. 'I had to go out on an errand to help my family.'

Wab sniffed. 'You might think to help the family who are sheltering you.'

'Of course – if there's anything I can do …'

'It's a bit late.'

There was clearly no pleasing her. Meryt apologised again and slipped past her, through to the courtyard and on to the roof. Dedi was combing her hair with a preoccupied expression on her face, and only smiled wanly as Meryt approached.

'Dedi, I'm sorry I wasn't here this morning. Your mother is angry with me ...'

'She is angry with everyone. We all are.' Dedi's voice was abrupt.

Meryt was taken aback, and sat down quietly to wait for her friend to expand. Dedi put down the comb and smoothed her hair with her fingers, and Meryt was reminded of the cat she had stroked earlier. It was almost as though Dedi were trying to calm her own agitation; and Meryt reflected that if Userkaf's intention was to unnerve Nebnufer and his family, he was managing rather well.

'At least Neben remains loyal to me,' said Dedi, letting her hands fall by her side.

'Were you with him last night?' Meryt remembered that her friend had disappeared once the party had broken up.

Dedi nodded. 'Yes. He took me away from here because he did not like to see me so upset. There is a secret place that we go to, sometimes.'

Meryt did not enquire further. What Dedi and Neben did together was another area in which her friend was much more worldly-wise than she. 'I am glad he is so good to you,' she said tentatively. 'You need good friends at times like these.'

'Yes.' Dedi sighed. 'Good friends among men. But I fear they are not enough when the gods have abandoned you.'

'Whatever makes you say that?'

Dedi played with her bracelets, fingering one that had little amulets strung all around it. 'Userkaf is gaining power,' she said. 'Half the men left with him last night. The unrest goes much further than Father had imagined. Userkaf is not a troublemaker with a few rowdy friends. He has the support of half the gang, and we do not understand why. What is all this, if not a sign that the gods are with him?' She raised her beautiful eyes to Meryt's, and Meryt saw the depths of the fear and confusion that lay there.

It was difficult to know what to say. After all, Kenna had said something very similar. Userkaf's confidence gave the impression of power and there were few men who did not respond to that.

Meryt frowned. There had to be some comfort that she could give. 'Remember the findings of the council,' she said eventually. 'And the oracle. They did not side with Userkaf. You must not give in to your fear, Dedi.'

Dedi picked up her comb and flung it down in fury. 'That is easy for you to say!' she exclaimed. 'It is not your marriage and your family's whole life that is at stake!'

Meryt recoiled from her friend in astonishment. She had never seen Dedi explode like this, ever. And almost at once, anger gripped her too, for until now Dedi's life had been charmed. She had little idea of the struggles faced by Meryt every day. Meryt had always borne their differences with good grace, but the pressure of her own predicament now made her lash out. 'How dare you!' she retorted. 'I do not even have a family of my own and certainly no prospect of a happy marriage. Have you forgotten that, or are you too spoilt?'

Dedi gasped. 'You ungrateful wretch. We have taken you in and sheltered you when who knows what has driven you here. We have trusted that your ill fortune will not follow you but I begin to wonder if it has. Why will Senmut no longer have you in his house, Meryt? What have you done to deserve such a thing?'

Meryt began to tremble. 'It is not my doing,' she cried. 'There are forces of evil around us but I am not under their sway!'

Dedi stared at her, her hair dishevelled and her breathing fast and shallow. She leant towards Meryt so their faces were close. *'What do you know about the forces of evil?'* she demanded, between gritted teeth. 'What do you know? Are you part of the misfortunes that are falling upon us?'

'No!' Meryt was frightened now. Dedi's lovely features seemed twisted and strange, as though something were eating at her from within. 'Of course not! Dedi, you said you trusted me!'

Dedi leant back again, the line of her mouth thin

and bitter. 'I don't know,' she said, almost to herself. 'I can't be sure any more … '

Meryt stood up. She couldn't bear it. She looked out over the rooftops and up at the sky. There were a few wisps of cloud stretched out towards the horizon and she wished she was up there with the sun-god Re on his journey to the west. Why not, after all? She was Meryt-Re; beloved of Re. But for once, his familiar presence did little to comfort her. He seemed distant, aloof, far removed from the daily events on the earth below. She turned to go down the staircase.

'Where are you going?' Dedi's voice was sharp.

Meryt looked back at her friend, her heart heavy. 'I don't know.'

Dedi's anger seemed spent, for she reached out her hand. 'I'm sorry, Meryt. Don't leave us.'

Meryt shook her head. 'These are bad times, Dedi. I don't wish to bring further anguish to your family. If people fear me then it is better for me to go.'

'It is not you that I fear. Not really.'

'If you feared me, you would not be the first. You know that. And maybe I am getting used to it. There is someone I need to see. It isn't Teti this time but someone who may hold the key to the problems of your family.'

Dedi looked incredulous. 'Hold the … who? What are you talking about?'

'I can't tell you,' said Meryt. 'In any case I may be wrong.'

'You can't say that.' Dedi stepped quickly across

the roof and grabbed Meryt's arm. 'Tell me, Meryt!'

But Meryt said nothing, for standing at the bottom of the staircase, with Nebnufer between them, were two members of the Medjay police force.

 # CHAPTER TEN

'Father!' Dedi stared down at Nebnufer, her eyes wide with shock.

'Don't worry,' Nebnufer told her. 'We need to come up to the roof to talk, my child. This will affect the whole family, so you can stay if you wish.'

Meryt quickly decided to make herself scarce. She slipped out of the house, leaving Nebnufer to climb up to roof with the two policemen, followed by Wab and his sons. The Medjays' visit was bound to be something about Userkaf's goings-on, and she hoped that they put an end to his antics once and for all. Meanwhile, she walked determinedly to the southern end of the village. She would play her part, if she could.

Outside the gate, Meryt positioned herself so that whichever way Nofret returned from her job in the embalmers' workshops, she would be able to spot and waylay the girl. She waited for what seemed like an eternity, tossing limestone pebbles from one hand to the other and tracing patterns in the dust. Foremost in her mind was her dream about Kha. She thought of Teti's words: *You must let your mind go. It will lead you to the truth if you allow it to* ... She went over the dream again. There was the amulet, lying in the dust. It was so hot that she could not touch it, and the gold began to melt away, leaving only the fragments of precious lapis lazuli and glass. But as she reached to grasp them, they too disappeared, leaving nothing on the ground at all.

Let your mind go. Meryt thought instead of Kha, standing in the moonlight, dressed in nothing but rags. *He has nothing*, she thought. *It is not he who receives the amulets. Nofret's story is a lie.* She thought of Userkaf – arrogant, wielding the power of the gods. If Nofret was stealing the amulets for her master, he was using them for despicable ends. He had great magic at his disposal and Nebnufer's downfall was his aim.

And yet ... and yet ... Meryt shook her head. Userkaf was not the sort of man to understand the fine workings of magic. He was a man of flesh and blood and wine. A man who longed for wealth and status and fine linen on his back.

Suddenly, the truth was so clear that Meryt could scarcely believe she had not seen it before. A sacred amulet was an object to be feared and respected. In the hands of the right person it could bring protection or destruction in equal measure. But this amulet was more than that. It contained enough gold and lapis lazuli to pay the wages of many men for months ... She thought of the traders she had seen at

208

the gate. Such men could easily dispose of precious objects, for they dealt in them all the time. Userkaf was not interested in the amulets' power; their value was enough to set the village alight.

Meryt jumped up as she spotted the little figure of Nofret trudging towards her in the late afternoon sun. The girl had her head bowed and did not see Meryt until she ran into her path and spoke to her.

'Nofret.'

Nofret stopped in her tracks. 'What is it?' she asked.

Meryt drew herself up tall, and assumed a dreamy expression. 'The gods have spoken,' she said, in a low voice. 'They have come to me in my dreams and revealed the truth. Do you wish to hear it?'

Nofret took a step back. 'Why … yes, of course I want to hear it,' she said, her nostrils flaring nervously.

'Come then,' said Meryt. 'We'll go up the hillside and I shall tell you.'

Without a word, Nofret fell into step behind her and they walked silently through the eastern cemetery to the top of the hill. There, Meryt did not sit down, but turned to face the servant girl with her arms folded. Her heart was beating fast, for she could not be completely sure of her ground.

She took a deep breath. 'You lied to me,' she stated, as coolly as she could.

Nofret's mouth dropped open. 'What do you mean?'

'The gods have revealed the truth. You lied to me,' repeated Meryt, studying the other girl's face. 'You lied to me about Kha. He is innocent. Did you think that you could get away with such a falsehood?'

Nofret stared at her, and Meryt could tell that her mind was working quickly. Then, to her astonishment, the servant girl laughed. 'The gods do not reveal such things so easily,' she said.

Meryt's confidence wavered. Nofret had seemed nervous at first, but now all signs of her fear had gone. But she was not going to give up yet. 'You are a strange girl, Nofret,' she said. 'On one day you come to me for protection from the gods. On another you say they do not speak to me. Which is it that you believe?'

The servant girl pursed her lips, and shrugged. But Meryt caught a look of uncertainty on the other girl's face, and took a step towards her. 'What if I told you that I know what becomes of the amulets?' she asked.

'You can't possibly know that!' Nofret's voice was scornful.

Meryt smiled. 'Can't I?' She turned to face the great River Nile and the mortuary temples, a slight breeze lifting her hair. 'I have seen the amulets fall apart,' she said, resuming her dreamlike voice. 'I have seen the value of their gold and of their lapis lazuli. I have seen the traders at the village gate and I have seen the gentleness of painter Kha.' She spun around quickly to catch the look on Nofret's face.

'So tell me what you make of that, Nofret, servant of Userkaf!'

Nofret looked incredulous. 'The gods revealed this?'

'Yes,' said Meryt. 'They did.'

The servant raised her eyebrows, and fell silent. She wandered away from Meryt and sat down on a rock with her back turned. Meryt began to feel frustrated. Perhaps she had gone about all this the wrong way, for it had not had the effect she intended. She had hoped that Nofret would crumble when she heard about Meryt's dream, and give away more information – perhaps even enough to blacken Userkaf's name. But instead she had clamped her mouth shut like the jaws of a jackal around its prey.

She marched over to her. 'So what are you going to do, Nofret?' she demanded. 'You can see that I know the truth. The gods will not protect you now.'

Nofret gave a cynical smile. 'You know little, Meryt-Re,' she said. 'You have seen that the amulets are sold to traders. It would not take the powers of a pharaoh to work out such a thing. You think you are clever but you will not catch me out like that.'

Despite her relief at having been right, Meryt was stung. 'You play with fire,' she exclaimed. 'You are a common thief and you stand in defiance of the gods.'

'There's something you don't understand,' said Nofret. She stood up and looked Meryt in the face. In the depths of her eyes, Meryt saw more than defiance and fear; there was a curious deadness there too. 'I am a servant girl. A slave.'

'I know that,' said Meryt, puzzled.

'But you do not know what it means.' Nofret twisted her lips into an almost pitying smile. 'My life cannot get any worse than it already is. I have nothing to lose.'

And with that, she pushed past Meryt and started back down the track to the village gate.

Meryt felt nonplussed, and a little lost. Her plan had failed, more or less; Nofret's admission, such as it was, had got her nowhere. She was going to have to think the whole thing through much more carefully.

I have nothing to lose. Strange, powerful words that somehow shook Meryt to her core, for she could not say the same for herself. Despite the difficult times she was going through, she loved Set Maat and its people. She loved the tomb of her father and the knowledge that she came from a long line of craftsmen. She loved Tia and Dedi and Kenna, little Mose and Henut. When times were good she even loved Senmut, in her own way. Deep down she knew she had faith – faith in Teti, faith in her friends and faith in the future.

But Nofret had nothing. *Nothing to lose.* And yet, Meryt thought slowly, if she had nothing to lose then she surely had something to gain.

Meryt began to make her own way back, and as she reached the eastern tombs she thought she could hear more of a hubbub than usual. Curious, she quickened her pace and saw as soon as she passed through the gate that the main street was thronging with people.

'What's going on?' she asked the Medjay guard.

'Haven't you heard? Nebnufer has been arrested.'

'*Nebnufer* has been arrested!' Meryt was shocked. She thought of the two men she had seen in Nebnufer's house. Somehow she had imagined that it was Nebnufer himself who had summoned them. Surely this couldn't be right! 'But what for?' she asked.

'Stealing tomb equipment, that's what I heard,' said the guard. 'The top Medjay men went round to his house. They found a pile of new copper tools in his storeroom – government stock. He'll have some explaining to do by the sound of it.'

Meryt could scarcely take it in. '*Stealing!*' she exclaimed. 'That's ridiculous. As if Nebnufer needs to steal anything.'

The guard shrugged and grinned. 'Well, that's what they found,' he said. 'Guess it's in the vizier's hands now.'

Meryt felt cold inside. She had no doubt that Userkaf was somehow at the bottom of this, but once the matter was referred to the vizier it would be difficult to show it for what it was – or certainly to prove anything. The situation had escalated beyond her wildest imaginings.

She walked quickly towards Dedi's house. To her dismay, there were clusters of people gossiping outside it. *Nebnufer*, she heard. *Userkaf. Sennedjem.* She decided not to disturb the household, and to return later. *The kenbet is meeting* … Everyone was talking about it. She broke into a jog, weaving her way through the crowds. And then she felt a hand on her elbow, and spun round.

It was Tia who stood there. 'Meryt, I'm so glad I found you.' Her eyes were sunken with weariness, and a faint twitch irritated the skin beneath her left eye. Meryt thought she had aged beyond her twenty-seven years, and she reached out to touch her aunt's arm.

'You look so tired,' she said.

Tia's eyes filled with tears, and she struggled to blink them away. 'I've left Senmut with Baki,' she said. 'I told him I was going to make an offering to Peshedu.'

Meryt thought quickly. Whatever was happening at Nebnufer's house, it would have to wait. 'Let's go to Peshedu's tomb anyway,' she said. 'There, you can rest.'

Her aunt nodded, and Meryt took her arm. Together, they walked slowly to the western gate and the cemetery that now stood in shadow, long since abandoned by the morning sun.

'How is Baki?' Meryt asked, when they had left the milling people behind. 'Is he any better?'

Tia's bottom lip trembled. 'He is knocking on the door of the Next World,' she said, her voice anguished. 'I am so afraid. I don't know how long he has left.'

214

Meryt's heart filled with guilt. If only she had made sure that her cousin received the linen charm when Teti had given it to her. She hoped desperately that Mose had done what she had told him. 'Did Mose give you the balm from Teti?'

'Yes. Thank you, Meryt. I used it on his wound, but I fear it will not be much help.'

Meryt frowned. 'I don't understand. Whatever you believe about Baki, this balm has come from Teti and she is sure it can cure him.'

Tia shrugged and was silent, breathing heavily as they climbed the hill. Meryt supported her until they reached the chapel courtyard, where her aunt leant against the wall in relief. 'Let's sit,' she said. 'I need to rest.'

She walked slowly to the chapel entrance and lowered herself to the ground just outside it. Meryt joined her and waited until her aunt's breathing steadied, and she seemed ready to talk. 'When did you last come here?' she asked.

'Yesterday,' Tia told her. 'And someone else had been here again.'

Meryt thought of Heria, hurrying down the hill back to the village. 'I know who it is,' she said. 'But I don't know why she comes.'

Tia looked at her sharply. 'She? Who is it?'

Meryt studied her fingers. They still smelt slightly of the fragrant tallow that she and Dedi had used to make the perfume cones. 'Heria,' she said.

'Heria!' Tia's eyes filled with wonder.

'So you don't know why either?' said Meryt.

Tia shook her head. 'No idea. She knew your father, of course.' She sighed and lapsed into silence again, playing with the string of amulets that she wore around her neck. Meryt watched her. Tia was clearly exhausted, and troubled to the core of her being. She wondered whether to question her, but could see that she needed to speak in her own time.

'Meryt, there is something I need to tell you,' her aunt said eventually. 'That's why I came to find you.'

Meryt's heart began to thump harder in anticipation, and she nodded. 'It's about Peshedu, isn't it?'

'Yes.' Tia swallowed, wringing her hands together. 'I don't know how … how …' she trailed off, her eyes filling with tears once more.

'Mose told me that you have angered him in some way,' said Meryt, trying to help her. 'But you are so gentle and good. I can't imagine what you might have done.'

'Oh, Meryt.' Tia's tears began to fall in big, heavy drops. 'I have done so much. I doubt you will forgive me, when you know.'

'*I* forgive you!' cried Meryt in amazement. 'What has it to do with me?'

She had to wait for several minutes before Tia could speak again. When she did, she spoke in little gasps, as though she were afraid to let the words out. 'If it were not for me, you might still have a father, Meryt,' she said. 'And now Peshedu is punishing me for this with the death of my own dear son.'

'No!' Meryt shook her head in bewilderment. 'Peshedu died of the coughing disease. That is what you have always told me. Is this not true?'

Tia made a little motion with her shoulders that was not quite a shrug. 'Perhaps,' she stuttered. 'But he might … he might have lived if it were not for me.'

'Men rarely recover from the coughing disease,' said Meryt quietly. 'I have always accepted this, Tia. You know that.'

'Yes. Yes. But he was getting better. I know he was, for I was the one who nursed him and implored the gods for his recovery. And then …' Tia stopped, and wiped her eyes with the edge of her dress. The khol she always wore made a black smudge on the clean white linen, but she didn't seem to care.

'And then?' Meryt prompted her.

'The priests of Ptah had given me a spell,' Tia carried on, her voice barely above a whisper. 'I was to repeat it seven times a day at his bedside. But I grew careless. We were short of grain, for Peshedu's treatment had cost us much, and Senmut began to complain that I cared more for my brother than I did for him. I did as much weaving as I could manage, and one day, news came that Paser the scribe wanted three new kilts. Peshedu was sleeping, so I left him and ran to Paser's house with the kilts. I forgot that it was time to repeat the spell. Paser kept me waiting for … for … half the afternoon.' She took a deep, shuddering breath. 'And when I returned, your father was …was …'

Tia could not finish her sentence, and Meryt felt a strange stillness. She imagined her father, lying on his sick bed, drifting towards the Next World for lack of the magic that could have saved him. The darkness that must have slowly crept up on him. The terror of dying untended and alone ... She had never felt so close to her father's death before – or to his life, that precious, precious life. It was as though the world were slowing down, going backwards, as Tia continued to speak. 'He left me for the Next World without a word. I could only think that he was punishing me for abandoning him in his hour of need. He has never given me peace from that day to this.'

Meryt stared at Tia, unseeing, as the vision of a different world flashed before her – one in which she lived happily in her own father's home, without Baki to taunt her or Senmut to fill her with guilt. In the house of her uncle she would have been only an occasional guest, the daughter of a respected sculptor in the Great Place and a playmate for her cousins, not a burdensome orphan to be resented and despised. She would have been happy, wanted and loved.

She tried to speak, but the words stuck in her throat.

'I tried to appease him,' Tia carried on. 'I made sure of his life in the Next World. All that he left behind was yours, but you were only two years old. I swore that I would care for you for your whole life if I had to. So he was given the best embalming and funeral. We paid for many amulets to be placed among his wrappings, and his tomb lacked for nothing. I hoped it would assure him that I never meant any harm.'

Meryt bowed her head. She felt almost sick. Her limbs began to shake. With a strangled cry, she buried her head in her arms and started to sob.

'Meryt … Meryt … Don't. Hush, please don't. I'm so sorry. I'm so, so sorry,' Tia's voice begged, but it could make no difference now. Meryt rocked to and fro, lost in her own world of grief. 'Hush, hush, please, don't,' Tia repeated, and Meryt felt an arm around her shoulders.

She couldn't bear it. 'Leave me alone!' she cried, without looking up. 'There is nothing you can do for me now!'

Tia said nothing more, and Meryt could not say when she felt the touch of her hand leave her shoulders. All she could feel was the life of the father that she had lost – snatched away from him as he lay abandoned and alone.

But some time later, as darkness began to fall, Meryt looked up to find that her aunt had gone. She crept into the chapel and laid down to one side of the altar, where she was sheltered from the cool evening breeze. She curled into a ball and waited for the velvety blackness of night to cloak her. Soon, the heavy weight lying in her chest pulled her down, down, into a dreamless sleep from which she never wanted to wake.

When at last Meryt opened her eyes, she didn't know where she was. A shaft of sunlight was beaming on to her face and she sat up, shielding her gaze from its glare. She looked around, taking in the offerings on the altar and the beautiful paintings on the dome of the chapel. It did not take long to remember what had happened the day before, and she sat still, wishing she could find the hidden entrance to the tomb itself and join her father for ever. In the Next World, they would never be parted and there would never be another death to face alone.

But then she felt angry, for life could have been so different. Peshedu might have lived. And to add to this pain, Tia's words crept back to haunt her: *I tried to appease him … I swore that I would care for you for your whole life if I had to.* Now, Meryt was alone, with the knowledge that the woman who had shielded her all her life had done so only out of guilt. The bitterness of it was like the taste of a tamarind in her mouth.

She felt her stomach rumble in hunger, and looked at Tia's most recent offering. What good could it do anyway, lying there on the altar? It was only to beg forgiveness for Meryt's own predicament! Peshedu would hardly blame her for eating it. She picked up a loaf and tore off a chunk, then helped herself to a handful of dates. She stared at them, daring herself to take the first bite. When she did, a strange sense of recklessness came over her and she ate hungrily, ramming the food into her mouth with savage, bitter glee. As she did so, Meryt thought of Nofret's words. *I have nothing to lose.* Suddenly, she knew exactly what the servant girl had meant.

As the day grew brighter, Meryt's thoughts drifted to the moment before meeting Tia. It seemed an eternity ago, but then she remembered: the buzzing crowds, Nebnufer's arrest, and talk of a council meeting. Despite herself, she felt curious.

She left the chapel and began to walk through the cemetery to the western gate, looking down at the village as she did so. From the sound of it, the bustle on the streets had returned to normal; people were going about their morning business. She glanced up and spotted a group of men walking up the path that led to the Great Place, and guessed that they were men from Sennedjem's gang. They reminded her of Senmut, and the house that could never be her home again.

It was too painful a thought to dwell on. Pushing it away, she walked through the gate and made her way to Dedi's house. The street outside was now quiet. The door, which was usually left ajar, was firmly shut. She looked around, and caught sight of a neighbour's head peeping at her from behind her front door, then quickly retreating again. Meryt felt chilled, a sense of foreboding filling her as she raised her hand to knock.

At first, no one answered. Then, after a long, long pause, Dedi's brother Yuya opened the door, his expression wary.

'Oh, it's you, Meryt,' he said. 'Dedi's not here. Mother's taken her away for a few days. All the women have gone – the servants too.'

Meryt stared at him. 'Gone?' she managed to stutter.

Yuya nodded. 'They're staying with relatives to the south,' he said. 'It's not exactly pleasant around here at the moment, Meryt. You know what neighbours are like.'

Meryt felt lost. For a moment, all she could think was that she had nowhere to stay. 'Oh ... well, thank you,' she murmured, then looked at Yuya beseechingly, unsure what to do.

He did not return her gaze. 'They'll be back in time for the trial,' he said abruptly, and shut the door.

The trial. So things had moved on. The council must have decided that they could not deal with Nebnufer themselves, for serious matters such as theft of government property were always dealt with by the vizier.

Meryt turned away and wandered down the street, feeling desolate. It felt as though no one in the world cared where she was, or what she did. Was there nowhere she could go to feel safe? She could not live in her father's chapel for long. There was Kenna's house, of course, but she had already thought that through. It wasn't an option. Such a thing could only happen if they were more than just friends ...

There was only one place left to her. She would have to turn to Teti.

As soon as the *rekhet* opened the door and gave one of her big, warm smiles, Meryt felt the floodgates open and she was swamped with tears.

'Meryt, whatever's happened?' Teti held out her arms and Meryt leant into them, choked with sobs.

'Come in, come in.' Teti led her through the house to the courtyard and sat her down on the reed matting, still holding on to her hands. 'Take your time. Cry as long as you want.'

Meryt did not need any encouragement. She wept for everything – for her lost mother and father, for Tia, for the home that she had lost, for her love for Kenna, for the disgrace that rested on Nebnufer and all his family, for despair at what the future might hold. At last, she grew still, and Teti handed her a piece of linen to dry her eyes.

'Dear, dear!' exclaimed Teti. 'It is as though the world has ended. Or perhaps, for you, it has?'

Meryt looked at her questioningly through her red-rimmed eyes. Nothing escaped Teti, she knew. But the look in the older woman's eyes was also questioning, and Meryt could see that she had not divined the whole truth. She gulped back her tears, and began to talk.

Everything came pouring out all over again – the long, uneasy presence of her father in the household, Ramose's proposal and Heria's visits to Peshedu's tomb, Meryt's banishment by Senmut and Tia's confession the night before. 'And as if all that were not enough,' she hiccuped, 'I went to Dedi's house and they have gone. Nebnufer must stand trial for something I am sure he never did and no one knows

223

about the stolen golden amulets.'

Teti's face went still. 'What stolen amulets?'

Meryt's lower lip wobbled. She hadn't meant to mention the amulets; she held their power in too much respect – and besides, she had sworn by all the gods and her ancestors not to speak. But now, Teti was regarding her intently and she was overcome with recklessness all over again. 'The … the amulets from the embalmers' workshops,' she said. 'That's how Userkaf is bribing the men. Or at least I think so, but I can't prove anything because Nofret denies it now.'

Teti held up her hand. 'Wait, wait,' she said. 'More slowly. You say that golden amulets are being stolen from the embalmers' workshops. That is a serious charge. Who is stealing them?'

Meryt hesitated, already wishing that she could take her admission back. But it was too late now. 'Nofret,' she said. 'Userkaf's servant girl.'

'How did you find out?'

'I bumped into her on the hillside path and she dropped one. Then she asked me for protection from the gods and told me lies about the painter Kha. I had a dream and saw that he was innocent and I tried to force her to tell me the truth, but it didn't work. Now there is nothing I can do.'

Teti drew a deep breath. 'So that's it,' she muttered, almost to herself. She took Meryt's hands and held them firmly in her own. 'Listen to me, Meryt. The gods have given you a heavy burden. We will come to your family in a minute, but for now we must talk of the amulets. You must know that such objects are not to be played with lightly.'

Meryt nodded. 'I haven't told anyone else,' she whispered. 'I promised Nofret I wouldn't.'

'And you said you had a dream, about Kha.'

'Yes. I saw that the amulets were broken down in great heat and that Kha is just a poor man. Then I saw traders at the village gate and gradually I saw what it all meant. Or I thought I did. When I challenged Nofret she admitted that the amulets were sold to traders but she would not admit anything else.'

Teti became silent, her brow furrowed, but she held on to Meryt's hands just as tightly. At last, she spoke. 'This is powerful knowledge. The fate of the village rests on it,' she said slowly. 'And the gods have put this knowledge in your hands. I cannot take that from you, but I will try to protect you, if I can.'

'Protect me from what?' asked Meryt miserably. 'I have told you what has happened. Surely my life cannot get any worse.'

Teti's face darkened. 'The forces of chaos are greater than you can imagine, Meryt,' she said. 'They are wielded by the god Seth himself, the enemy of Horus and the god of mischief and vengeance. When he unleashes his weapons, problems such as yours are as nothing, I can assure you.'

Her words reminded Meryt of the warning that she herself had given Nofret, and she knew that they were true. She swallowed. 'So what should I do?'

'I will make you an amulet,' said Teti. 'And I will consult the gods myself. You ...' She paused, and stroked Meryt's hands. 'You must do as the gods direct you.'

'But ... how?'

'They have brought you this far,' Teti answered. 'They will guide you, if you allow them to.' She looked deep into Meryt's eyes, and smiled. 'And now, we must talk of your family. Did Baki receive the treatment that I sent?'

Meryt nodded, her head bowed.

'But you do not know if he has begun to recover?'

This time, Meryt shrugged, for the issue seemed hopeless, and to think of the family carrying on without her filled her with pain. But Teti's next question touched the core of the matter and she was forced to look up.

'Do you really believe that Tia has not loved you all these years?' asked the *rekhet*. 'Think before you answer. It is always hard to see beyond your bitterness and anger, but you must try.'

Meryt felt the tears welling up once more, for Tia had cared for her as far back as she could remember and had been the only mother figure she had ever known. Her care had always been deeper than Senmut's and until now, Meryt had never doubted that it was founded on love. And yet ... and yet ... 'She *had* to love me,' she burst out. 'She had no choice.'

'There is always a choice, Meryt,' said Teti quietly. 'I have seen mothers who have rejected their own flesh, and fathers who wished to dash their children's heads against the stones.'

Meryt let the words sink in. She thought of Tia's long-suffering love for her children and her endurance of Nauna's jibes ... how she had always stuck up for Meryt. How, as Meryt had grown up, they had become allies – even friends. And slowly, as she thought it through, her anger turned to a swelling sadness. 'You're right,' she mumbled. 'Tia has loved me, Teti.'

'There ... there, you see,' said Teti, her voice full of tenderness. 'You have a good heart, Meryt. It is big enough to find forgiveness, if you try.'

CHAPTER ELEVEN

For the rest of the day, Teti gave Meryt jobs to do around her house. There was a pile of grain to be ground to flour, for Teti did not qualify for help from the government servants; there was a batch of beer to be made and a hole in the mud-brick wall to be repaired.

'When you have much to think about, it is sometimes best to keep busy,' said Teti, as Meryt began work on the grain. 'Solutions present themselves in their own way and you cannot always force them.'

Meryt smiled wanly. She was not sure if it was true, but in any case, it was a comfort to feel part of someone's household for a few hours. She bent her head over the grain, her arms soon beginning to ache from the unaccustomed effort. Nes the servant girl had to do this every day, moving from house to house, she reflected; and Meryt did not envy her. It made her realise how lucky she had been, all these years.

But as the rhythm of the work absorbed her body, her mind started ticking over, as Teti had said it might. By the time the afternoon sun had begun to dip, she had worked out what she was going to do.

'Teti,' she said, as the *rekhet* carried a basket of linen across the courtyard, 'I would like to go back to the village for a little while, if I may.'

'Of course,' said Teti.

'But ...' Meryt took a deep breath. 'I was wondering if I could return here to sleep.'

Teti smiled. 'You will always be welcome here, Meryt-Re,' she said. 'I thank the gods for bringing me a helper. And I do not just mean someone to grind the grain.'

Meryt looked at her uncertainly, unsure what she meant, but Teti had turned away to tend to the linen. She stood up and slipped quietly out of the house.

Now that she had a purpose, Meryt walked briskly to Kenna's house. One of his sisters came to the door and grinned shyly at her.

'He's carving a *senet* set on the roof,' she told Meryt. 'Do you want to go up and find him?'

Meryt smiled briefly. 'Thank you,' she said, and hurried through the house – aware, as ever, that the women's whispers were following her. She hated it, and knew for sure that she could never beg for help from a family such as this.

Kenna was sitting in a patch of afternoon sun, humming a tune as he whittled away at the little *senet* pieces. The sets that he made were much in demand among his friends and neighbours as gifts, and he spent many hours perfecting them. Meryt paused at the top of the staircase to watch him, but he heard her and looked up.

'Meryt!' His eyes lit up. 'You disappeared again. I looked for you during the council meeting. I thought you would be with Dedi but ...' he shrugged, and placed his copper carving knife on the ground. 'Well, you know where you were. Come and sit.'

Meryt walked over to where he sat and squatted down beside him. 'You have almost finished this set,' she commented. The chequered board lay next to him, made in the form of a box with a little drawer in it to hold the pieces. Kenna had just been giving the finishing touches to one of the pawns, which he placed in the drawer.

'Yes. Just two more pawns to go, and the throwing sticks – but they take no time at all,' said Kenna, clearly satisfied with his work. He smiled. 'So, what brings you here?'

'I need you to help me again,' said Meryt.

Kenna became serious at once. 'Of course. Anything.'

'It's nothing too difficult – just the same as before. I need to see Mose,' she explained. 'I will wait outside the northern gate, as I did last time.'

Kenna frowned. 'So you are still not living with your family. And things cannot be easy in Nebnufer's house. I wish you would tell me what's going –'

'I can't,' Meryt cut across him. Then she smiled gently. 'Not yet. I'm sorry, Kenna. I'm fine, that's all

230

you need to know. I am staying with Teti.'

'Teti!' Kenna looked startled. 'Meryt, it is one thing to consult the *rekhet* in times of trouble but quite another to stay under her roof. Are you not afraid?'

Meryt was puzzled. 'No. Why should I be afraid? She's good to me. I trust her.'

Kenna picked up the *senet* set, and sighed. He pulled the drawer out and pushed it back in, then smoothed the chequered squares of wood with his finger. Meryt saw his discomfort, and it grieved her that her friend did not understand the ways of the *rekhet*. But she also knew Kenna well enough to understand the reason why; he preferred not to dwell on people's troubles if he could.

'What happened at the council meeting?' she asked him, changing the subject.

Kenna put the box down again. 'Have you not heard? The Medjay showed the council the bag of copper tools that they found in Nebnufer's store-room. The council asked him if he had anything to say. He made a simple statement, saying that he was innocent of the theft but could not yet prove it. So it was decided that he would be suspended as foreman until the matter could be heard by the vizier.'

'Suspended!' Meryt thought of the men she had seen climbing to the Great Place that morning. 'But work is carrying on in the tombs, all the same.'

'Yes. Sennedjem has returned with his men, out of loyalty to Nebnufer, some say. It makes a change for his gang to be doing more than Nebnufer's.' He

231

grinned. 'Father is making the most of his days of idleness.'

'So none of Nebnufer's gang have gone back?'

Kenna shook his head. 'They have been given leave while the council decides how to proceed. There is a rumour that Userkaf will be promoted to foreman until Nebnufer's trial is over. Many of the men support him.'

Meryt's mouth dropped open in shock. 'Userkaf as *foreman* …!' she exclaimed.

'Yes. Makes sense, I suppose,' said Kenna. 'It will suit him. He has never been the most patient of draughtsmen, after all.'

Meryt stared at him, trying to take it in. So that had been the purpose of it all! The position of foreman was coveted by all, of course, for it brought with it wealth and status and many contacts among government officials; but Meryt never imagined that anyone would go to such lengths to obtain it. It was breathtaking. In Kenna's own words, it made sense – but far more sense than he was aware of.

She thought of Teti's words: *You must do as the gods direct you. They will guide you, if you allow them to.* She chewed her lip. There had been no guidance as yet, but an idea was beginning to form and she wanted to think about it. She scrambled to her feet. 'I had better get going,' she said. 'I would like to see Mose before nightfall.'

Kenna nodded. 'I will fetch him right away.'

'Thank you, Kenna.' Meryt felt wistful. 'Maybe

some day, I will be able to repay you for all you have done for me.'

'Don't say such things,' replied Kenna, looking wounded. 'It's nothing. I only wish I could do more.'

As she walked back to the northern gate, Meryt was thinking hard. What she could not get out of her mind was the night of Nebnufer's party and the image of Kha, offering her a glass of water. She thought of his gentleness, the kindness in his eyes, the way he had seemed quieter than everyone else. And then, later on, he had disappeared. The explanation seemed to hover at the edge of her mind but she could not quite see it.

She reached the village wall and leant against it to wait for Mose. Perhaps there was more to be gleaned from her dream about the painter. Meryt put her fingertips to her temples and closed her eyes to go through it again. There he had stood, alone in his ragged loincloth on the Peak of the West, with the moonlight shining upon him. There he had stood, alone ... alone ... Meryt thumped the wall with her heel. Had she hit upon the answer?

She stirred as Mose's familiar voice greeted her. 'You look far, far away, Meryt,' he said, and she opened her eyes to see her cousin smiling up at her.

'Mose! Oh, I'm so glad to see you.' She waved at Kenna, who was already retreating to the village gate. 'There are many things I need to ask of you.'

Mose placed his hand in hers, and they walked a

little further down the wall before squatting to talk.

'Baki is getting better,' Mose informed her. 'I placed the charm under his head, as you told me to, and I gave Mama the balm. They are beginning to work.'

Meryt looked at him quickly. 'Really, Mose? Are you sure?'

'Yes,' said Mose. 'He is not so hot now and he has started to ask for food again.'

His words had a strange effect on Meryt. On the one hand she felt a rush of relief and astonishment. On the other, the news was like a crushing blow, because she could no longer share in the family's happiness.

She bit her lip. 'And how is your mama?' she asked.

Mose was silent for a moment, his young face struggling. 'There is something wrong,' he said eventually. 'But we don't know what it is. She is happy about Baki but something else troubles her.' He shook his head solemnly. 'I wish you would come home, Meryt. I think she misses you.'

Meryt looked up and saw a falcon circling above, its graceful, pointed wings outstretched as it soared on the gentle breeze. The bird was silhouetted against the sun, which seemed to form a golden halo around it. Her heart beat a little faster. The sun-god Re was embodied as a falcon, for he was a facet of the falcon god Horus, the king of all the gods. Could it be that the gods were guiding her, as Teti had said they would?

She reached for the scarab amulet that she wore around her neck, and pulled it over her head. 'Take this,' she said to Mose, and placed it in his hand. 'Give it to your mama.'

'But you always wear that, Meryt,' exclaimed Mose. 'It is your protection. You will not be safe without it.'

'Don't worry about my safety, Mose,' she said. 'This amulet was my father's, but I want Tia to have it now.'

As Mose stared down at the amulet, Meryt felt the empty space where it had always lain. She did feel oddly exposed, but the sun was now warming her neck and she felt quite sure that she was doing the right thing. Her heart felt lighter, and she closed Mose's hand around the amulet and smiled. 'Tell her it is sent with my love,' she said.

Mose seemed nonplussed, but he nodded and rose to his feet. 'I will,' he promised.

'And if she wants to know where I am, tell her I am staying with Teti,' she added. 'I hope she will come and find me. Take care, Mose.'

'See you soon, Meryt.' Mose turned and trotted off towards the gate with his side-lock bobbing in the last rays of the golden afternoon sun.

When he had gone, Meryt's thoughts quickly returned to Kha. Part of her wanted to act on her instincts at once, but another part warned against it. Mose had been right to point out that she had no protection. She would first return to Teti, and ask to take another look at the *Dream Book*.

Teti welcomed her back into her home, and together they cooked an evening meal. When they had eaten they sat on the roof to eat slices of water-melon, and as darkness fell, Meryt described her dream about Kha and the golden amulet. 'I think I understand most of it,' she said. 'But there is one thing that puzzles me. The amulets are burning up in the heat and the gold is melting away. But when Kha stands alone on the mountain, he is bathed not in sun but in moonlight.'

Teti nodded. 'This is something the *Dream Book* can answer. As it happens it is a good sign,' she said. 'But you are right to be cautious.'

She fetched the papyrus and another lamp, and read each entry carefully to herself, muttering over the words. 'Here,' she said at last. '*If a man sees him-self in a dream with the moon shining: Good. He is being pardoned by his god.*'

'Why ...' Meryt shook her head in disbelief. 'That's perfect.'

Teti gave her a querying look. 'What do you mean?' she asked.

'It is more than I could have hoped for,' said Meryt. 'But I would like to sleep on it before I act, and speak to Kha before I tell you what I think – for fear I am wrong.'

Teti looked amused. 'Very well,' she said. 'You are growing wise, Meryt-Re. But I'd like you to have greater protection all the same. Wait here.'

Her words reminded Meryt of the emptiness around her neck where her amulet had been, and she wondered how Tia had responded to her gesture. She thought of how her aunt had been so anxious over Baki's care, scarcely leaving his side from the moment he returned from the priests. It made sense. Meryt realised how deeply Peshedu's death must have haunted her. What a burden to carry for all these years ... no wonder her aunt often seemed tired and restless. Meryt felt her heart swell with sympathy.

Teti reappeared at the top of the stairs, and Meryt saw at once that she was dangling another amulet from her hand.

'This is for you,' said Teti. She sat down next to Meryt and slipped the string over Meryt's head. 'It is from my store of protective amulets and I have pronounced a special blessing over it.'

The amulet was larger than the scarab, and weighed more heavily around Meryt's neck. She looked down and fingered it, fascinated. It was a little dwarf-like child with bandy legs, similar to the household god, Bes, but without his lion's mane, shaped in faience and glazed a light golden brown.

'It represents our lord Horus the Child, to protect you in your innocence,' said Teti, 'but it also contains the protection of Ptah, for it is in his world that you tread.'

Meryt smiled. She liked the funny little object, and

she thought she could already feel its strength weaving a web around her. 'Thank you, Teti,' she said. 'I shall treasure it. It has come at a good time, because today I gave my scarab to Tia.'

Teti's eyes grew wide, and Meryt saw something new in their regard. It was respect. 'The gods guide you well,' she said. 'To pass on one's own protection to another is an act of great power. It will not go unrewarded, I am sure.'

'I don't want a reward,' said Meryt shyly. 'It just seemed the right thing to do. And there is still much to be done about Nebnufer.'

Teti played with one of the wicks, teasing away the ends with her little tongs. The flame flickered, casting shadows on her face, and when she spoke it was in a low, serious voice. 'And there I cannot help you,' she said. 'I have seen that you must travel this path alone. But you will do so well, Meryt-Re. You need not be afraid, for the gods are with you.'

It was a comfort to think of Teti's words later that night when Meryt lay alone under the stars, thinking of what she must try to achieve the next day. And yet, even though she felt confused and uncertain about the future, she knew that she had lost her fear. Her fist closed around her new amulet and she smiled up at the velvety black sky, tracing patterns from one star to another. Perhaps there was hope, after all.

She did not remember falling asleep. When she woke, she felt a heaviness on one leg, and realised that Teti's cat had snuggled up to her in the night. She stroked it absently, staring out at the pink streaks of dawn that were rising in the east. She shifted the cat gently to one side and stood up to stretch before padding down the staircase to the courtyard.

There was no sign of Teti anywhere, and Meryt guessed that she had gone out to gather herbs. She sat and ate a piece of bread with some of the *rekhet*'s salty goats' cheese, chewing slowly. There was no hurry. Now that the darker season was drawing in, most of the village would only stir slowly – especially the men who had been granted leave from work. But when the sun had gained a little strength she set out, heading into the village and taking an alley that led to the north-eastern corner, beneath the wall.

She found the house of Kha the painter and knocked on the door. It was his wife who opened it. 'He isn't here. What do you want with him?' she asked suspiciously.

'It is only about his work,' Meryt reassured her. 'I wish to consult him, that's all.'

The woman looked Meryt up and down, then shrugged. 'He is moonlighting. In the tomb of Paser,' she said, pointing up at the western hillside.

'Thank you,' said Meryt politely. 'May the gods be with you.'

She felt the woman's stare on her back as she made her way west, but did not turn round. Taking the western gate, she made her way around the tombs until she found the section that Kha's wife had pointed out. She did not know this part of the cemetery well and she had to ask a passing stonemason where the painter was working.

When Meryt found the right tomb shaft, she looked around. The chapel that would stand over the tomb had not yet been built. A low mud-brick wall marked out the courtyard boundary, but that was all. Meryt peered down into the shaft, which had been dug into the rock almost vertically. A steep, narrow stairway had been hewn into the rock, and she could see that the darkness would soon engulf her. She took a deep breath and lowered herself down backwards into the shaft, gripping the steps above her with her fingers as her feet found ones further down. When her feet touched a layer of solid rock she realised she had been holding her breath all the way down, and her legs were shaking.

'Who's there?' called a voice out of the gloom ahead of her.

A flickering light showed somewhere below. The passageway she stood in was not big enough for her to stand in upright, and Meryt bent over to creep forward a few steps. There must be another stairway down into the tomb chamber, and she was terrified of tumbling down it accidentally. With her hands, she groped along the ceiling, but all at once the flickering light grew brighter and a man's hand appeared, placing a lamp near her feet.

Meryt peered down the next shaft. Standing below her was Kha.

'It's … it's Meryt. The lyre player from Nebnufer's party,' she managed to say.

Kha looked astonished. 'Whatever are you doing here? The tombs are no place for a girl.'

'I need to speak to you,' said Meryt nervously. 'Please don't send me away.'

The painter stared up at her, puzzlement in his eyes. 'Well – if you wish.'

Kha lifted the lamp and guided her feet down the steps as she began to descend once more. The second shaft was not as deep, and when she reached solid rock again Kha led her forward into the tomb chamber itself. The passageway opened out before her, and Meryt gasped in delight. It was beautiful. Following the design laid out by a draughtsman, Kha had completed the ceiling and two of the walls with intricate paintings in vibrant colours that took her breath away.

Kha smiled at her response. 'You have never seen inside a tomb before?'

Meryt shook her head, gazing at the paintings in wonder. Of course, she had seen plenty of chapels, but somehow it was different standing here in a chamber below the earth, seeing the freshly painted scenes by the flickering light of a lamp.

'See, here Paser greets the gods in the next world,' Kha explained. 'And here, he and his wife tend the fields in paradise, where the crops are always lush and plentiful.'

Meryt longed to reach out and touch the paint, but

instead she smiled and said, 'It must be a pleasure to work on something so sacred.'

'It is easy to forget that,' Kha confessed, with a little laugh. 'Nothing seems sacred when you do it every day.'

'That's not true!' exclaimed Meryt. 'I see the bust of my father every day and it still seems sacred to me.'

Kha studied her, his smile dying. 'You are a strange young woman, Meryt-Re,' he murmured. 'First I was struck by how well you play the lyre. Now you have entered my workplace, where young women never intrude. What is it that has brought you here?'

Meryt let her eyes wander over the paintings for a moment, uncertain where to start, then bowed her head. 'I have dreams,' she blurted, before she could stop herself. 'I see things that others do not see.'

She looked up, and saw that wariness had come across the painter's gentle features.

'And what have your dreams been telling you?' he asked quietly.

Meryt took a deep breath. Now that she had started, there was no point in holding back. 'What I know concerns the draughtsman Userkaf,' she told him. 'He is using power that does not belong to him.'

Kha's eyebrows shot up. He stared at Meryt intently. 'Go on.'

Meryt paused. She knew she had to choose her words with great care. 'You are his friend,' she said. 'You know him well.'

Kha folded his arms. His friendliness had gone. 'What are you trying to say?' he demanded. 'Yes, I am a friend of Userkaf's. You are treading on slippery ground, young Meryt. What is it that you want from me?'

A gust of wind blew down the shaft and the lamps sputtered, casting eerie shadows around the tomb. Meryt felt a shiver run down her spine, for she could not escape while Kha was standing in front of the shaft. How foolish she had been! Perhaps Nofret's tale was true. The man who stood before her might be dangerous – and she was trapped with him in a tomb that could all too easily become a place of darkness. She looked around, mute with fear, knowing there was no other exit.

'I …' Her voice came out in a squeak and she cleared her throat. 'I have seen that the gods have pardoned you.'

Kha took a step towards her, and Meryt backed away. 'Pardoned me for what?' he demanded. 'What is it that you know?'

There were beads of sweat on Meryt's forehead, for there was much that she believed, but little that she actually knew. She decided to take a gamble. 'Userkaf offered you riches,' she said, the words coming out breathlessly. 'Bribes. He offered them to others too. But you were the only one to refuse.'

Her heart thudded painfully against her chest as she watched his reaction. Kha's face remained neutral and calm.

'And what else?' he asked.

Meryt wondered whether to mention the amulets, but an instinct warned her not to. 'Just that the gods have pardoned you,' she repeated. 'Please do not harm me, Kha.'

'Harm you!' The painter shook his head.

Meryt let out her breath in relief. So she was safe, at least.

'I am more concerned that you may harm yourself,' the painter continued. 'What you talk about is a serious matter.'

Meryt fingered the new, heavy amulet around her neck. She nodded. 'I know,' she said. 'I did not ask for the gift of dreams.'

Kha stroked his chin. 'The gods must surely be with you,' he admitted. 'It is true Userkaf has bribed many of the men. In return, they give him their support. He has done well, for his offers are generous.'

'But you stood alone, and refused the temptation.'

'Yes, I refused,' said Kha. 'But Userkaf has my support, all the same.'

Meryt frowned. To usurp a foreman appointed by the vizier was against all the principles of truth and justice by which they lived. If Kha was trying to undermine him, he was defying the will of the gods despite refusing the bribes. 'Is Nebnufer such a terrible foreman?' she asked. 'Does he deserve this treachery?'

Kha said nothing but looked uneasy, and Meryt realised she had touched his conscience. The image of her dream flashed before her once again: the painter standing alone wearing a ragged loincloth, his painter's palette worn out. And suddenly she knew what she had to say. 'You imagine that Userkaf will be a good foreman, don't you?' she said. 'You think he will treat you all better than Nebnufer, and act with wisdom and justice. This is foolishness. Userkaf's tools are betrayal and deception, and that will never change. How do you think he will treat someone who refused to accept his bribes?'

She paused. Kha was standing very still, and she knew that her meaning had hit home. 'The gods have pardoned your treachery,' she carried on. 'But the pardon brings with it a price. Nebnufer's future depends on the vizier and what is said at the trial. It rests in your hands, Kha.'

Kha's expression grew cold as he realised what she was saying. 'You are telling me to speak out,' he said. He snorted, and shook his head. 'Userkaf is my friend. So are the others. What they are doing is wrong, but ...' he spread his hands. 'You do not know what you are saying, young Meryt,' he finished.

Meryt moved towards the tomb shaft. Kha allowed her to pass, and she placed her foot on the first narrow step. 'I cannot make you do anything,' she said, meeting the painter's gaze. 'All I can say is that I have seen that the gods are with you. Do not be afraid to do what you know is right.'

Then, after one last look around the half-painted

tomb, she turned and began to clamber up the narrow shaft towards the daylight.

The morning air seemed fresh and wholesome as she emerged in the unfinished courtyard. Meryt took deep, long breaths and stretched her limbs. She hadn't noticed it at the time, but now that she was above ground she realised that the air in the tomb had been hot and oppressive from the mixture of stale breath and burning linen wicks. She sat in a patch of sunlight and closed her eyes, glad that she was not a man, and would never have to work in the tombs.

So she had been right. Userkaf had bribed his fellow-workmen to gain their support, having sold the precious amulets to traders. It did not answer the question of the stolen copper tools, but it was a start. She could only hope that Kha would act on what she had told him, for without the evidence of a workman Nebnufer stood no chance.

The sound of sandals crunched on the limestone pathway and a shadow fell across her face. She opened her eyes, and gasped.

'Ramose!'

The stonecutter was looking down at her with a perplexed expression. 'I have often hoped to come across you, but I never thought it would be here,' he said.

Meryt scrambled to her feet. 'I was just going,' she said. 'I only came to … to …' she trailed off, not wishing to reveal the reason for her visit.

Ramose lowered a bag of tools from his bulky

shoulders, and shook his head. 'I am sorry I cause you such fear,' he said. 'I never meant to. Please don't go.'

He seemed so mild and unthreatening, and Meryt's curiosity began to get the better of her. 'It is not *fear*, exactly,' she said slowly, toying with her amulet.

'No. You just don't want to be near me,' said Ramose, wiping a bead of sweat from his forehead. 'It hasn't been difficult to work out. I am not the kind of man you thought you'd end up with. Right?'

Meryt hung her head in embarrassment. 'I ... suppose so,' she admitted, then felt doubly awkward – both for herself and on his behalf. How could he expose himself this way with her? Didn't the man have pride? 'I'm sorry, Ramose.'

'Well, you needn't worry,' he said. 'It wasn't what I really wanted either.'

'Wasn't ...!' Meryt's mouth dropped open. 'What do you mean?'

Ramose met Meryt's gaze for a second, then looked away hastily and scratched the back of his head. 'I would have been good to you, though,' he mumbled.

'You would have ... *What?*' Meryt closed her mouth again with a snap, a sense of outrage building up inside her. She thought of the agonies she had been through: the prayers to the goddess Hathor, the offering to her father, her fear of Senmut and the endless hours pondering her dream. 'My whole life rested on this and all you can say is that you would have been good to me, as though I were a … a … donkey or a she-goat!'

Ramose looked up, his big, doe-like eyes defensive. 'I tried to talk to you,' he said. 'You ran away. I wanted to let you know the truth.'

'The truth! That I'm the best wife you could find,' said Meryt bitterly. *'She'll do*, is that what you thought?'

The stonecutter's features twisted with hurt. 'No. It wasn't like that.'

'So what was it like?' cried Meryt. 'Do you know what I've been through because of this? My uncle Senmut wanted to get rid of me. You came along with your offer and he jumped at it. I had to fight tooth and nail for time to think about it and then … and then …' Her voice quaked as she thought about Baki. 'And then he found another excuse and got rid of me anyway.'

'I'm sorry,' said Ramose, his face sorrowful. 'I do mean it, you know.'

But Meryt was angry, and a momentary streak of cruelty rose within her. 'Do you always do what your mother tells you?' she asked.

Ramose recoiled as though he'd been slapped, and Meryt regretted her words at once. The stonecutter bit his lip. 'You don't understand,' he said. He tried to smile, but he now seemed too upset.

'Why?' asked Meryt, more gently. 'Please tell me.'

The stonecutter took a deep breath. 'The offer was genuine. I would have married you in honour of

248

your father. It was him that I loved, you know.'

Peshedu. Meryt stared at the stonecutter as his words sank in, taking her breath away. How could this be? What was Ramose talking about? She shook her head, bewildered. 'You ... you knew him?' she whispered. 'But you are only young.'

'He died when I was seven,' said Ramose. 'Until then I loved him well.'

Meryt licked her lips, which felt suddenly dry. She was lost for words. 'And ...?' she managed – for surely there was more.

'We both did.' Ramose scuffed his sandal against a boulder, staring at his feet. 'Mother and I.'

"You ...' Meryt gulped at the words.

Ramose looked up again, his expression frank. He seemed relieved to have got things off his chest. He picked up his bag of tools as though the matter were closed. 'Well, now you know,' he said, with a brief smile. 'May the gods be with you, Meryt-Re.'

And he walked off towards the northern end of the cemetery.

# CHAPTER TWELVE

Meryt watched the stonecutter disappear down one of the tomb shafts, feeling slightly light-headed. She was not sure which had been the greater shock – the revelation that Ramose did not really want her, or the thought that her father and Heria had … what? What? She stamped her foot in frustration and began to hurry away from the tombs, scattering stones as she leapt down the path.

She did not want to face the heaviness that Ramose's words had created in her chest. To know that he would not pursue her further should have brought her relief – and it had, to some extent. But the thought that he had never wanted her in the first place was a blow, an unexpected blow, for if Ramose did not want her – bumbling, podgy Ramose – then what hope could there possibly be for her?

It was all too much. She passed through the western gate and stamped along the streets in fury. 'How dare he,' she muttered to herself, trying to ignore the choking feeling in her throat and the stinging tears at the corners of her eyes.

Best to forget it all right away. He was only an ugly useless stonecutter! She would follow Teti's advice: in times of trouble, keep your hands working. She would go to the *rekhet*'s house and make herself busy for the rest of the day.

Teti had returned from her early morning foray and was chopping herbs as Meryt walked in.

'Can I help?' Meryt demanded, her voice abrupt, for she did not want the *rekhet* to see her distress.

Teti looked up and smiled. 'Later, perhaps.' She nodded in the direction of the staircase. 'You have a visitor.'

Meryt was not in the mood for any more surprises. She gazed at the staircase resentfully, as though it might move and engulf her.

'Go on up,' laughed Teti. 'He is harmless, I assure you.'

'He?' Meryt squinted up at the edge of the roof, where a little figure now stood looking down at her. It was Mose. He waved and beckoned, a happy smile on his lips.

Despite herself, Meryt was pleased to see her cousin. She grinned, and climbed up the steps to greet him with a hug. 'Mose, it's good to see you. Is everything well?' she asked him. 'Did you give your mama the amulet?'

Mose gazed up at her, his eyes dancing. 'Yes,' he said. 'It made her happy, Meryt. She sent me to find you.'

'Oh!' Meryt felt gladness swell up, followed quickly

by doubt. 'Could she not come herself?'

Mose grinned at her. 'She doesn't need to,' he said. 'I've come to fetch you instead.'

Meryt was not sure she had heard correctly. She frowned and stepped back. 'Why? Has Senmut gone back to the Great Place?'

Her cousin shook his head. 'He is still here.'

'But …'

Mose looked up at her, his young eyes full of understanding. 'Mama says you needn't be afraid.'

Meryt pursed her lips. Mose had obviously got things wrong. She led him further on to Teti's roof and sat him down on the mats. 'Listen,' she said firmly. 'Your papa has said that I mustn't go back to your house. You know that, don't you? I'm glad that Tia is happy about the amulet, but that doesn't mean I can come home.'

Mose looked troubled. 'You don't trust me,' he said in a small voice.

'Oh, Mose.' Meryt reached out and hugged him. 'Of course I trust you. But …'

'You think I'm too young.' A flash of resentment appeared in Mose's eyes, then disappeared again, replaced by the usual calm. 'I know Papa was angry with you. But Baki got better when you sent him the spell and the balm.'

'But your papa doesn't know about that.'

Her cousin nodded. 'He does. I told him.'

'You *told* him!' Meryt thought of Senmut trampling the linen charm in the dust and drew back from Mose, horrified. 'I told you not to, Mose!'

Mose gave a heavy sigh. 'I will be glad when I am grown up,' he said gravely. 'Then people will stop thinking I know nothing. Mama told me that it wasn't your fault that Baki was sick. I thought she was right. So I put the charm under his head and I gave the balm to Mama. When Baki started to get better, I told Papa why.' He squinted up at Meryt. 'How could that be the wrong thing to do?'

Meryt was speechless. 'Well ...'

'It is better that he knows the truth.' Mose nodded to himself. 'And now you can come home.'

He stood up and took Meryt's hand to pull her to her feet, then began to lead her confidently towards the steps. Meryt followed uncertainly, then pulled back. 'Wait. I can't ... I can't just go home like that.'

Mose frowned. 'Why not?' he asked.

It was hard to resist his childlike determination. Full of doubt, Meryt followed her cousin down the steps to the courtyard. Teti looked up from her herbs and smiled.

'Teti, should I go?' Meryt asked her.

The *rekhet* cocked her head on one side. 'The gods are with you,' she said. 'Let them lead you on. They seem to guide you well, Meryt-Re.'

'I hope so,' murmured Meryt, embarrassed. She wished she could talk it through with Teti for longer, but Mose was already tugging her away towards the doorway.

Mose trotted quickly to the village gate. Whenever

Meryt slowed down, he chivvied her along as though she were a wayward sheep. In spite of herself, Meryt was impressed by her little cousin. He had the makings of a fine young man. But then, as they neared the family home, Meryt's heart began to beat faster. She dragged her feet and resisted her cousin's hand.

'I'm not sure I can do this, Mose,' she protested, as he pulled her determinedly forward. 'What if …' She didn't finish her sentence, for in the doorway of the house she spotted Tia.

Her aunt was peering out, her face full of apprehension. Meryt met her gaze, and they both stood still.

'Tia.' Meryt whispered her name, terrified that Mose had made a horrible mistake and that she would be sent away again, just as her hope was beginning to rise.

But Tia's face split into a smile, and slowly, she held out her hand. Meryt's heart gave a bound. She let go of Mose and placed her fingers in Tia's.

'Come in,' said Tia simply.

Meryt stepped into the front room. In front of Peshedu's bust, arranged neatly on the floor, were three loaves, a golden melon and a plump gourd. Next to them were Tia's incense burner, a little box of incense and a little bowl containing embers from the oven.

'Where is Senmut?' asked Meryt, hovering in the doorway.

'He is with Baki, on the roof.' Tia looked at Mose.

'Go and tell them we are here,' she instructed him.

Meryt backed towards the street in fear.

'Stay. He will not banish you again,' Tia assured her. She lowered herself down next to the offering, clutching her growing belly. 'I will take you to him and you will see. But first I must offer to Peshedu. You can join me, if you wish.'

Meryt hesitated. This all seemed so sudden. She noticed that Peshedu's scarab now rested around Tia's throat, and she reached up instinctively to touch the child-dwarf that had replaced it.

Seeing her gesture, Tia's eyes filled with tears. She closed her hand around the scarab and looked away for a moment, biting her lip. Then she swallowed, and smiled. 'Something happened the moment I touched the scarab,' she said in a low voice. 'I felt as though a burden had lifted and I knew the blessing of forgiveness. Thank you, Meryt.'

Meryt knelt beside her aunt and silently took her hand.

'I was still afraid you would not come,' Tia carried on. 'But I promised Peshedu that if you did, the first thing I would do would be to offer my thanks.'

Meryt squeezed Tia's hand. She could find nothing to say, but watched as Tia reached for the incense and the burner. Trying to block out her fear of Senmut, she sat quietly while her aunt performed a simple ritual before the bust.

When it was over, they sat for a few moments in silence.

'It has been so hard recently,' said Tia eventually. 'The closer you have come to adulthood the more I have felt my guilt, and your father's anger. I was sure he would punish me through Baki – and I was right. I did not want you to marry Ramose against your will and yet Senmut thought it was the best solution for us all.'

'Against the will of Ramose, also?' murmured Meryt.

Tia sat upright with a jolt. 'Whatever do you mean?'

Meryt sighed. 'Are you really saying you didn't know?'

Tia's mouth had dropped open. 'Know what?' she stuttered. 'No. I don't know anything. Heria approached Senmut about the marriage and she has always been the one pushing for it. I thought Ramose a coward but I never imagined …' She shook her head. 'How did you find out?'

'He told me himself,' said Meryt. 'He said …' The words stuck in her throat as she gazed up at the bust of her father, his handsome features so calm and still.

'What?' Tia touched her arm.

'He said he would have married me for love of Peshedu.'

Tia's eyes widened. She leant forward on to her knuckles, her forehead creased into a frown. 'But he was only a boy when he died,' she said slowly. 'Younger than Mose.'

Meryt nodded, and threw Tia a meaningful look.

'Yes. But his mother knew Peshedu well.'

'Ha!' The laugh burst from Tia's lips like a shout. 'Heria! And my own brother! I never heard of such a thing.'

'Can it be true?' Meryt scrutinised her aunt's face, not sure whether she wanted it to be true or not; she didn't know what it might mean.

Tia had become thoughtful, casting her mind back, searching her memory for clues. 'Well … perhaps,' she said. 'Perhaps it can. If it is, I shall make it my business to find out.'

There was a scuffling in the doorway, and Meryt looked around. It was Mose standing there, his hands behind his back and his face scrunched up as though trying not to laugh. Then came a muffled giggle from the next room, and she guessed that Henut was not far behind.

'We wanted to say …' began Mose, as his little sister's face peeped around his legs.

'Wanted to say welcome home!' squealed Henut, jumping out from behind him. She leapt towards Meryt, presenting a very squashed and wilted lotus flower in her grubby fist. 'We got them for you.'

Mose shuffled towards her shyly with his own lotus, which was slightly less bruised though no less wilted. Meryt took both the flowers, sniffing them in turn. She swallowed the lump in her throat and smiled. 'Thank you,' she said, as Henut wrapped both arms around her thighs.

Their happy greeting made Meryt all the more

aware of what lay ahead, and she looked across at Tia nervously. Senmut, Baki and Nauna had made no attempt to come and find her, and despite what Mose had told her she found it hard to believe that they would welcome her.

'Let us eat,' said Tia. 'It is a little late for breakfast, but today is a special day.'

She led the way through the house to the courtyard. Mose and Henut escorted Meryt on either side, oblivious to the tension that was building up inside her. They reached the courtyard and stopped. Senmut and Baki sat on the reed matting in the shade, while Nauna milked the goat. Baki grinned, but Meryt knew instantly that it was the provocative grin of old. She felt a jolt of fear.

Senmut looked up at Meryt and gave a nod of acknowledgement. She smiled stiffly, and allowed Mose and Henut to lead her to a sunny patch on the mats.

'I made some fresh cheese,' said Tia, her tone determinedly cheerful. 'There is a new batch of bread and the gardeners brought some cucumbers.'

Meryt watched as Nauna filled some cups with warm goat's milk. The older woman had not greeted her, but offered Meryt the first cup of milk, which she accepted graciously. It might be only a little thing but it was a start, at least.

The family was quiet as Tia bustled around, placing the cheese and bread in the centre of the floor and shooing away the cats. She added a bowl, a knife and two cucumbers, then joined the circle and began to chop them up.

Meryt realised she wasn't hungry. She had already eaten a breakfast of bread and cheese in Teti's house. But Senmut raised his eyes to hers and handed her a chunk of bread, and she did not like to refuse it.

'You need to eat,' he said gruffly. 'You have grown too thin.'

Baki sniggered, but Meryt felt the goodwill in Senmut's words and allowed their warmth to comfort her.

'Thank you, Uncle,' she said quietly. 'I will eat as much as I can.'

The meal continued, interspersed by Henut's happy chatter and Nauna's complaints that the goat no longer yielded enough milk. Baki, who had stayed quiet at first, began to talk about his new-found status as a man.

'I will soon start receiving wages, won't I?' he asked, of no one in particular. 'We will have extra grain. Extra everything. We'll be rich.'

'Not yet,' said Senmut. 'Your recovery is not yet complete. You will stay here for another two weeks.'

'Two weeks! But I am better.'

'The walk to the Great Place is long and arduous,' said Senmut. 'Make the most of your freedom, Baki. You have a whole lifetime in which to work.'

'Yes. Unlike some people,' said Baki nastily, throwing a glance at Meryt.

Meryt stiffened, and concentrated on chewing her

bread. There was an awkward pause, which even Henut did not try to break.

At last, it was Senmut who spoke. 'Do not say such things, Baki,' he said, his voice strained. 'Meryt brought the balm that healed you. For this you should treat her with respect.'

Meryt looked across at Mose, who gave her a little smile. He had been right – and she had been wrong to doubt him. But all the same, she thought she caught an edge of fear in Senmut's voice. She tried to meet her uncle's gaze, but he looked away again hurriedly and reached for the bowl of cucumber. She sighed. Things might have changed, but not as much as she had hoped.

The meal over, Senmut disappeared to while away the afternoon with friends. Nauna headed out to gossip with neighbours, and Baki challenged Mose to a game of *senet*. Meryt was left with Tia and Henut to clear up in the courtyard. Meryt saw that her aunt had started to tire more quickly than in the past, and told her to go and rest.

'I can't,' protested Tia. 'Nes is coming to grind the grain. I need to keep an eye on her.'

'Leave it to me,' said Meryt. 'I'll look after her. You look tired.'

Tia placed her hands in the small of her back, and sighed. 'Well, it's true my back is aching,' she admitted. 'Thank you, Meryt. Come and wake me when Nes has finished, won't you?' Then, taking Henut with her, she went to lie down on the roof.

Left alone in the house, Meryt looked around for something useful to do. It felt strange, being back. She could no longer take her life in the house for granted. Now, she viewed the everyday chores and family mealtimes with fresh eyes. They had seemed so insignificant – until they were taken away.

She had started scouring a pot when she heard Nes's soft knock on the door. After bringing the servant girl through to the courtyard to start work on a sack of grain, Meryt scrubbed the pot until it was spotless. She put it away in the storage cellar, then watched Nes settle into a rhythm as her strong, wiry arms ground away. Meryt thought of grinding the grain for Teti, and remembered how her arms had ached.

'Would you like me to help when you grow tired?' she asked, with a smile.

Nes stopped grinding for a moment and stared at Meryt as though she were mad. Then she grinned, and shook her head. 'I'm fine.'

'But wouldn't you like a break sometimes?' persisted Meryt.

The servant girl shrugged. 'I don't let myself think about it,' she said. 'This is what I do. It's my job.'

Her resignation surprised Meryt. Nes had none of Nofret's defiance. Maybe, when you were assigned to grinding grain, you had to stop thinking about alternatives; if you sat wishing for something better it would only make you miserable. But Nofret ...

Nofret was different. Meryt had a funny feeling that she often dreamt of other ways of life, and it was time to tackle the issue head-on.

Meryt waited for Nes to finish her work, then woke Tia and headed out on to the street. She walked quickly to a house in the southern end of the village and, before her nerves could get the better of her, knocked on the door.

It was Userkaf's wife who answered, a haggard-looking woman of Tia's age. Meryt had heard that she had already borne seven children, three of whom had died in infancy.

She took a deep breath. It would be best to come straight to the point. 'Hello. Is Nofret there, or at the embalmers' workshops?' she asked.

'Nofret?' Userkaf's wife looked at her askance. 'The servant?'

Meryt nodded. 'We are friends,' she hazarded. 'I would like to speak to her.'

Userkaf's wife pursed her lips. 'I can't spare her at the moment.'

'It would not be for long.' Meryt gave her a pleading look, and saw the flicker of a response in the older woman's eyes.

'It had better not be. She must be back in time to help me cook.' Userkaf's wife turned away, and called back into the house. 'Nofret!'

Meryt waited by the big water jars that stood outside the house. As ever, neighbours peered out of their houses, drawn by the sound of voices. She ignored them, trying to think through what she was going to say to the servant girl. *I have nothing to lose*, Nofret had said. She was prepared to risk everything for her master. But why? There could be only one possible reason ...

She stirred as Nofret's face appeared in the doorway.

'What are you doing here?' demanded the servant girl.

'I need to speak to you,' said Meryt. 'Come quickly. Your mistress said you could leave your work for a while.'

Nofret looked annoyed. 'You make trouble for me, Meryt-Re,' she said.

'Not as much as you make for yourself,' Meryt retorted. 'I am trying to help you. Come, before your time is up.'

Reluctantly, Nofret followed Meryt as she walked the short distance to the village gate and along the winding southern path.

'Let's climb up towards the Great Place,' said Meryt. 'Then we can sit and look down on the village.'

'If we must,' said Nofret ungraciously. 'But it is hard work climbing up there. I don't know why we can't just sit alongside the path.'

Meryt ignored her. She had already turned up the steep, rocky path that led around the Peak of the West and over the cliffs to the great valley of the kings' tombs that lay beyond. As she did so, she looked down at the panorama that began to unfold below – the sprawling western cemetery, the cramped houses and the village temple-chapels at the northern end. When she could just see the massive mortuary temples and the River Nile too, she stopped, and looked back to see Nofret labouring up the path behind her.

They stood in silence, getting their breath back. Then Meryt made a sweeping gesture with her arm, taking in everything that lay before them.

'This is my home,' she said. 'This village. I have always lived here.'

Nofret remained quiet, as Meryt thought she might.

'I hope to stay here, one way or another,' Meryt carried on. 'And I hope that in some small way I shall help to keep our lives governed by truth and justice, the principles of *maat*.'

'Why, good for you, Meryt-Re,' said Nofret in a cynical tone. 'What a happy future you have laid out before you.'

Meryt turned towards the other girl. 'The strange thing is ...' she said slowly, 'I have a clearer picture of your future than I do of mine.'

Nofret tried to mask her startled look. 'And what future is that, Meryt-Re?' she asked.

'You think you have it all worked out,' said Meryt. 'Stealing the amulets, telling me that story about Kha. But you haven't done it all for nothing. Userkaf has offered you a reward, hasn't he? He even gave you gifts to keep you happy in the meantime.'

Nofret's mouth closed into a stubborn line. She said nothing.

'Of course he did,' reasoned Meryt. 'As you said, you had nothing to lose – and everything to gain. And I know what that *everything* is to you, Nofret. It's your freedom.'

The words hit their mark and Nofret's mouth dropped open. 'How do you know?' she cried.

Meryt gave a little shrug. 'This does not take any special magic to work out,' she said. 'Why else would you risk your life with such defiance?'

At last, Nofret's guard was broken. Her eyes flashed in pride and anger. 'Yes!' she shouted. 'And that freedom is now very close, so do not provoke me, Meryt-Re!'

'I am not provoking you,' said Meryt. 'I told you. I want to help, that's all.'

Nofret snorted. 'I suppose you are going to say that I would be better off remaining a slave in your beloved village,' she said scornfully. 'I know what freedom means. It might mean hardship and poverty but it will be of my own choosing – and that is what I prefer.'

Meryt shook her head. However wonderful freedom might seem, a person still had to eat. 'What has he offered you, exactly?' she asked.

Nofret hesitated, narrowing her eyes. 'He has a small piece of land, by the river,' she said. 'There is a little hut there. I could grow vegetables, and sell what I do not eat in the market.'

'He has offered you this?' Meryt spoke quietly, for her heart now went out to the servant girl. She saw the dream in Nofret's eyes – the dream of a life of tranquillity where she could work hard for her own ends, no longer at the mercy of her masters. But for all her fiery defiance, she must be truly desperate to believe that Userkaf would give her such a thing.

Nofret must have seen the sympathy in Meryt's eyes, for her own began to fill with fear. 'Yes,' she whispered. 'He promised that if I stole enough of the amulets ...' the words died on her lips.

Meryt stood still, and gazed out over the view.

'What have you seen?' demanded Nofret. 'What have the gods shown you?'

A thought flashed through Meryt's mind – a memory. She saw Teti, her eyes large and troubled as she tried to offer comfort to the three women who sat huddled in her front room. Meryt knew instinctively that there had been little hope; and now, suddenly, she understood the nature of Teti's work. It meant sharing people's grief as well as their joy, and shouldering their burden with them.

'The gods showed me the painter Kha,' she said. 'They showed me that your story was false. But I saw more than that. Kha is loyal to Userkaf, but it will not do him any good. Your master uses people, but he gives nothing in return, for he is driven by ambition and greed.'

Doubt crept across the servant girl's features. 'But he gave me the shawl and the collar ... He promised ...'

Meryt looked at her. 'Think, Nofret.'

The servant's shoulders sagged as the truth of Meryt's words began to dawn on her. It was a harsh realisation, and she seemed to shrink in disappointment and pain. But then her spirit fought back, for a moment. 'I can threaten to expose him!' she cried.

Meryt nodded. 'Yes, you can,' she said. 'But it depends what you hope to achieve. If you think it will be your freedom, you are much mistaken. Userkaf will not take kindly to threats from a servant girl and in any case, you are his thief. Surely you can see what this means?'

This time, Nofret was silent. She looked at the ground and traced a pattern in the dust with the toe of her sandal. Eventually, she looked up. 'I will not be his slave all my life. I would rather *die*,' she said in a low voice.

Meryt swallowed. What proud, desperate words ... but as she looked at the other girl's hunched, scrawny shoulders, Meryt saw the depths of misery that filled her life and realised they were true. She took a deep breath. 'If you really mean that ...' she began.

Nofret's eyes filled with tears, and she began to weep. 'I do mean it,' she sobbed. 'He promised. It was my only hope. What else do I have to care about?'

Meryt took a deep breath, and touched her arm. 'There is something you can do, Nofret,' she said. 'You do not have to threaten to expose him. You do not have to speak to him at all. But remember what you have said: *you have nothing to lose*. If you speak the truth before the court, you may find greater mercy at the hands of the vizier than you would at the hands of your master.'

She said the words with hope, but at the same time her heart was cold, for she knew that the penalty for theft was harsh – and for the theft of precious amulets, the court might demand the highest penalty of all. She placed her arms around Nofret's shoulders, and waited for her sobs to subside before guiding her back down the path towards the village.

'Take time to think,' she murmured as they reached the village. 'Should you decide to act, do not be afraid. On the day, I do not think you will be alone.'

Nofret disappeared into Userkaf's house without a backward glance. Meryt felt full of sorrow that life could be so cruel, and she wandered back home slowly. She wondered what the servant girl would do; what Kha would do. She had done everything in her power and the matter was now in the hands of the gods. Her fingers closed around her new amulet and she muttered a solemn prayer. 'May the gods be with us all,' she murmured. 'And may they be merciful to those who deserve it.'

But as she drew closer her thoughts took a more positive turn, for *home* was such a beautiful word and she now appreciated it more than ever before. She stepped over the threshold with gladness, humming a tune. After briefly touching the bust of her father in the front room, she walked through to the next.

And there, sitting on the floor next to Tia, was Heria.

'Oh!' exclaimed Meryt. She stared at the two women – first at Heria, quickly, then at Tia. All at once, she wanted to flee.

'Come and sit,' said Tia, giving Meryt a meaningful look. 'Heria wishes to speak with you.'

Meryt pursed her lips. She was not sure she wanted to hear what Heria had to say. After all, hadn't she almost forced Meryt into a marriage she did not desire?

'Please,' said Heria. 'You have nothing to fear.'

Reluctantly, Meryt lowered herself down on to the mats, close to Tia, glowering at the other woman. 'What do you want with me?' she asked ungraciously. 'You must know that I am not going to marry your –'

She stopped as Tia nudged her arm in warning. 'She is here to tell us the truth,' said Tia. 'I went and fetched her myself.'

Heria looked embarrassed. 'I only wanted to help,' she said. 'I hope I can show you that.'

Help? thought Meryt, frowning. *What kind of help was that?* But she waited for Heria to continue.

'When your mother Simut died, Peshedu was left on his own, as you know,' Heria carried on. 'Tia helped to raise you but she soon gave birth to Baki. So Peshedu employed a wet nurse to give you milk and look after you. He was often alone and seeking company. That is when I got to know him. I had been a widow for two years and I was worried for Ramose, who had no father to guide him. We visited Peshedu at quiet times to avoid the gossip of the neighbours and we grew to love him well. I would have become his wife if … if he had not fallen sick.'

Heria stopped for a moment and wiped her forehead. She had begun her story quickly, but her sentences were gradually growing slower. Meryt threw a glance at Tia, who was listening as intently as she was herself.

'I was so young myself – fifteen when Baki was born,' said Tia thoughtfully. 'I never had any idea …'

'We had decided to keep our love a secret until Meryt was weaned,' Heria told her. 'I had no milk of my own to offer her but I would have taken her as my daughter later on, just as Peshedu was happy to treat Ramose as his son.'

'But you were nowhere to be seen once Peshedu fell sick,' said Tia, a hint of accusation in her voice. 'That was when I needed help most of all. Baki was still no more than a baby and hated being left with Nauna while I cared for Peshedu …'

Heria's eyes flashed defensively. 'What could I do?' she cried. 'I feared the worst. I had a son, but no father to care for him or give him an apprenticeship. I could not care for Meryt as well. I needed to find a husband.'

Meryt stared at Heria as the picture of yet another life opened up before her – a life in which she had been raised by Peshedu and the woman sitting here before her. 'Ramose would have been my brother!' she stuttered, instinctively leaning closer to Tia.

Heria nodded. 'I know I let you down, Meryt-Re,' she said. 'I let your father down too. I chose Paneb the stonecutter to provide a future for my son.' She paused. 'But I still wanted to help. I did not care for you as a girl, but Ramose could have cared for you as his wife. I even went to Peshedu's tomb to ask for his blessing on you both.'

So that was it. The offerings in the tomb, the proposal of marriage … all the fruit of Heria's love for Peshedu. Meryt bowed her head, wishing for a moment that she had she never been born. All these years, the adults around her had fretted over her care and her future, burdened by guilt.

But then she felt Tia's arm around her shoulder, and heard her aunt speak. 'The past is the past, Heria,' she said. 'I too have carried a burden for many years, but I know my brother has forgiven me. Think of this: if you had taken Meryt into your home, I would not have cared for her myself. And that would have been my loss, for she is now a daughter to me. And more than that – a friend.'

Meryt's heart gave a bound. Since returning home, she had known that Tia loved her more than anyone ever had, but it was still wonderful to hear her say it out loud. She looked up at her aunt and wanted to hug her, but did not – for in the doorway stood her uncle Senmut.

271

She had no idea how long he had been standing there. She wondered if he had heard what had been said, and dreaded his anger. But Tia saw him too, and smiled. 'Senmut. Come and sit with us. We have been learning more of Peshedu.'

'And of a woman's foolishness,' said Heria, with a sigh, as Senmut moved forward silently to squat at Tia's side. 'I am sorry, so sorry. From what Tia has told me, I have caused trouble for us all.'

'I heard what you have to say,' said Senmut. 'But what of your son? Is it not time he found a wife?'

Meryt looked at her uncle anxiously. Everything had changed since Baki's illness, and her time away from the family home. She had hoped that Senmut's views on Ramose would have changed as well, but she couldn't be sure. The issue of her future still remained.

Heria gave a little smile. 'Ramose is a good man,' she said. 'But he has lived too much in my shadow. He does as I tell him, even now. I dare say he would find a wife of his own choosing if I gave him a little more room.'

'And Meryt is not that woman, in truth,' Tia put in quickly.

Heria shook her head.

Senmut sighed, and scratched the back of his head. 'Well,' he said, looking at Meryt. 'It seems that the goddess has spoken.'

CHAPTER THIRTEEN

Two weeks passed. Senmut returned to the tombs and Meryt found that life at home was soon much as it had always been, except that she loved and valued it more than before, for there was now a bond between herself and Tia that could never be broken. However, there was still a thorn that seemed to prick her deeper every day: despite his close shave with the Next World and the cure she had brought him from Teti, Baki was as difficult as ever. Meryt marvelled at his attitude, secretly furious that he could still treat her with such disrespect.

One morning Meryt came down from the roof to find Baki drinking the last of the goat's milk. It was now in short supply, for the goat's udders were slowly drying up.

'Baki!' she exclaimed. 'You could have left some. It is important for Tia to drink the milk. You know that.'

Baki grinned. 'I will tell her you drank it,' he said, a wicked glint in his eye.

Meryt snatched the milk jar from him, biting her

tongue. It was not worth responding to such childish taunts, but she was itching to clip him around the ear all the same, or fight him as she had always done. But since his ritual their fights had stopped, and Meryt thought it best not to start them again. She turned away.

But Baki put out his foot in front of her, and she tripped. The milk jar flew from her hands and cracked against the wall, breaking neatly in two.

Her cousin's peal of laughter rang around the courtyard. 'Shall I tell her you broke the milk jar too?' he hooted, and this time Meryt's rage was too great. Not trusting herself to speak, she flung the broken pieces into one corner and stormed from the house.

She made for the place that she now went whenever she needed to find peace. It was no longer the polished limestone slab on the top of the Nile-facing hillside, or the chapel of her father's tomb. It was the house outside the village wall where Teti the *rekhet* lived.

'Meryt! Good to see you,' Teti greeted her, on opening the door.

Meryt tried hard not to scowl. 'May I come in?' she asked.

Teti opened the door wider, looking amused. 'Did a cat steal the milk this morning?' she asked.

'Don't mention milk,' muttered Meryt darkly, following Teti through the house. But now that she was here she felt calmer already, and looked with interest at the necklace that Teti was stringing in the courtyard. This was one of the ways in which Teti managed to survive – many villagers were prepared to pay not only for her skills of divination but for the charms and trinkets that she made.

'Help yourself to some fruit, or beer,' said Teti. 'I would just like to finish this off.'

Meryt fetched a couple of dates and sat munching them as Teti added two tiny clay amulets to the neck-lace, which was made mainly of beads. The amulets were lizards, creatures that Meryt loved to watch as they slithered between the crevices in the rocks. She and Kenna had often played with them, and had sometimes seen the marvel of a lizard regrowing its tail when it had been lost. Because they could do this, a lizard amulet was a powerful symbol of new birth.

'Was it the children that annoyed you?' the *rekhet* asked presently, throwing Meryt a glance.

Meryt shook her head. 'It was Baki. Who else?'

Teti's face grew serious. 'I sense trouble brewing for him. A man cannot live in defiance of those around him any more than he can live in defiance of the gods.'

It was a comfort that Teti thought so. Meryt played with a date stone in her mouth, pondering something that had puzzled her ever since Baki's recovery. She had told Teti all about her reconcilia-tion with Tia and Senmut, about going to find Kha in the tomb of Paser and her encounter with Nofret on the road to the Great Place. But she had one question left to ask of the *rekhet* and she decided to ask it now.

275

'I sense trouble for him as well,' she said. 'But I am not sure why. He likes to make trouble but there is something darker about him as well.' She paused, throwing the date stone into a corner. 'I have often wondered what magic it was that touched him, Teti. I don't think it was Peshedu. Do you know what it was?'

The *rekhet* held the finished necklace up against the light. The sun glinted through the coloured beads that sat between the earthen lizards.

'You have learnt much, Meryt-Re,' she said. 'It is good that you like to ask questions. You will go on to learn so much more.'

Meryt didn't understand what she meant. 'But that has nothing to do with Baki.'

Teti lowered the necklace and laid it out before her. 'There are many kinds of magic in this world,' she said. 'We can master some of them. But there are times when you have to let the gods keep their answers to themselves.'

'So you don't know?' Meryt pressed her.

Teti cocked her head on one side. 'No,' she said, with a smile. 'I don't.'

It was puzzling, but when Teti said she didn't know something, Meryt knew she had to accept it. She stayed in the *rekhet*'s house until the heat of the day had passed. When she left, she noticed a little train of three donkeys approaching the village, and she shielded her eyes from the sun to watch them approach. The first donkey was laden with goods and was led by a Nubian servant. On the second sat a tall woman, her back stiff and straight, while on the last sat a girl of Meryt's age.

There was something familiar about the last two, and Meryt craned her neck to get a better look. As they began the last ascent, she suddenly realised who they were.

'Dedi!' she cried, bounding down the track.

She heard her friend call to the servant, and the donkeys came to a halt. Dedi slid down to the ground as Meryt rushed up to her, then stopped abruptly to bow her head to Wab.

'Hello, Meryt-Re,' said Wab gravely. She called to the servant. 'Carry on. Dedi will catch us up in the village, I'm sure.'

The servant nodded and took the third donkey's lead rope in his hand. As the little train trudged into motion again, Dedi flung her arms around Meryt's neck. They hugged without speaking for several minutes.

'I've missed you so much!' exclaimed Meryt, when they pulled apart.

'Not as much as I have missed you,' said Dedi soberly. 'I have been stuck with relatives all this time. And all they want to do is speak of the wages the men get in Set Maat, and of course the trial.'

Meryt took her arm, and they began to walk slowly to the village gate. 'What of the trial?' asked Meryt. 'I have heard that the vizier arrives tomorrow.'

Dedi nodded. 'Yes. But he will stay on the east bank and see to the affairs of the great temples before he comes here. We expect the trial to take place in two or three days' time.'

Meryt clutched the amulet around her neck and felt suddenly nervous. For the last two weeks she had concentrated on enjoying life at home, and had ignored the looming village crisis – for there was nothing more she could do. She had sown what seeds she could; she could only hope that they bore the fruit she had intended.

'I trust the gods will be with your father,' she said quietly. 'These are difficult times, Dedi. But the rule of *maat* must prevail.'

Her friend's composure was beginning to crumble. 'Let's not speak of it,' said Dedi, her voice shaking. 'If we do, I know I shall cry. I just want to feel glad to be home, and among friends.'

'Of course.' Meryt squeezed her arm, and they lapsed into silence as they passed through the gate. She could not help but notice that the Medjay guard stared at Dedi, his beady eyes curious, and she felt a flash of anger. Did the foreman's family not have enough to endure without everyone gawping? She frowned, and shook her head. She could tell that the next few days would bring a trial in more ways than one.

Nebnufer's family kept a low profile for the next two days, and Meryt did not like to intrude. The village was alive with chatter and gossip; even Wab and

Dedi's movements gave rise to speculation about how the family was coping, and Meryt could not blame her friend for trying to avoid it. Instead, her thoughts turned to the trial itself. She decided that the person she wanted by her side on the day was Kenna – happy, dependable Kenna, who would help to calm her nerves.

She went to ask him the day before, and found his family home in a high state of excitement about the arrival of the vizier. The men were sitting in a huddle in the middle room, drinking beer and discussing the future of the gang. Meryt sat with Kenna in the front room and asked him what was going on.

'Father says that Userkaf had already petitioned the vizier's department for the position of foreman,' explained Kenna. 'Everyone is talking about it, for Userkaf might make some changes to the gang.'

'But the trial has not yet happened,' objected Meryt.

'No. But everyone seems to think that Nebnufer will be found guilty,' said Kenna. 'I feel sorry for Dedi and her brothers.'

'Yes. But we mustn't assume the worst – not yet.' Meryt shivered, for the worst was something she did not allow herself to think about. She thought instead of Kenna's face when he spoke of Dedi. Was it her imagination, or had he shown less yearning than before? It was possible. Infatuations could quickly blossom, and quickly fade. Or so she had heard.

She remembered that she had not yet told him

about Ramose, but decided it could wait. Better to get the trial over first, for it would surely affect them all.

'Will you watch the trial with me?' she asked him. 'I want to be near the front, so that I can see clearly.'

'Of course,' said Kenna. 'Let's get there early. I'll come and collect you.'

Meryt nodded. 'Thank you, Kenna.' She sighed. 'I shall be very glad when the whole thing is over.'

The next morning, Meryt felt sick with anxiety about the trial. No one in her home seemed particularly concerned, for Senmut's future was safe on Sennedjem's gang and Tia had never been interested in the goings-on of the *kenbet*. But Meryt could scarcely do her chores for nervousness. She dropped the pots that she set herself to scour; then tried to lose herself in sweeping out the house but found that she was simply stirring up dust.

At last, she heard Kenna's voice in the doorway, and propped up the broom.

'The first of the vizier's messengers has arrived,' announced Kenna. 'They say that the vizier's procession is making its way past the temples. It will call at the Fields of Djame before it comes here.'

They hurried along the main street, which was already buzzing with people. Meryt kept a keen look out for Nofret or Kha, but she spotted neither as she and Kenna jostled their way forward. Outside the village walls by the cluster of chapels the mats were already laid out in the shade, but few people were sitting yet; most were gathering along the track that led to the valley, eager to see the vizier's chariot proceed up the hillside in all its pomp and finery.

Meryt and Kenna picked a spot on the foremost edge of the mats and settled down to wait. In the distance, Meryt heard the sound of horns and trumpets, and wiped her hands down her linen dress. They were already damp with sweat.

'Is anything the matter?' Kenna asked her. 'You're very quiet.'

Meryt tried to smile. 'I am worried for Dedi's family, that's all.' She did not want to tell him about Nofret or Kha; the matter was in the hands of the gods now.

Kenna stared at his hands. 'I have tried not to dwell on the consequences,' he admitted. 'The whole thing feels unreal, like a strange kind of game. But if Nebnufer is convicted of theft as everyone says he will be …'

'Don't,' said Meryt, for they both knew where his thoughts were leading. 'I know what you mean. I have not allowed myself to think of what might happen. May the gods be with him.'

They stood and craned their necks as the sounds of the procession grew nearer.

'The vizier's chariot approaches!' cried a voice, and there was a flurry of movement as villagers rushed to find seats on the matting, jostling each other for space. Meryt and Kenna sat down again hurriedly as the fanfare sounded closer, and Meryt spotted Teti on the fringes of the crowd. It made her feel a little better to know that the *rekhet* was there.

The members of the *kenbet* appeared first. Sennedjem led the way, followed by the other four – Paser, Montu, Amenakht and Hori. But instead of sitting as they usually did, they stood in a row to greet the vizier, the second most powerful man in the whole of Egypt.

There was a hush as the procession reached the square. First came the horn-blowers on foot, followed by fan-bearers and a small troop of the vizier's personal guards. Next came the vizier's chariot, pulled by two magnificent horses and driven by the great man himself. Two high officials rode in plainer chariots behind him, and were followed by an entourage of lesser officials on donkeys.

The horses and chariots came to a halt, and a murmur rippled around the crowd, for such a sight was to be marvelled at. The vizier's chariot was lightly built and partially gilded; the panels were covered in delicate carvings, painted in brilliant colours and inlaid with precious stones and glass. It was one of the most splendid objects to have ever reached the walls of Set Maat, but the villagers were equally impressed by the finely bred horses, who stood with their necks arched and their nostrils flaring.

The guards took hold of the horses and the vizier stepped down, raising his hand in greeting. The villagers gazed at him in awe, for this was a man who knew what it was to stand in the presence of the king:

surely his face must shine from the splendour of it? His gaze was majestic, taking everyone in as his officials joined him, and the guards led the chariots and donkeys out of the way. Two fan-bearers stepped forward to shelter the great man, their fans made of the most enormous feathers that Meryt had ever seen.

'They are from the ostrich bird,' she heard someone whisper. 'The king's men hunt them in the Red Land. Just one of their eggs can feed the whole of the king's court.'

Meryt was staring at the feathers, trying to imagine the bird they came from, when Kenna nudged her and nodded to one corner of the square. There stood Nebnufer and Wab, standing quietly with Dedi and their sons behind them. A Medjay guard stood discreetly to one side; and Meryt was glad that Nebnufer was being allowed his dignity, at least.

The vizier greeted the members of the *kenbet*, who all bowed low before him. Then he walked slowly to an ornate wooden chair in the centre of the court area with his fan-bearers behind him. His entourage of scribes and judges were taken to plainer chairs on either side, while the *kenbet* of Set Maat sat right at one end. When everyone was settled, Sennedjem rose to his feet, bowed low before the vizier once more, and began to speak.

'My lord the vizier – life, prosperity, health!' he began. 'We have requested your presence to find justice in our village, which has hit upon troubled times. The foreman Nebnufer, appointed by your predecessor eleven years ago, has been accused of stealing government supplies and of mismanaging his men. On the latter charge, we did not find him guilty. The charge of theft is a serious one, and this we hand over to you.'

He turned to the Medjay guards. 'Bring out the evidence and the witnesses.'

Sennedjem sat down and the vizier settled back into his chair, stroking his chin, as the chief of the Medjay police force carried forward a linen bag. He bowed, then opened up the bag and laid out an array of brand-new copper tools, which glinted in the light of the sun. There were chisels of several sizes, ranging from the largest used by stonecutters for hewing out the tombs from the rock, to the finest used by sculptors to define the delicate lines of reliefs; hammers and adzes; and two fine carpenters' saws. The chief of the Medjay held up each in turn, pointing out the special government seal that had been stamped on to the copper.

'The seal of the Great Place,' he said solemnly each time, handing them to the vizier one by one. The vizier nodded, clearly growing impatient as the police officer went through the bag methodically until there were no tools left.

At last the chief had finished, and stood up straight to speak. 'My lord, my men found these tools in the storeroom of Nebnufer the foreman,' he said. 'As you know, tools such as these have no place in the village. They are delivered directly to the Great

Place for their consecrated use in the tombs. We arrested Nebnufer at once.'

He bowed again, then picked up the tools and stepped back into the crowd.

'The next witness!' called Sennedjem.

It was Userkaf himself who stepped forward. He bowed lower than anyone, and took the liberty of looking around at the crowd before beginning to speak. 'My lord the vizier – life, prosperity, health!' he boomed. 'I am a draughtsman on Nebnufer's gang and I have suffered for many years. He drives us hard. Not only this, but he does not abide by the rules of *maat*. He is dishonest and punishes us for no reason. Men on the other gang are given the freedom to look after their sick and to worship their gods on feast days, but we are always forced to work. And our work is made harder in the tombs when he refuses to replace our worn-out tools. He makes the Guardian of the Tools hold them back until the ones we are using have no life in them.'

Meryt felt winded at the audacity of this man who could stand before the gods and his fellow workmen and tell such blatant lies. But Kenna leant towards her.

'It's true, you know,' he whispered. 'Nebnufer will never change the tools when he's asked to. That's what Father says.'

Meryt was horrified. Surely Kenna did not believe the words of the draughtsman? She stared at her friend as Userkaf finished his speech.

'And so,' the draughtsman concluded, 'I for one

am not surprised that tools have been found in the foreman's home, for no doubt he uses the surplus for his own ends.'

He bowed again with a flourish, then stepped back to make way for the next witness. Meryt's mouth was dry. She watched dumbly as five more of Nebnufer's gang stepped forward and confirmed what Userkaf had said. Finally, a male servant from Nebnufer's own household stepped forward. He bowed before the vizier twice, as though to make sure he had done it correctly.

'My … my lord. Life – life, prosperity, health,' he stuttered, his gaze fixed firmly on the ground. 'I … am a servant of the foreman Nebnufer.' He hesitated, and seemed tongue-tied, transfixed by the enormity of the occasion. As his silence continued, people began to mutter, and someone laughed.

'Speak, man!' cried someone from the back of the crowd.

Titters rippled around the square, and the chief of the Medjay shifted, frowning.

The servant coughed. 'I saw my master with … with the bag of tools,' he muttered, so quietly that he could barely be heard.

For the first time, the vizier spoke. 'Stand tall. Look the crowd in the eye. Repeat what you have said,' he ordered.

The servant jumped nervously, and pushed back his shoulders. 'I saw my master Nebnufer with the bag of tools,' he said, his eyes wild as he surveyed the crowd. 'In ... in the house. Near the storeroom. I saw him with it in his hand.' He held his own hand up, as though to show how Nebnufer had looked. Then he clamped his mouth shut and gazed at the floor once more with his hands behind his back.

'Is that all?' asked the vizier.

The man nodded. Meryt felt anger rising inside her. *Bribes, bribes, bribes,* she thought to herself; but there was nothing she could do.

'Let him go,' said the vizier, with a sigh.

The servant scurried off, and the next man to stand was Sennedjem. 'That concludes the evidence, my lord,' he said. 'But Nebnufer himself wishes to speak.'

The crowd was still as the foreman stepped forward. After a deep bow to the vizier, he went over all that he had expressed before the *kenbet*: his appointment by the former vizier, his faithful service to the government, his belief in fairness and *maat* for the men. 'I do not encourage my men to be wasteful,' he acknowledged. 'If there is still life in the tools, then I insist that they use them. It is too easy to blame a blunt tool for idleness.'

There was a murmur among the workers in the crowd, and Meryt sensed anger in their midst. She began to see that Nebnufer did not have goodwill on his side. Userkaf and his followers were muttering, but she knew that not even the likes of Kenna's father liked to be accused of idleness. The grumblings grew louder as Nebnufer tried to carry on.

'Quiet!' cried the chief of the Medjay.

'As for the bag of tools,' said Nebnufer, when the hubbub had died down. 'I have no need of them. I have a farm in the valley where I smelt tools of my own. Recently I held a party for my men, and I believe the tools were brought into the house on that night.'

The grumblings began to rise again as Nebnufer spread his hands before the vizier. 'That is all I have to say, my lord.'

Nebnufer retreated back to Wab's side and the vizier looked across at Sennedjem.

'These are all the witnesses, my lord,' said the second foreman. 'The case is complete.'

The vizier frowned. 'Is no one going to speak in favour of the king's foreman?' he asked. 'He has served for eleven years. Are there no witnesses who can answer for him?'

Meryt felt her limbs begin to tremble. Where were Kha and Nofret? She looked around, scanning the crowd, but there was no sign of either. Had her plan completely failed? Perhaps she should stand herself, and tell the court what she knew ... She swallowed as Sennedjem spoke.

'My fellow foreman has been my friend and ally all these years,' he said, his voice tinged with sadness. 'I believe him to be a good and honest man. But in the matter of these tools I cannot speak, for I know nothing of them.' He scanned the crowd, his expression hopeful. 'People of Set Maat, you hear what the

288

vizier is asking. Is there no one who can defend the man accused?'

Kenna looked at Meryt in amazement as she began to rise to her feet. 'Meryt …!'

But then she stopped, for out of the corner of her eye she saw a movement – a man, elbowing his way forward. She breathed a sigh of relief, for it was Kha.

'Workman Kha,' said Sennedjem in surprise, as the painter made his way into the square. 'What do you have to say?'

Kha bowed both to the foreman and the vizier. 'My lord the vizier – life, prosperity, health,' he started. 'I come with a confession and a plea for forgiveness from the gods.'

Meryt held her breath until she thought her lungs would burst.

'What Userkaf says is true,' continued the painter. 'Nebnufer works us hard and does not like to supply us with new tools. The Guardian of the Tools is forced to listen to him and we resent his interference. But that is where the truth of his story ends.'

There was a gasp as the crowd took his words in. Meryt saw Userkaf exclaiming angrily to his friends, but the chief of the Medjay called the court to order.

Kha carried on. 'For many months there has been a plan to usurp Nebnufer. One man has been at the heart of it, and that is Userkaf.'

Another gasp. Meryt let out her breath slowly, for she could hardly believe that her plan was beginning to work.

'Those who did not agree were bought by Userkaf with bribes. He has promised much and given much, though I cannot name the source of his wealth. All I can do ...' he paused, and looked around, beads of sweat standing out on his face. 'All I can do is tell you the source of the tools. I know that Nebnufer did not steal them. The thief was Userkaf. They were placed in Nebnufer's house on the night of his party – as Nebnufer has claimed.'

The words hung in the air amidst a thick silence. Kha's confession was sensational, and even the vizier now sat on the edge of the seat.

'And how can you be sure of this?' asked the vizier. 'How do you know that they came from Userkaf's house?'

Kha looked as though he might topple over. He wiped his forehead. 'May the gods and the king forgive me,' he murmured, and touched the amulets that he wore around his wrists. 'I know, my lord, because I fetched them myself.'

This time his words were met with a roar, and Meryt felt faint. She had been wrong. She had made a mistake. She had misinterpreted her dream for she had never, ever anticipated this. She closed her eyes for a moment, thinking of the night of the party. Kha had been there at the start with his wife ... he had brought her the cup of water ... and then ... and then he had disappeared ...

She opened her eyes again as the vizier's voice spoke above the crowd. 'Tell us more of the bribes,' he said.

290

'I received nothing,' said Kha. Meryt breathed out. So she had been right about that, at least. 'I wanted Nebnufer gone and I was happy to see Userkaf replace him. But I did not want to anger the gods by taking a bribe, for I felt that the wealth on offer was tainted. But Userkaf demanded an act of loyalty. So I carried the tools to Nebnufer's party while Userkaf caused a distraction.'

The vizier's eyes were blazing. He stood, and the crowd grew quiet. 'Villagers of Set Maat!' he cried. 'I have never heard of such corruption in your midst. And yet perhaps there is more. Perhaps there are many who have accepted a bribe. But if there are bribes, the wealth must come from somewhere.'

He gazed around at the crowd, raising his hand and pointing at random villagers, who quailed and looked away.

'I know where it comes from.'

The thin, small voice seemed to rise in the air from nowhere. *Who said that? Where?* could be heard around the crowd, but Meryt already knew. She looked straight at the thickest part of the gathering, which was slowly parting to reveal a small, cowering figure. It was Nofret.

Userkaf gave a bellow from the sidelines. '*That* useless scrap of a servant!' he screamed. But he was helpless to stop her now. The Medjay held him back as she walked forward timidly to stand in front of the vizier.

291

At the sight of the scrawny twelve-year-old girl, a silence fell. The court officials stared at her in disbelief, though none seemed more amazed than the vizier himself. Without a bow or a greeting, she launched into a speech.

'I don't care what you do to me,' she said, her voice high and shaky. 'I have suffered enough as a slave for the last five years. My first master beat me daily. I was bought from him by Userkaf, who does not beat me but makes me work double the time, both in his home and in the embalmers' workshops.'

The vizier shrugged, for this was nothing unusual. But Nofret looked around. As she realised how carefully the crowd was listening to her, she drew herself up taller, and her eyes began to spark with anger. 'What he has done is the cruellest of all,' she carried on, her voice becoming shrill and piercing. 'He promised me freedom. He promised me land of my own. And I believed him.' She turned to face him, pointing at him with her bony finger. 'You thought I was stupid, Userkaf,' she said, and tears began to fall down her cheeks. 'And you were right. I did what you wanted me to do because I didn't see that you would never keep your promises.'

'And what did he want you to do?' The vizier's voice broke through the murmur of the crowd, stilling it.

'I stole from the embalmers' workshops,' said Nofret. 'Amulets. Golden amulets. I knew how to access the stores because my father had taught me how to steal as a child.' She stood with her shoulders shaking, a poor, broken figure of a girl, wracked with sobs. 'I gave the amulets to my master and he sold them to passing traders. That is all I know.'

Meryt found that her whole body was tense. She was clutching Kenna's wrist, so tightly that he had to gently prise off her fingers. She met his gaze briefly and saw the wonder in his eyes as the truth of the tale unfolded.

'You say your father was a thief,' commented the vizier, raising his eyebrows.

Nofret nodded, wiping the tears off her cheeks with her arm and sniffing loudly. 'I don't care about that either. He may have been a thief, but I loved him. And now you will send me to join him in the Next World.'

She bowed her head, almost as though she expected to be whipped upon the spot. There was a moment of uncertainty. No one seemed sure what to do. And then Sennedjem stood, and walked over to the servant girl. He placed a hand upon her shoulder and led her back towards his own chair, and told her to stand there next to him.

He addressed the vizier. 'I believe that is all, my lord,' he said. 'We can adjourn.'

The crowd stirred and shuffled and rearranged themselves while the vizier and his officials were led through the village gate to the house of Sennedjem, where they would be attended on by his sons and servants while they discussed the case and came to a decision.

Meryt saw Nebnufer and his family being escorted back to their house. To her satisfaction, she also noticed that all the witnesses were being guarded by members of the Medjay. She hoped that, at last, the forces of *maat* were holding sway.

She and Kenna decided to keep their places by the edge of the square. The vizier was a busy man; they would not have to wait all day.

'They say he is a merciful vizier,' murmured Kenna, at her side.

Meryt nodded. 'I hope it is true.' It was impossible to avoid the verdicts that would soon be made – and the punishments that would follow. She still felt nervous, despite the testimonies of both Kha and Nofret, for so much had come to light so suddenly that she did not know what the vizier would make of it. She feared for Kha, and thought once more of her dream – there he stood on the hilltop, dressed in rags … she had been wrong about some of it. Might she be wrong about his punishment too?

'Anyone would think it was you who was on trial,' said Kenna. She looked up and saw that he was studying her. 'You are shaking, Meryt.'

'I … I have much to tell you, Kenna,' she said. 'These past weeks have taught me so much.'

He nodded. 'I know.' He smiled at her gently. 'I have seen it. I would like to understand, but I fear that it is beyond me. I am only a simple messenger.'

'You are far more than that!' The words escaped Meryt's lips before she could stop them. 'I don't know what I would do without you.'

'Perhaps you would lean on Ramose,' said Kenna, with a lopsided grin.

Meryt stared at him. Even now, he spoke of it so lightly! How would he respond when he knew that the marriage was not taking place? She opened her mouth to tell him when the blast of a fanfare sounded and drowned out the words as they formed on her lips.

Some of the villagers had drifted away from the square and were chattering together in little groups. Now, they hurried back, jostling for position as the vizier's entourage appeared once more. One group of Medjay officers stepped forward with Nebnufer and his family, while another prodded Userkaf and his friends to the edge of the square. Kha and Nofret had a guard of their own and stood together.

The vizier took his seat, and Sennedjem stood to address the crowd.

'People of Set Maat – life, prosperity, health!' he began. 'The vizier has reached his conclusions. Listen, and receive the rule of *maat* at his hand.'

A deathly silence fell. Somewhere in the village, a donkey brayed, its squeaking call echoing along the cliffs. A gust of wind flapped the vizier's tunic, and he brushed an arm across his eyes, frowning at the dust. And then he stood.

'People of Set Maat,' he said, 'I have considered the case of Nebnufer your foreman. He works hard, and he demands the same of his men. But I see nothing in him that is not fair and true.'

The crowd gasped and muttered, then grew quiet again as the vizier raised his hand.

'I do not find him guilty of this theft. A foreman he is, and a foreman he will remain.'

The gasps grew louder, and Meryt's eyes filled with tears of happiness. She looked over at Nebnufer and his family. The foreman and his wife stood tall, dignified in justice just as they had been in accusation. But Dedi, Meryt saw, was leaning on her brother Ahmose, weeping with relief.

'Bring forth the witnesses!' Sennedjem's voice called out.

The Medjay pushed forward Userkaf and the vizier regarded him coldly.

'I have heard your complaints, Userkaf the draughtsman,' he said. 'You are an ambitious man and your greed has been your downfall. I might not have believed your servant girl, but for this: I was at the embalmers' workshops only this morning. The loss of amulets has not gone unnoticed.'

He paused, and Meryt lowered her gaze. There was a glint of something hard and cruel in the great man's face that she could not bear to look upon any longer.

'You have stolen from the king's officials. You have stolen from the Great Place. You have tried to bring down a man appointed by my office. These are heavy crimes for which you must be punished.'

It was as though the whole crowd were holding its

breath. Meryt still could not look up. She felt sick.

'Take him out into the desert and impale him on a stake.'

The silence was broken by a woman's wail, howling across the square. Meryt glanced upwards, and caught a glimpse of the wife of Userkaf hurling herself across the reed matting towards her husband, who had fallen to his knees in shock. The Medjay grabbed her and dragged her away. Others pulled Userkaf to his feet. Meryt forced herself to watch as the draughtsman was led away and his followers were brought before the vizier as a group.

'Cut off their ears!' he cried. 'That will teach them not to listen to troublemakers!' The crowd gasped again, then sighed and breathed easier, relieved that it was their ears and not their lives that they were losing.

And then it was Kha's turn. The vizier eyed him with interest, playing with the fat gold rings that adorned his fingers, then rubbing his hands together. 'Kha. Painter Kha. You are an interesting case,' he said. 'You chose to aid the ringleader and then you thought better of it.' He stroked his chin. 'I cannot decide if you are a coward or a man of courage. A thief or an honest man. To be punished or rewarded.'

Meryt was looking away again. This was too much. She was glad she was seated for she was sure her legs would not support her if she stood.

'I tend to think you should be punished so that you do not make the same mistake again. One hundred lashes!'

Meryt felt dizzy. She had never imagined that Kha would be punished. She had been so sure of his innocence. *He has been pardoned by his god.* What did this mean, if not that he would walk away untouched? But then she thought of what he had done, and knew that his punishment was light. A hundred lashes could be endured and he would return to his work in the tombs, a poor man, but alive – scarred – but free …

She made herself look up again to see Nofret step forward, her thin face pinched and tight with fear. Meryt's eyes blurred with tears and she bit her lip, blinking them away to see the expression on the face of the vizier.

There was a faint sneer on his lips. Rather than stand, he sat back down on his seat, and looked Nofret up and down. He eyed her scrawny body with disdain.

'I have better things to do than deal with servant girls,' he said, with a shrug. 'She is a common thief. She must be punished but she is not worth the effort of a lashing. Let one of the village men take her and use her as he sees fit.'

Meryt felt a wave of horror, for everyone knew what *that* meant. It was as good as a death sentence, or possibly worse. She looked around the crowd at the faces of the men, many filled with greed and lust. Some even licked their lips, and she felt the nausea rising in her stomach all over again. But there was a pause, for the villagers were reluctant to push themselves forward in front of such a great man.

And into that pause, someone spoke.

'She is mine.' The man spoke clearly, stepping into the square with his head held high.

It was Nebnufer.

The vizier raised an eyebrow, and gave a sort of smile. He spread his hands. 'And much fun may you have with her,' he said, in a cynical tone.

But Nebnufer did not move. 'I shall not use her badly, my lord,' he said. 'I consider she has done a great thing for me today. She may even have saved my life. For that I will give her to my daughter Dedi as a maidservant and I shall teach her the ways of *maat*.'

The vizier made an arch with his fingers, studying the foreman through narrowed eyes. Then he turned to the crowd. 'Do the villagers think well of this?' he asked.

In the roar of approval that followed, the villagers rose to their feet and shouted praises to the vizier, the voice of their god and king. Meryt and Kenna rose with them and joined in, clapping with joy.

The vizier's entourage did not linger. At a click of the great man's fingers, the chariots were brought forward and he was soon on his way, heading back across the river to the east bank. Exhausted, the villagers began to disperse. The fate of Userkaf flashed through Meryt's mind and she pushed it away. The punishment of the gods was just. Instead, she thought of Nebnufer and his family, Nofret, and the happy future that was now assured for Dedi and Neben-Maat.

The thought of this reminded her of Ramose. As she and Kenna wandered through the village gate, she knew the time had come to give Kenna the news at last.

'I was about to tell you something, just as the vizier came back,' she said.

'Were you?' Kenna grinned. 'Go on then.'

Meryt took a deep breath. 'I am not going to marry Ramose,' she said.

'Is that it?'

'Yes!' she exclaimed. 'Why? Did you expect more?'

Kenna shrugged, and laughed. 'I thought you were going to say you knew something about all that business with Nofret.'

'Oh!' Meryt stared at him, feeling her cheeks growing hot. She was about to turn away in frustration when Kenna touched her arm.

'I'm glad,' he said. 'About Ramose, I mean.'

'Are you sure?' Meryt stared at him indignantly.

'Look at it this way,' said Kenna. 'I need company when I go to the market. Who would I take with me if you were to marry?' His eyes smiled down at her.

And Meryt smiled back.

# MAPS AND GLOSSARY

This book is a story, so none of the characters really existed. But the village of Set Maat is a real place (you can still visit its ruins at modern-day Deir el Medina) and it was built especially for the Egyptian kings' tomb-builders to live in. The village thrived for about 300 years during the New Kingdom, when kings were no longer buried in pyramids but preferred tombs hidden in the rocks. Much has been learnt about the villagers of Set Maat – how they lived, which gods they worshipped, what they ate and even how hard they worked. Many of these facts are woven into Meryt-Re's story.

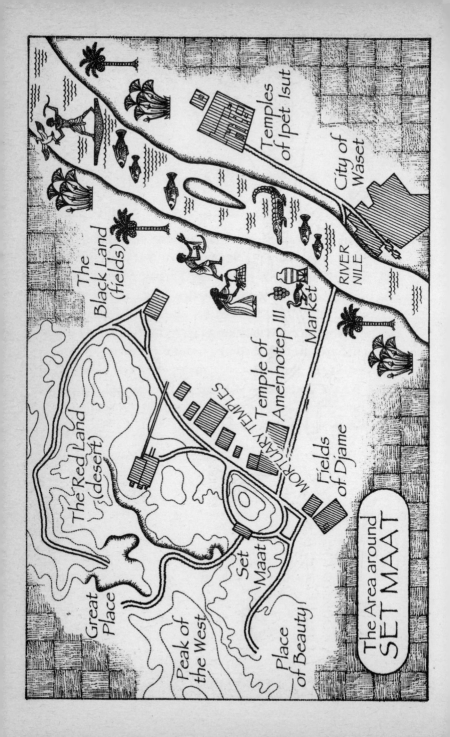

The Area around SET MAAT

Great Place

Peak of the West

The Red Land (desert)

Place of Beauty!

Set Maat

MORTUARY TEMPLES

Temple of Amenhotep III

Fields of Djame

Market

The Black Land (fields)

RIVER NILE

Temples of Ipet Isut

City of Waset

SET MAAT

Great Pit

Road out of the Village

Kha's House

Hill overlooking Nile Valley

Village Shrines

Harmose's House

Meryt-Re's House

Kenna's House

Teti's House

Userkaf's House

Ded's House

Route to the Great Place

Paser's Tomb

The Western Cemetery

Peshedu's Tomb

The Eastern Cemetery

Route to the Place of Beauty

GLOSSARY

Ahmes Nefertari A real queen, the mother of Amenhotep I, who was worshipped in the village of Set Maat as a goddess. She lived roughly 350–400 years before Meryt-Re's time.

Amenhotep I One of the first kings of the New Kingdom, who was worshipped in the village of Set Maat as a god. The villagers regularly consulted his oracle.

Amenhotep III A New Kingdom king who built a magnificent mortuary temple on the plains below the village of Set Maat.

Amen-Re A combination of Amun, the great god of Waset, and the sun god Re. In the New Kingdom he was worshipped as king of the gods.

Ammut the devourer A monster who waited in the Next World to gobble the hearts of people who had not led a good life. She had the head of a crocodile, the front paws of a lion and the hindquarters of a hippopotamus.

Bes A dwarf-like god with a lion's mane who was believed to protect children and women during childbirth.

blessed spirit of Re A name given by the villagers to relatives who had died.

Black Land The fertile land close to the Nile. See **Red Land**.

carnelian A red or reddish-brown semi-precious stone that was found in the Egyptian desert. It was often used in jewellery.

Deir el Medina The modern Arabic name for the village of Set Maat. It means 'the monastery of the town'.

Dream Book An Egyptian guide to interpreting dreams. It was very old indeed – even in Meryt-Re's time, it was considered ancient.

deben A measurement of copper. There was no money in ancient Egypt – people bought things with grain or just swapped one item for another. But they estimated how much things were worth in copper *deben*. For example, a good-quality shawl was worth about eight *deben*.

emmer wheat The particular kind of wheat that the villagers received as wages and used to make bread.

faience A kind of glazed ceramic material made mainly from quartz. It was used to make pottery and jewellery.

Fields of Djame The ancient Egyptian name for the site of the great mortuary temple of Ramesses III. This temple was the centre for administration on the west bank of the Nile at the time of Meryt-Re's story. Today, it is called Medinet Habu.

Great Place The villagers' name for the valley where the kings' tombs were built. Today we call it the Valley of the Kings.

Hathor The cow-headed goddess of love, beauty and music.

Hatshepsut A queen of Egypt who built a wonderful temple dedicated to Hathor in the cliffs not far from Set Maat.

Horus One of the oldest Egyptian gods. He was the ancient falcon-headed king of the living world, who defeated his evil uncle Seth to avenge the death of his father Osiris. Egyptian kings were believed to be the living manifestation of Horus.

Horus the Child The ancient Egyptians worshipped

Horus in several forms, not just as a falcon. As Horus the Child, he was revered as the young son of Isis and Osiris.

Ipet Isut The ancient name for Karnak, the big temple complex on the east side of the river at Waset. It was dedicated to the worship of Amen-Re, his consort Mut and his son Khonsu.

Isis One of the most ancient and powerful Egyptian goddesses, wife of Osiris and mother of Horus. She embalmed the body of Osiris in order to bring it back to life.

kenbet The name for the village council of elders in Set Maat.

Ken-Her-Khepeshef A man who actually lived in Set Maat before Meryt-Re's time. He was a scribe, and collected a big library of ancient teachings.

khol A black powder used as eye make-up.

lapis lazuli A semi-precious stone often found in ancient Egyptian jewellery. Only rich people could afford it, as it came all the way from modern-day Afghanistan.

lotus A beautiful blue waterlily that grew in the River Nile, now known as the Egyptian Lotus, the Blue Lotus or the Blue Waterlily. The Egyptians believed it had magical and medicinal properties.

maat The principle of truth and justice that underpinned Egyptian beliefs. There was also a goddess by this name.

Medjay The police force of ancient Egypt.

Men Nefer The oldest capital city in ancient Egypt. The site is now known by its Greek name, Memphis, and is situated about 10 miles (15 kilometres) south of the modern capital, Cairo.

Meretseger A cobra goddess worshipped by the villagers of Set Maat, who believed she lived in the western mountain behind the village. Her name means 'she who loves silence'.

Mut A goddess, the consort of Amen-Re, the great god of Waset.

Nefertari A very beautiful queen of Egypt. Her husband, Ramesses II, built her a wonderful tomb in the Place of Beauty.

nefret **flower** A flower that was used in magical rituals. Experts still don't know exactly what kind of flower it was, so they use its Egyptian name.

New Kingdom A period of ancient Egyptian history that lasted from 1552–1069 BC. Meryt-Re's story is set roughly a hundred years before the end of the New Kingdom.

Next World The place that all ancient Egyptians believed they would enter after death.

oracle A god or shrine that offered prophecies and advice, usually through its priests. There was an oracle of Amenhotep I at Set Maat, which the villagers consulted about all sorts of issues that affected their daily lives.

Osiris The great god of the underworld. In Egyptian mythology, he was the king of Egypt until he was murdered by his brother Seth. His wife, Isis, brought him back to life to rule the underworld.

ostracon (pl. **ostraca**) This is not an Egyptian word, but a Greek term for bits of pottery and limestone flakes that were used for writing on in ancient times.

Peak of the West The mountain behind Set Maat and the home of Meretseger, the cobra goddess.

peret One of the ancient Egyptian seasons, the 'time of

emergence' (October to February). There were three seasons. The others were *akhet*, when the river Nile flooded the valley (June to October), and *shemu*, the harvest time (February to June).

Per Ramesses The capital of Egypt in Meryt-Re's time. It is situated in the north of Egypt in the Nile Delta.

Place of Beauty A valley to the south of Set Maat where many officials, queens and other members of royalty were buried. Some of the tombs were as beautiful as those of the kings (see **Nefertari**). It is now called the Valley of the Queens.

Place of Truth The meaning of Set Maat.

Ptah A very ancient creator who was the god of craftsmen.

Ramesses II A great king of Egypt who ruled for 67 years (1279–1212 BC) and built many temples, tombs and palaces.

Ramesses III A king who tried to follow in the footsteps of Ramesses II (1186–1154 BC). He built a massive mortuary temple at the Fields of Djame, but he had many problems during his reign.

Re (also known as **Ra**) The sun god, who travelled in his barque across the sky every day.

rekhet The Knowing One or Wise Woman in the village of Set Maat. Very little is known about the role of the *rekhet*, but people turned to her for advice and to foretell the future.

Red Land The desert, seen as wild and dangerous by the Egyptians. It was the land of Seth, the enemy of Horus. The Black Land was much safer – it was the fertile area close to the Nile, where nearly everyone lived.

red ochre A red pigment that was used in ancient

Egyptian make-up.

scarab The dung beetle, which makes big spheres of dung and rolls them along the ground. The Egyptians believed that at dawn, as the sun rolled over the horizon, the sun god Re took the form of the scarab god Khepri.

senet A very popular board game in ancient Egypt.

Sekhmet A fierce lion-headed goddess of war, destruction and disease. However, she could also prevent these things. She was the wife of Ptah.

Seth The god of chaos and destruction, the evil brother of Horus. He was represented as a strange dog-like creature. Although he was feared, many people also worshipped him.

Set Maat Meryt-Re's village; the village of the Egyptian kings' tomb-builders. It means the 'Place of Truth' and is now known as Deir el Medina.

side-lock The tuft of hair that Egyptian children grew on one side of their head. The rest of their hair was shaved off.

sistrum A musical instrument, rather like a rattle.

Sobek The crocodile god, a protector of the king.

Tawaret A goddess of childbirth and pregnancy, usually depicted as a pregnant hippopotamus.

Thoth The ibis-headed god of scribes and writing.

Tutankhamun A minor New Kingdom king, buried in the Great Place (now called the Valley of the Kings). The discovery of his tomb in 1922 has made him famous.

udjat The eye of Horus, damaged by Seth in their final battle. It was healed by Thoth and became a powerful symbol of protection.

vizier The Egyptian king's second-in-command. Sometimes there were two Viziers, one for Upper and one for Lower Egypt (ie, north and south).

Waset The ancient name for the area that is now roughly Luxor and its surroundings, the location of this story. The Greeks called it Thebes and many books still refer to it as this.

ACKNOWLEDGEMENTS

I would like to thank Dr Morris Bierbrier, former assistant keeper in the Department of Egyptian Antiquities at the British Museum, for reading through the manuscript and answering my endless queries. His comments were invaluable, and his own book, *The Tomb-builders of the Pharaohs*, was one of several specialist books about Deir el Medina that I could not have managed without. However, any historical inaccuracies in the novel are mine, and mine alone.

Thanks to my agent, Rosemary, my editors, Emma and Helen at Bloomsbury, and all the friends who saw me through the penniless and nail-biting months of the first draft, especially Gill, Anna and Sue – the Farina's crew! Thanks to Lesley and Rosie for commenting on the completed novel. And a big thanks to my sister, Sal, for her unwavering belief in me.